MORE

THAN

MAYBE

ALSO BY ERIN HAHN

YOU'D BE MINE

MORE THAN MAYBE

ERIN HAHN

WEDNESDAY BOOKS
NEW YORK

First published in the United States by Wednesday Books, an imprint of St. Martin's Publishing Group

MORE THAN MAYBE. Copyright © 2020 by Erin Hahn. All rights reserved. Printed in the United States of America. For information, address St. Martin's Publishing Group, 120 Broadway, New York, NY 10271.

www.wednesdaybooks.com

Designed by Anna Gorovoy

Library of Congress Cataloging-in-Publication Data

Names: Hahn, Erin, author.
Title: More than maybe / Erin Hahn.
Identifiers: LCCN 2019051882 | ISBN 9781250231642 (hardcover) |
    ISBN 9781250231666 (ebook)
Subjects: GSAFD: Love stories.
Classification: LCC PS3608.A444 M67 2020 | DDC 813/.6—dc23
LC record available at https://lccn.loc.gov/2019051882

Our books may be purchased in bulk for promotional, educational, or business use. Please contact your local bookseller or the Macmillan Corporate and Premium Sales Department at 1-800-221-7945, extension 5442, or by email at MacmillanSpecialMarkets@macmillan.com.

First Edition: July 2020

10 9 8 7 6 5 4 3 2 1

For Mike, who stole my heart
at seventeen and has yet to give it back.
I must've done something right.

And also for every girl who wishes they had a Phil.
Here. You can borrow mine.

MORE

THAN

MAYBE

I don't believe in fate. I believe in music.

I've heard there is one person out there for everyone. One missing half to complete your whole. The fates will magnetically pull the two halves together through some orchestrated coincidence, and that's it. You're all set.

Bollocks, that. I met my other half three years ago, and as far as I know . . . she has no idea.

I don't have time to wait on fate to make its move. For the fender bender, or the missed lift to the roof, or the swapped locker combination. It's the end of senior year, and I can't afford to leave things to a happy accident any longer.

I need music. Give me angsty lyrics, the heartfelt plucking of strings, passionate and world-weary pleas. Give me the banging of keys, the staccato of backbeats, the gift of swing and swoon.

If I slice open my heart and put the rhythm to song, will she hear it?

The fates can get fucked. I've got to try.

1

LUKE

Spring rains, my arse. I shrug in my leather jacket, trying to simultaneously make my coat longer and myself smaller.

Growing up in London, you'd think I'd be immune to rain. You'd be wrong. Michigan in March is shite. I shift my longboard to my other hand and bury my fist in my pocket, working to get the feeling back in my fingers.

I should have called my brother for a ride, but I was downtown with Zack working on our English project at the library, and I've been itching to longboard since the weather started to thaw. It was barely a trickle when I left, swerving my way down the massive hill toward the club. But within minutes, I was huddled under a bus shelter, pouring rain beating down around me.

My phone buzzes, and I tug it out, willing my digits to work. I balance my board between my hip and the corner of the shelter, using the damp toe of my Converse high-tops to hold it in place. Someone next to me squeaks when I bump them with my backpack. "Bugger," I mutter. "So sorry."

I tap my screen.

CULLEN
Have you left yet?

I roll my eyes at my brother, composing something snarky in my head before tapping out:

LUKE
Yeah, but I'm stuck in the rain.

CULLEN
Where?

I wipe at my fogged-up glasses and squint, trying to read the sign. Useless. I turn to the college-aged girl I'd accidentally knocked into.

"Excuse me, what's the cross street here? Bloody can't see a thing."

Her face does this comical annoyed-to-charmed thing that happens when most people hear my accent. I know it, and I use it. I'm not ashamed.

"Oh em gee. You're British, right? We're at University and Huron. I love—"

"I am. Thanks very much." I cut her off. Which is rude, I know. But desperate times and all that.

LUKE
University and Huron.

CULLEN
Want me to come get you?

I think about it. I have no idea when the next bus comes or where it's headed. The rain has me disoriented.

"Hold on, you look super familiar. Do I know you?"

I bite the inside of my cheek, the bus shelter feeling

suddenly smaller. Two people sitting on the bench glance up from their phone screens.

"I don't know," I hedge. "Probably not."

"Maybe something about your voice?"

"Maybe," I start before she gasps theatrically, her hand going to her chest, where the symbols of some sorority dangle off a gold chain nestled between the layers of her Ravenclaw scarf.

"You're Luke Greenly. *The Grass Is Greenly!* I thought I recognized your accent, but it's the hair, too. I follow you on Insta!"

"Ah." I scramble for more words, but all I can come up with is, "Thanks."

"I'm sorry things didn't work out with Lindsay," she says.

"That's . . ." Jesus. This. *This* is why I'd told Cullen I didn't want to do Instagram. "Thanks," I repeat dumbly.

A car honks out of nowhere, startling us. My board clatters to the ground. Through the murky shelter, I see my best mate's familiar red Jeep Wrangler and give a sigh of relief.

Perfect timing.

"Sorry, I have to go!" I shout, grabbing up my board and dashing out into the rain before she can say more. I tug open the door of Zack's car and swiftly shut it behind me.

"Thank Christ," I say. I take off my glasses and unzip my coat so I can wipe down the lenses on something dry. "Did Cull call you?"

"Nah," Zack says, flipping his blinker and pulling out into traffic. "After you left, I heard the rain beating against the roof and figured you were dumb enough to skate. And sure enough . . ."

His phone vibrates, and the corner of his mouth lifts. "There's Cullen, I bet."

"You're a pair."

"And you are welcome," he says in a singsongy voice.

"Thank you," I say, more sincerely. "You saved me from a sorority girl."

He tsks, turning down Liberty and coming to a stop at a light. Even in the monsoon, hordes of bicyclers in full-bodied neon rain suits swoosh by in front of us at top speed. Typical Ann Arbor.

"She said she was *sorry about Lindsay.*"

His dark brows join in the middle as he looks at me. "Huh. Did you know her?"

I adjust my board between my legs. "Nope."

His lips twitch.

"Laugh it up. Har har."

"I told you Lindsay was bad news."

"Barely. If I remember, you said, 'You need a girlfriend, Luke.'"

"But I *also* said, 'Not that one; she's thirsty.'"

I grunt. "I thought that would work in her favor. At least in your eyes. You seem under the impression I'm a monk."

"You are."

"Just because I'm not in a sickeningly healthy, committed relationship at the moment doesn't mean I'm celibate."

He snorts. "Aren't you?"

"Not totally," I complain.

"Yeah," he says dryly, turning down a side street. "I saw."

I rub my face in my hands, knocking my glasses off course and readjusting them. A week ago, my ex-girlfriend secretly recorded us making out and posted the high-lights in her Instagram story.

Which I didn't even know was a thing until there it was. I woke to a hundred comments and a pit in my stomach. We ended on far-too-amicable terms, which she tearfully posted about the following day.

Cullen thought it was hilarious and good press for the podcast, *of course.*

"In my defense, I assumed you would go after—"

"Don't," I cut him off.

His fingers tap on the steering wheel.

"You haven't told my brother, have you?"

He glances at me. "No. I swear. I told you I wouldn't, and I won't."

I sink back into my seat, grimacing at the cold drips still easing down the back of my neck.

"But you've been doing this pining thing for-the-fuck-ever. Have you even introduced yourself yet?"

"Like, formally?" I ask. "We've talked. Sort of. She knows who I am."

"Does she? You sure about that? Or does she know who Cullen is and therefore knows you're the other twin?"

"Wow," I say. "*Wow.* Just because *you* fell madly in love with Cull the second you met him and forgot for a *solid ten minutes* his twin was your *best mate* doesn't mean everyone else does."

Zack shrugs, flashing an easy grin. "You could have them falling at your feet just as easily, you know. If you could drop the sullen artist act for a night."

"What sullen artist act?"

He doesn't respond, turning in to the cramped parking lot of the Starbucks next to the Loud Lizard, where we record our show.

He points to his phone. "Cull asked us to pick something up."

"Green tea latte?" I ask, amused. "I'm not ordering this time. He's your boyfriend."

"He's your brother. You share DNA."

"Yeah, but *you* share—"

He holds up a hand and unclicks his seat belt. "Enough. I'll do it. But he's getting full fat, and I don't want to hear it when he's a whiny bitch about calories."

"I'll take a cake pop," I try.

"Fuck off."

I watch as Zack runs through the rain. "Love is catching the flu to order an overpriced, high-calorie beverage for your boyfriend," I say under my breath, digging out my phone.

I scroll through my Instagram, immediately deleting and blocking Lindsay. I can't undo the damage, but I can stop it from perpetuating. I'm not a monk, but Zack and Cullen are right. I barely date. And this mess is exactly why.

Well, okay. It's part of the reason. The rest is far more complicated.

I skim through the row of pictures, barely taking them in. They aren't who I'm looking for, until—there's the one.

It's an anonymous shot. In the foreground, a plastic cup of cherries in some sort of mixed drink. In the background, a jukebox. Underneath, it reads, *Cherry, cherry, chick-a-cherry Cola-*chef kiss*-BTM #sundayafternoon #damntheman #behindthemusicblog*

My fingers hover in reply for a full minute. I almost respond at least twice a day. But responding on Insta would require me to open a whole new anonymous account, and that would be akin to admitting I'm lurking.

Which is why I don't follow her private account, only her blog one. It's a privilege I haven't earned.

Instead, I scroll Twitter and answer a few podcast questions until Zack returns, shaking out his sandy hair like a wet puppy. A six-foot-three point guard of a puppy.

"What act?" I ask, not willing to drop the previous conversation.

He sighs, long suffering, and plops the steaming cardboard cup in the center console. I see Cullen's name scratched in black Sharpie, followed by *nonfat / no whip* marked under preferences, and a knowing smile crosses my lips. We're barely three months apart, but when it comes to relationship stuff, Zack acts a decade older. Like his relationship with my brother ages him in golden retriever years.

"Look," he says, "you're going to be late. It's not a big deal. I happen to be very impressed by your artsy side. It's gonna make you millions one day. But you do realize not everyone knows who Adam Duritz is? And that's not a bad thing."

"I never said it was," I protest.

He glares.

"*You* know who he is," I hedge, petulant.

"Because you've beat me over the head with his lyrics since the first day we sat together at lunch. At the time, I thought it was super weird. Still do. Endearing," he clarifies, "but weird. My point is, maybe tone that down around girls."

I wouldn't need to for her, I think but don't say. He smirks.

"Or," he adds. "Stop playing around with girls who don't know who Adam Duritz is and"—he turns his gaze meaningfully toward the club—"ask out the one who does."

"I don't mention Adam Duritz that much," I grumble. "I mean, yeah, he's talented as fuck, but—"

"Don't care. Get out." Zack shoos at the door. "Don't forget the latte."

I grab the drink, and my free hand finds the door handle, pushing it open. I grapple for my board, dropping it to the ground. "Thanks for the ride." I flip up my hood and hook my backpack over my shoulders while trying not to drop the drink.

"You're welcome, sweetums!" he shouts as I slam the door in his face and push off into the rain.

2

Is it *actually* murder if it's a coworker? Like, is there some kind of fine-print situation for that? Because I'm gonna kill Kazi. That hippie-dippy granola brain should be the one dealing with the drunk coeds pretending they know how to skank to the latest Interrupters song, but no. He had to pick up an extra shift at Whole Foods, and I'm stuck here on a Sunday night, cleaning something sticky off the perpetually sticky concrete floor.

"Oops! Shit! Vada, sorry!"

I stand, rolling my shoulder and glaring at one of the

regulars. But taking in his bloodshot eyes and loose grin, I decide it's pointless to gripe.

"No problem. I'm in the way." Technically.

He starts waving his arms in circles over his head like one of those garden pinwheels and kicks out his feet in a disjointed beat. "Come on, Vada! Dance with me, darlin'!"

"Not now, buddy!" I try to smile. Fucking Kazi. I sidestep the group of terrible skankers and dodge a few guys failing at making a mosh pit before ducking under a drink tray and sliding behind the bar. I slap the dingy gray rag full of germs and sour beer into a bucket of lukewarm bleach water and scrub my hands in the small employee sink.

"Vada, I thought you'd left!" Bearded Ben is my favorite bartender. He's a student at the University of Michigan and has wholly embraced the lumbersexual look. Like, he's shown me his facial wax collection, and it's ridiculous. Tonight, he's curled the edges of his mustache Captain Hook–style, and I'm having a hard time looking anywhere else.

I sidle up to him and start to fill a plastic cup with my usual snack of maraschino cherries. "I thought so, too," I say, tugging out the beverage gun and filling my cherry cup with lemonade. I prod it with a skinny straw and spear one of the cherries before popping it in my mouth.

"Kazi?"

I nod.

"Don't you have a dance or something tonight?"

I make a face around the fruit. "Dinner with Marcus."

"Ah," he says, deftly flicking the caps off two bottles and sliding them down the dinged-up bar toward a couple.

"No biggie. Just my future." Except my dad *did* show up today. Three hours ago. But not to discuss FAFSA forms. To drink and cause a ruckus. You know, typical Sunday-afternoon shenanigans. Poor Ben had the privilege of cutting him off. It went splendidly, thanks for asking.

Ben twists his mustache and takes a moment to reroll his flannel sleeves up his hairy forearms.

"Sorry," I say. "I made it awkward." He shakes his head, but I cut him off. "I did. It's okay. I was being dramatic. Marcus cares about two things," I explain, ticking my fingers. "Free booze and making Phil look bad." I drop my hands, shrugging. "My dream of college in California and I aren't even on his radar."

I know he wants to say something, but Ben's a trust fund kid. He works here purely for the aesthetic and because sometimes our boss, Phil, lets his bluegrass band play a set when we have last-minute cancels.

"That's bullshit, Vada, I'm sorry," he finally says before going to take another drink order. I feel my lips roll up, warmed by his cussing. It's like when my best friend, Meg, lets one slip. They both try so hard not to swear because of their personal beliefs, so when one of them does let a *fuck* out, it feels earned.

Still, I want to pout about my asshole dad for a little longer, so I do. I grab a fresh rag, wiping down some tables and scrubbing a little more vigorously than the lazy Sunday-afternoon crowd warrants.

The Loud Lizard is an institution. In the early '90s, Nirvana and Smashing Pumpkins played here. The bar sits at the midpoint of the dance floor, and there's a small raised stage at the front for bands. Along the sides and over the entrance sits a balcony that fits in a half circle facing the stage. It's VIP seating, but I like to call it the "old folks' lounge." It's where you go if you want to listen to live music but don't want to stand. I can't fathom it. I can't *not* move when music is playing.

Anyway, this is my happy place. Sticky, sour-smelling, loud, and crass. These weirdos are my people. We speak a common language of lyrics and chest-thumping beats.

And outdated, ska-music dancing.

I slouch against the ice chest, another rag discarded, eating a maraschino as Phil rounds the bar and closes the flapping door behind him. He runs a thick hand through his receding hair and slumps next to me, crossing his arms over his broad chest.

"I should have called the police on him last time."

I grunt, rolling my eyes, and take another stab with my straw. Phil's lips twitch under his whiskers at my sullen display. We've been through this before. I would've called the cops the first time Marcus showed up, reeking of Jim Beam and self-righteousness, and I certainly would have called them any number of times since. Phil's the hold-out. For all his grousing, he's too pure when it comes to my mom and her skeevy ex, a.k.a. Marcus, a.k.a. my dad. I suspect it's out of affection for my mom. They've been dating for over a year, but he claims he's been in love with her since high school. It's why I can't give him shit about being her *boyfriend*. That level of Captain Wentworth pining deserves a break. Besides, my mom's a catch.

"No one ever dates the drummer," he always says. Instead, my mom fell for the redheaded lead singer, got pregnant out of grad school, and is forever tied to a narcissistic insurance salesman with a fondness for free whiskey and making everyone around him as miserable as he is.

"You going to reschedule your dinner?"

I shrug. "I'm not sure it matters. He's not giving me money."

He straightens. "But you're going to ask him." The music blessedly changes as the band on deck cues up their set.

"Yes, Phil," I respond dryly. "I'm going to give him the chance to break my heart and ruin my dreams. He deserves that much."

He presses his lips together, and his eyes glint behind his frames. Phil's what would have happened if Kevin Smith hadn't made his fortune making cult slacker films. Thick, dark beard and smudged glasses, Red Wings jersey paired with faded jeans. He's as revered as this venue in the eyes of the locals. Phil has what's known in the music industry as a "knack." He can tell from one listen if a group is going to make it big.

He's my mentor and one of my favorite people. Some kids have an old soul. I have a middle-aged, overweight, receded-hairline soul.

"Where's Kazi?" he asks, wisely switching the subject.

I grunt again. "Running late. Called an hour ago to say Whole Paycheck was getting in a shipment and needed all hands on deck."

"And you offered to stay."

I sigh, tossing my cup in the garbage. "I couldn't leave Captain Hook on his own with the ruffians."

Phil huffs, eyeing the skankers like they're something stuck to the bottom of his Vans. "They aren't even doing it right."

I narrow my eyes, following his. "Is there a right way to do that?"

He snorts. "Just ask," he insists, back to Marcus. He's

lucky I speak fluent Phil and can follow along. "You have a plan B."

Yeah. Plan B. See, I have this plan. When I was sixteen, I begged Phil for a job. I couldn't work in the bar yet since it was illegal, so Phil let me hang around his office as an administrative assistant of sorts. I took over his music review blog, *Behind the Music,* and sometimes, we snuck me into shows on a strictly "journalistic basis." When I turned eighteen, the real work began. I still blog, but I also work the bar, so I'm here for the shows. Phil's teaching me everything he knows and lets me tag along to meetings if I'm not in class. Which, high school is pretty inconvenient, but whatever. Three months left. This summer, Phil is even allowing me to take over production of one of the shows during our annual concert series, Liberty Live.

All because my dream is music journalism. You know those reporters who follow musicians around on tour and get the inside scoop and create lists of the top artists of all time and whatever else? That's my passion. I was made for it. I've already been accepted into the music journalism program at UCLA, but I need more. Everyone in California was born into the industry. I need a leg up.

Phil and Liberty Live are my in. It would be easier if the sperm donor in my life would help with the loans, but I can't even get the guy to tip when he spends all afternoon with his worthless butt on one of our stools.

Phil's watching the dance floor with glassy eyes. It's been a long weekend, and by Sunday night, we're all tired.

"Go on. Me and Ben got this. I'll drop in before I head home." We both know I mean I'll wake him before I take off, since he's dead on his feet and has an old, cracked leather couch in his office begging him for a nap.

Phil yawns into his elbow and ruffles my hair. "If Kazi's not here in thirty minutes, let me know. I'll fire him. For real this time. And don't you be taking any more of his shit."

"I don't mind—"

His eyes narrow behind his glasses. "Uh-huh. Don't think I didn't notice how relieved you were to be needed here. I appreciate it, but you can't hide forever. Your mom is going to want to make sure you're okay after this afternoon."

Phil closes his office door behind him just as a door in the back opens, and a few beats later, Cullen Greenly saunters up, leaning in the spot Phil vacated.

"Greenly."

"Carsewell," he says.

"What's the topic tonight?" Cullen and his brother, Luke, rent Phil's sound booth to record their weekly podcast, *The Grass Is Greenly,* in return for advertising. It's a pretty good gig, in all honesty. The sound booth sits vacant the rest of the week, and the podcast has really caught on with college students in the last six months, bringing a younger crowd in for our shows.

"Remember the viral video of the kiss-cam couple at the Pistons game where the woman kissed the mascot instead?"

"Vaguely."

"That."

I grin. "You're gonna fill fifty minutes with that?" I can't say I've ever understood talk radio.

Cullen scratches nonexistent scruff. "Usually do. We'll layer in the rest with my brother's latest dating disaster and a bit of nonsense filler using our 'disgustingly hot British accents.'"

It's embarrassing, but he's not wrong.

My phone buzzes, and I leave Cullen to Ben, who's me-andered over to show off his new beard balm, probably.

MEG

$$$$$$$$$$$$$$$$$I know
you won't get this until after,
but I'm sending you good vibes
for the father-daughter talk
$$$$$$$$$$$$$$$

I inwardly groan. Speaking of too pure for this world. Meg would offer grace to Trump.

VADA

Save your vibes. It's off.

MEG

Oh, man, really? Tell me he didn't
forget! You've been planning this for
over a month.

VADA

More like he showed up three
hours early.

MEG
NO! Again?

VADA

Again.

MEG

Are you still at work?

VADA

For a bit. Waiting on Kazi's
sorry organic ass to show up.

MEG

I'll be at your place in thirty. New
epi of America's Funniest tonight.
Chinese or Mexican?

I grin. One of Meg's best qualities is how well she can read a situation. I don't need to rehash the shitty afternoon, and I don't feel like a hug. What I need is food and *AFV*.

VADA

Chelas. Extra hot sauce,
please.

MEG

You got it, babe.

I slip my phone back in my pocket, and the door opens again, causing my heart to flip-flop in my chest. Luke Greenly walks in, looking wet and harried and straight from my nerdiest daydreams, carrying his longboard under his arm and a cardboard coffee cup in his hand. Luke and Cullen aren't identical twins. Cullen is tall and wiry with dark hair. Luke's broad shouldered and fair with longish pale blond hair, currently plastered to his forehead despite the hoodie under his black leather jacket.

He's also got light gray-blue eyes behind bold black frames, contrasting his twin's un-spectacled dark brown ones. Yet somehow, when they're together, they *look* the same. They move in a similar way. And, yeah, their accents are yummy.

(I would never, ever admit it, but I play their podcast recordings before bed. Luke's voice is extra soothing. Deep, lyrical, and crisp.)

The owner of those golden vocals approaches, and I duck, prodding at my nearly empty cup in an effort to hide my flaming cheeks. The Loud Lizard is my territory, and I am cool and calm and not at all flustered by Luke Greenly. We've spoken exactly nine times since Christmas and I'm, regrettably, still nervous around him. Also, I'm still counting. So, that's . . . annoying.

"Hey-hey, Vada." Luke clears his throat.

"Thought we wouldn't see you tonight. Didn't you have plans?" Cullen asks.

"I did, yeah. But Kazi didn't show." Thank God Kazi is reliably unreliable. No need to mention my Marcus drama to the Greenly twins.

"Shocking," Cullen says drolly.

"Yeah, so I'm here. For a little longer anyway."

"Well," says Cullen, wrapping an arm around my shoulders. The music dies down as the band wraps up their set. Unless it's a special occasion, our live music usually ends early on Sundays, which is convenient for the Greenlys. The sound booth isn't exactly sound*proof* in this place. "D'you need a ride home?"

I shake my head and lean into him. "Nah, I brought my mom's car since I planned to meet my dad. Wanted a quick getaway." That part's true anyway.

Luke's full lips twist in a half grin, and he removes

his frames to give them a swipe on the dry edge of his hoodie.

I pull out the keys Phil left me and lead Luke and Cullen down a dark hallway, away from the noise of glasses clinking and instruments being loaded up. I unlock the sound booth and flick on a light.

"All yours, boys."

Cullen leans down and smacks a kiss on my cheek. "Thanks, doll."

I don't know the Greenly twins super well, but Cullen is definitely the outgoing one. He's also very, very gay. He's been with his boyfriend, Zack, for so long they won homecoming kings this past fall by a landslide. Maybe that's why I can talk to him so easily. Or maybe that's just Cullen. His superpower is making people comfortable.

But it's rare for me to see Luke without headphones or even hear his voice in person. I give him my best smile, but he only nods shyly as they pass. I inwardly sigh, all lust and longing and whatever else alliterative pining I can come up with. You know it's bad when *I'm* the social one. I wait for them to get hunkered down at the mics before I close the door with a soft click behind me.

Back on the floor, I fill another cup with cherries and settle in to people watch. We have the modern equivalent to a jukebox in the corner that can be fed off debit cards, and someone's clearly coming off a bad break because a second loop of Demi Lovato's "Sorry Not Sorry" has started. I skim the club for the culprit. My money's on the black-haired beauty with Cover Girl's Matte #5 stained on her one, two, *three* straws. "Get it, girl," I mumble under my breath. Demi is a perfectly respectable breakup diva. See also: Sam Smith and Ray LaMontagne.

The door flings open with a gust of icy air, and Kazi

appears in his pale, full-on dread-headed glory. I glance at my watch. Ohhhhh, he's late. Or, later. Phil's not gonna be happy.

I pass the keys to Kazi with a bored scowl. "You get to wake up Phil," I say. He winces, and I don't bother to hide my smile. "Also, he was expecting you half an hour ago, so."

Grabbing my jacket from behind the bar and feeling for my keys, I wave goodbye to Ben and head out into the night. My breath huffs out in front of me. I unlock my door with a beep and immediately lock it behind me, turning on the heater and heated seats full blast and letting the ringing in my ears from an afternoon spent in a noisy club dissipate.

But I don't like the silence. What I want is to walk back into the bar and perch on a stool and listen to breakup songs and banter with Cullen and let Phil preach at me. I want to help Ben pour drinks, cast dirty looks at Kazi, and wait for the moment Luke leaves and see if I can't earn one last shy smile from him. I want to stay here. I want to delay the moment when I have to face my hurt feelings—or worse, my mom's hurt feelings, because even after all this time, Marcus is still breaking two hearts with one drunken accusation.

After a minute, I release a slow breath and reluctantly pull my seat belt across my lap, backing out of my space to drive home. My real home, and not just the place that feels like it.

3

LUKE

"The moral of the story, dear listeners, is don't date your mail carrier's niece."

"Or nephew," I add into my mic, shifting forward in my chair as quietly as possible.

Cullen nods his dark head. "Cheers, Luke."

"I have regrets," I admit. "And to whoever is now getting my packages, I hope you enjoy season 3, part 1 *and* 2 of *Teen Wolf* on me." A lot went wrong with Lindsay and me, more than I would ever admit on our podcast. While I won't let Cullen mention Instagram-Gate, I do make *some* allowances for humor at my expense, and I'm all in over how Lindsay's aunt is our mail lady and my recent Best Buy packages have been coincidentally "lost."

"You could stream it like the rest of civilization," my brother suggests.

"That's hardly the issue."

"No." Cullen smiles, and it's all bright white teeth. "The issue is you need to not let government workers set you up with their family members."

"I'm too nice." I grimace.

"You're too nice," he agrees, gesturing wildly even though no one else can see it.

"Moving on," I say, switching gears before Cullen accidentally reveals too much for polite podcasting. "We're about out of time, and loyal listener Lola from Ypsi sent us her list of 'Marry, Kill, or Kiss.' To twist the knife in further, she offers Stiles, Derek, and Scott from . . . *wait for it* . . . MTV's *Teen Wolf*. Hilarious, Greenly."

"I thought it clever."

I roll my eyes. "Of course you did. Why don't you start this one off? I need to mull it over."

Cullen leans back in his chair. "Right. Well, so many good choices here. You know how I feel about Derek . . ."

"Not a secret." Cullen's many, many celebrity crushes are steady filler on our podcast even though he's been with Zack for more than three years.

"But I've had some time to think on it, and I'm gonna snog Stiles, marry Derek, and kill Scott."

"Wow, no respect for the True Alpha! I'm gonna say, kiss Scott, marry Stiles, kill Derek."

Cullen gasps theatrically, his hand on his chest as if I'd mortally wounded him. "Why would you kill my husband?"

"Jealousy?" I offer. "You know how self-conscious I am about my inability to grow stubble."

"I can respect that."

"All right, that's all we have for tonight. I'm gonna leave you with a little Twenty One Pilots to kick off your week. Thanks for joining me, Luke, and—"

"Me, Cullen."

"This has been *The Grass Is Greenly*." I switch out to play "Heavy Dirty Soul" over the top and tug off my headphones, raking through my hair.

Cullen taps around on his Mac screen. "And we're out. Not bad for a light news week."

"How long?"

"Fifty minutes, give or take. Should be plenty of material for the online version, including ads."

I roll back on my ancient, creaking chair and stand,

stretching my hands to the ceiling and cracking my neck to the right and left.

Cullen closes his Mac with a click and stuffs it away in his backpack. "You coming with me or . . . ?"

"Nah. If the rain's stopped, I can use the air." Cull's always teasing that my board is attached to my hip, but he doesn't now, and the look he's giving me? It's the same one I give him after he and Zack get into a fight. "It's nothing," I insist before he can start.

"I thought you didn't like Lindsay."

"I didn't. Not much anyway." I'm not lying. We barely went out. He lifts a single dark eyebrow.

"But?"

I tap my board against my hip, waiting him out. Thank Jesus Zack is loyal. The last thing I need is my brother meddling. "But nothing. I'll see you at home."

He glances at his phone and scowls. "Shite. Forgot Zack's coming over at eight."

I shake my head, smiling, and tease, "Please. You know he's not there to see you."

Zack and Cullen have been together since sophomore year, but we all know it's our dad, Charlie, he really loves. Or rather, his stories. Zack's a history nerd, and our dad was the lead singer of a pretty hyped punk rock bank called the Bad Apples in the late '80s and early '90s. Zack's the only one in the world who cares enough to listen to 1,001 litanies about his glory days "touring the countryside and sloshing through pints with my old pal Morrissey."

Shudder.

From the look on Cullen's face, his thoughts are mirroring mine.

"I'd better get back. Cut him off before he can really get rolling."

I take the long way home. It's cold, but the roads and walkways are mostly dry as I wind my way from the Loud Lizard to our cozy west-side neighborhood. Zack's Jeep is already in the drive, and all the lights are on. I push open the front door to a deceptively quiet house and prop my board against the back of a closet. My glasses immediately fog up at the temperature change, and I swipe them up on top of my head to deal with later. I could get contacts, but it feels like the cold freezes them to my eyeballs when I board. I've tried Lasik. It worked for about a minute, and a year ago, I was back in glasses because of my super-healing, super-broken eyes. I'm a medical wonder of devolution.

Shrugging off the rest of my things, I pile them by the door with all the various winter paraphernalia before heading to the kitchen where my mum is cleaning up after dinner. I walk over to the stove and pick up a slice of cold pizza off the stone and eat it while propped against the island.

"How'd the podcast go?"

I swallow and shrug. "Good. Cullen's got to work his magic, obviously, but we should have enough material."

My mum grins, scrubbing at the counter. Her blue-black hair is pulled back in a barrette, but loose strands fall in front of her eyes. She tucks them away, turning to me. "Cull filled me in on the *Teen Wolf* kiss, marry, kill. I'm with him. Derek all the way; he's scrumptious."

"Gross. He's at least twenty years younger than you are."

She gasps, feigning hurt, flicking me with her towel. "Take that back! He can't be more than fifteen years younger, tops. He's got that beard!"

"And now we see where Cullen gets his taste."

She resumes her scrubbing with a wink from behind her thin wire frames. "Well, he certainly didn't get it from his father, or Zachary would be out of luck."

My brother is the hashtag *pride* and joy of the family. Not that I mind. Could have been utter shite. Can be, even at school and stuff. But with a beatnik former British punk rocker for a dad and liberal studies professor for a mum . . . let's just say we wear our rainbows face-out in this family, and Zack's upgrade from best friend to best friend *and* boyfriend of their children was welcomed with wide open arms.

It's a tangled web we weave at the Greenly house, and all threads lead to Zack. The only one not impressed with him is our cat, and that's because she only tolerates humans on principle.

I grab another two slices of pizza, one for each hand, and head for the door to the basement. "Everyone downstairs?"

"Yeah."

I hesitate at the top of the basement stairs. It's not that I don't love hanging with Cullen and Zack . . . it's fine, but . . . *together*, they can be a lot. Usually, Zack's like me, quieter and pretty nerdy when it comes to music and the internet and the BBC Sherlock Holmes fandom. But I would be lying if I said things didn't change after Cullen and Zack started throwing around the L-word and losing their collective virginities.

They've officially crossed over into something decidedly

apart from me. I'm thrilled for them but also completely left behind.

Like, the two people in the world who know everything there is to know about me love each other, and I can't be sure at any given moment they aren't discussing me. I've gone from one meddling brother to two.

I'm still hovering, undecided, when my dad pops his bleached-blond head around the wall. My dad's pushing fifty, but like Paul Rudd, you can't really tell. He can't either, to be honest. He still wears enough metal in his ears to set off the detector in the airport, and I come by my preference for leather jackets honestly. In the right light, you could almost imagine my dad onstage cussing out the patriarchy. You could just as easily see him carving a coffee table out of a single piece of driftwood. He's a versatile fella in his early retirement.

"Oy! You coming down?"

"You watching *The Eighties* on CNN again?" I counter. Because of course he is.

"Fine, fine. I left my ale on the counter. Be a lad and toss it down?"

Mum points to the unopened bottle on the island. I exchange my slices for the beer, and, staring my dad right in the eye, I shake it once aggressively before throwing it down.

"Ungrateful lad, pain in my arse," he complains after deftly catching the bottle in midair.

"I learned from the best!" I close the door behind me and turn to my snickering mum.

"Oh, he's gonna make you pay for that one."

"Probably," I admit, feeling tired. My family is a lot.

I head up to my bedroom, closing the door behind me

before plopping on my bed and opening my laptop while taking a bite of pizza. My clock shows it's nearly ten. I've waited long enough. It's been up for at least an hour, so I won't look like a completely overeager idiot. Probably.

Behind the Music

By Vada Carsewell

I didn't choose the thug life; the thug life chose me. Well, okay, probably not. I'm a white girl from nowhere Michigan. But on Friday night, LBJayz struck hard and fast, and whatever they're selling, I'm buying. Forever. Front man Carlos "El Burro" Dominguez oozes star power, and his vocals burned in only the best possible way. "Fat Chopper" spins a dizzying backbeat that somehow manages to be both the good kind of fuck-you and the sensual awakening we all need.

Am I making sense? I don't even know, man. I'm a purist, born and raised on vitamin D milk and Pink Floyd, but I feel a conversion coming . . .

My eyes drink in her words, and I'm grinning ear to ear. She's incredible. I've been reading Vada's *Behind the Music* blog religiously for two years, and it sounds just like her. It's biting and real and brilliant. I don't think many people realize she's only eighteen. I've seen her blog referenced by top reviewers in the music industry. Of course, no one wants to give her or Phil credit; they're out of a little college town dive bar. But they definitely have *something*. I always retweet her article like a fanboy, but she probably thinks it's Cullen. I'm too self-conscious to tell her what a fan I am. At least publicly.

L8RSK8R comments:

Well, milk does a body good . . . No.

Pink Floyd, eh? I think my dad once played . . . God.

What's the best kind of fuck you could imagine? Pathetic, Greenly.

Great review. You've convinced me!

I groan, shutting my laptop, and check my watch. I could go downstairs. Chances are good Zack's still around. Instead, I move to my keyboard in the corner of the room and carefully plug in my headphones. No point in letting anyone else know I'm tooling around on this thing.

Or that I've *been* tooling around on it for two years. Or three. Give or take.

Ever since the Great Greenly Showdown of 2017, as far as anyone knows, I don't play. I don't sing. I don't write. I don't so much as fiddle around on the keys. The beautiful Steinway my parents bought me when I was eight sits out of tune in the front room, covered in a generous layer of time. I will go out of my way to cut through the dining room to avoid seeing it. It hurts deep down in my soul to see it dusty.

As long as I live under my parents' roof, and under the eye of my former music producer dad, that's how things have to be. Me, playing my cheap Casio-knockoff keyboard in my room, whisper-humming under my breath behind a locked door.

I've unlocked my door to my mum holding my laundry and studying me suspiciously on more than one occasion, but I'm pretty sure she thinks I'm watching porn.

Her knowing the truth would be worse.

If they got wind of me playing again, it would mean lessons and YouTube channels and flying into London to meet with a "friend" of my dad's. It would mean Lasik surgery. Again. And personal training and kale diets and expensive haircuts. It would be months away from my mum because her job won't let her travel. It would be forgoing college altogether.

It would mean singing someone else's songs.

Because even if they say you can write your own stuff, they don't mean it. They want you to sing whatever radio-friendly pop music they push in-house, and after you've been sucked dry and become too much of a liability, only then will they release you to write your own lyrics with an indie label for a tenth of the money.

Not that money matters. It's all of it. I don't need it. I like writing music. I like singing the songs I write. But I also like being me. Just me. Not "son of former punk rock icon Charlie Greenly." Not "Luke Greenly, Performer."

Just Luke.

Except, I can't stop.

I play a soft melody that's been dancing around in my consciousness. It's been there for a while. Slowly easing its way to the surface. I'm not ready to let it take over yet, though. I suspect it's going to carry me someplace I shouldn't go.

Soon, though.

Maybe.

4

VADA

High school is not my favorite. More like, it's item number one on my Things I Have to Do Before I Start the Rest of My Life list, except it takes four long years to accomplish. I've had a raging case of senioritis for the last three. I did get to drop Spanish after convincing my guidance counselor that, one, I have no need for the language credit, and two, my sad attempt at a C is bringing down my entire average. In lieu of Español, I chose dance and body movement.

I know, I know, the grungy bartender girl likes to dance? It's weird. But you know how some people feel music in their minds or hearts or whatever? They play an instrument or sing, or they write. Well, I've always felt music in my blood. It *moves* me. As a little girl, I studied ballet and lyrical, but I grew out of the pink tights and black leotards. I didn't love performing to someone else's song choice, and I never cared for the rigidity of repetitive barre exercises for hours and hours. I needed to *feel* the melody. My toes twitched, and my abs would contract without my permission. I couldn't wait for the moment my teacher would allow us to dance our own interpretations of the music.

I'd been eyeing this class for a while. It never fit in my schedule, but I was also afraid it might suck. Or, worse, *I* might suck. Because while I love to dance, I'm not prima ballerina material. But there is a certain freedom that comes with the last semester of your senior year. I can comfortably say *fuck all* to self-consciousness. Who cares if I look ridiculous? Next fall, I won't even know these people. I barely know them now.

There are three separate high schools in this town, and each one is ginormous. Mine alone houses thousands of students, built around a courtyard easily the size of a football field. After sophomore year, I stopped seeing a lot of my classmates. Our classes were held in opposite wings, we parked in different lots, and I'm not an athlete, so I never grew close to a team.

It sounds lonelier than it is. But I'd rather lose myself in a sea of strangers than find myself one-on-one with an acquaintance. One-on-one requires a level of commitment I'm not sure I'm capable of. It took Meg an entire year to crack my shell. Of course, now she can't get rid of me.

I've been attending Madame Marcel's body movement class since January, and I'm in heaven *most* of the time. But I can handle the eight counts she instructs us to follow for the first half of the period if it gets me to improvised movement, or IM, the second half.

"Before we move on to IM," she says, huffing slightly, a flush to her cheeks, "I want to talk to you about the end-of-the-year spring showcase." She motions with a grace borne out of decades of practice, and we all sit around her turned-out feet in silence. I stretch out my legs, wrapping my fingers along the inner arch of my foot and pressing my torso against my knee. This isn't the first we've heard of the showcase.

"I know it seems like there's plenty of time, but let me assure you," she continues, pinning us with her gaze, "it is the highlight of the performing arts department's year.

There are choral and band performers who have been working *years* toward this night. So, I ask that you be diligent and take this seriously, even if you do not plan to dance professionally after high school."

I switch legs. While I don't plan to make a career of dancing, I take this seriously. I've been considering music for weeks. I need the perfect song.

"Our senior composers have been given an assignment to observe the dancers and write something inspired by the body's movement. This year, I've requested they take it a step further. We'd like the movement and the composition students to collaborate. You will act as muses to their creations. Therefore, the composition students will be attending today's class to observe you. They will be given the opportunity, if inspired, to choose a dancer to partner with. Together, you will create a piece that speaks to both of you."

I straighten, not bothering to hide my grimace.

"If a match isn't in the cards, that's okay. Creativity is best not forced. If you aren't chosen, or if you are but don't feel comfortable collaborating, just say the word and you are welcome to proceed with your own performance piece. But we are hoping you will all reach outside your comfort zones and give collaboration a try."

No, thanks. I'm happy to take the out that's offered. Not to say anyone would want to work with me, but if they did, I can't even imagine a scenario in which I'd want to collaborate. I'm far too particular about my music. My shoulders sink comfortably back to their rightful place. No reason to get all hyped up over a "suggested assignment."

"Our piano composition director, Mr. Leonard, will be stopping in with his class sometime in the next thirty minutes, and we will see if we can make this senior show-case the best yet!"

Puh.

I stretch my arms over my head, impatient to move on to improvisation. Madame Marcel claps her hands, jar-ring us up to standing, and we make our way to the cor-ner of the spacious, mirrored room. "I want to start with some across-the-floor movement. Wherever the music takes you, dear ones."

I shake my hands at my sides, rocking my neck back and forth and closing my eyes. Despite the unwelcome collaboration news, this is my favorite part of my day. I've been looking forward to this ever since underperforming on the pop quiz in AP bio second period. I'm not here for the spring showcase. I'm here for the daily release. Roll-ing my shoulders, I imagine the tension sloughing off my back, shimmering to the ground, and slipping across the polished wood-planked floor and out the fucking door.

Behind me, I feel a rush of air and the low murmur of movement. I'm sure it's the composer kids, but I refuse to open my eyes. Let *them* be the awkward ones. This is my home court, and I claim the advantage.

The room falls silent, and I can imagine them settling in cross-legged against the mirrors facing us. My hands fidget, tugging at the fitted tank and yoga pants uniform we all wear for class. Baggy attire is forbidden. Madame likes to see exactly the way our bodies are bending and make corrections when necessary.

My eyes have stopped spasming in protest to open. But the first piano chords of Madame's playlist are starting up, and I need to be able to see so I don't hurt anyone. I open my eyes but refuse to look at the seated observers.

Madame's preferred dance posture of raised chin and lowered shoulders is convenient. I manage to look practiced and graceful rather than nervous.

Jet's "Look What You've Done" plays. It's a trudging march of a song. The cadence swings in a low militaristic drumbeat and swirls along the constant piano. I hardly notice the vocals, already lost to the rhythm.

It's my turn, and I let the cool detachment of the last verse push through my veins and pump into my fingertips. I drag my pointed toes along the floor, reluctant, while my limbs stretch to the four corners, spinning my body across the length of the room. As I near the end, I extend one leg in a flourish, stepping out of my turn abruptly.

By the next pass, one of my favorite bands is playing, and it's far more difficult to ignore the lyrics. Sleeping At Last's "Earth," and we're given over to our bodies.

"To the floor, dancers!" Madame calls. "Free movement."

It's all the instruction I need. I find my usual shaded corner in the back of the room, where the mirrors are too crowded to decipher and the sun streams in through the windows. I'm greeted by my shadow, and that's where my eyes are drawn.

Hello, old friend.

Instantly, the world is forgotten, and all I know is the way the beams of light crisscross my outstretched limbs.

My fingers twine with stardust, filtering the point where light and darkness kiss, and I turn underneath on the balls of my feet, springing to a plié in second position, my knees bent over my toes, my thighs dipping so deeply my palms trace the floor. I swing them up wildly as the tempo picks up for the crescendo of the song. Lunging to the side, my fingers grasp the sunshine once more, and my shadow scrambles to keep up as I spin, shaking off my melancholy.

My dad and his hurtful acts can't find me here. Worries about my future, about college and plan B and my mom and Phil and and and . . .

I am ready, I am over, I am untouchable and gracelessly graceful.

I am un-hurtable here.

As I twirl and stretch and drag and tumble in my small corner, my thoughts dissipate and dissolve. It's the part I love best—when I become the music and nothing else.

The song ends, and a switch is flicked off in my soul. When I'm finally cognizant of the glare of halogen lighting, I see my sunbeams have been swallowed by gray clouds. My classmates are gathering up their things, and the composers, if they were ever really there, are gone.

I find my small pile of belongings and cross to the doorway that swings into the ladies' locker room.

"Miss Carsewell!"

I stop at the door and spin to face Madame. She is waving a torn piece of lined notebook paper in the air. I gulp. I had assumed I wouldn't be chosen. I'm steeling myself to turn down whoever it is when she places the slip into my hands.

In a bold slash of black ink, spelled in capital letters, reads my name followed by another. I swallow.

Luke Greenly.

Luke was here? My Luke? Well, not *my* Luke, obviously. But the Luke I know? He saw me? Oh my god, he *saw* me. Holy hell, he saw me spazzing across the floor in my spandex and he picked me? He wants to write a song with me?

My knees bend, but I catch myself, stepping one foot back and steadying my grip on the paper. Madame waits for my answer. I was so ready to say no, but . . .

I hadn't counted on *Luke Greenly*. I had no idea he was in the senior composition class. This shouldn't change things. I barely know him. I'm still too picky about my music, and I'm still only here for my own therapy. I shouldn't say yes. I need to stick with my plan.

My mouth spits out a "Yes!" before I can register it. "Yeah. I'll do it."

Madame's face lights up. "Excellent! I'll let Mr. Leonard know. Do you know this student, or would you like me to get his contact information for you?"

"No! I mean—" I shake my head, trying to get my words and brain to match up. "I mean, *yes*. I know him. I'll work it out. Thanks."

5

LUKE

I never should've signed up for that senior composition class.

6

VADA

Dance is the last period of the day, so even though I hear the end-of-day bell ring out and the girls' softball team starts to arrive, I take my time in the locker room. I run a slow brush through my hair, detangling it completely, and with it, my nerves about Luke's request. I reapply my ChapStick and spritz on some fruity body spray. I don't have to be at work for another hour, but there's no point in stopping home to an empty house. After repacking my bag and zipping my puffy winter coat, I deposit a few singles into the vending machine near the entrance, and when my favorite purple Gatorade loudly fumbles down, I grab it, cracking the cap and gulping half down in one go.

I'm feeling more myself as I exit the building but am quickly thrown again by the sight of Luke—*my new partner, Luke!*—leaning against the outer wall, his ever-present longboard propped against his leg. He's got earbuds in, and his head bobs along with some unnamed music.

I can't help myself. I'm already reaching for his earbud when he registers my presence. You can tell a lot about someone by what they listen to when no one is watching.

Twenty One Pilots' mellow and painful "Car Radio." Huh.

"Huh," I say aloud. Because I'm relentlessly clever like that.

"Tyler Joseph is a brilliant lyricist," is all he says. Equally clever.

The song picks up, and in the tiny speaker, I hear the electronic backbeat kick in as Tyler's voice screams his sadness over and over. It's a strangely relatable song. Someone mourning the loss of their car radio because now they are forced to face their silent demons head-on whenever they're in their car.

Luke's quiet, his hand tapping the board at his thigh. His mouth opens and closes without saying anything.

"I sometimes wonder if radios and headphones represent the downfall of emotional health," I say because I am awkward and decidedly nervous about being alone with Luke. "Like, if I don't want to face something, which is pretty much always, I just"—I motion to the little toggle on the wire connecting the earbuds—"turn it up. So loud I can't hear myself think."

He nods, wavy blond wisps falling across his black frames. He tucks them behind his ear, but they only slip back out. "Ah."

My words tumble over one another, to fill the silence. "Of course, sometimes I don't know what I really feel until I hear it sung. Have you ever heard that Flora Cash song? 'You're Somebody Else'? Like, obviously they aren't singing about me. They've never met me. But it *feels* like they're talking about me. I can pretend they are anyway, and before I know it, I'm crying into my Gatorade"—I wave the bottle in my hand—"and questioning my self-image."

He blinks, no doubt overwhelmed by my verbal essay, but recovers, clearing his throat.

"I have heard it, actually. That line about seeing someone in a way they won't until they are older, right?"

"Hm?" Now I'm the one struck dumb.

He shakes his head, his long fingers tapping. "At least . . . that's the part that . . . erm . . . struck me."

My mind catches up, and my stomach unclenches a little. "Yeah. It's like everything you would hope for—" I almost say *in love* but cut off in time. It's not like I know anything about *that* anyway, with my zero boyfriends.

He shoves at his lenses with his long fingers and tucks his free hand back into his pocket, and I realize I'm still holding his earbud, music beating out a tinny rhythm between us.

I hold it out and he takes it, rolling it up carefully and stowing it away in his pocket.

"They're my mum's," he explains, changing the subject, *thank God.* "I lost my wireless ones somewhere on Fourth Street."

"Hazard of boarding, I imagine."

He glances down at the longboard at his hip. It's covered in rainbow stickers in growing obnoxiousness. The one on top is a giant unicorn with rainbows shining out of its butt. His cheeks turn red, and he drops the board with a clatter and clears his throat.

"Ah, that's Cullen. His idea of a joke. Not that it's a joke. I mean, I fully support . . . obviously. It's just . . . well, the unicorns are a bit . . . erm . . . over the top. One night while I was sleeping, Cullen snuck into my bedroom and covered it in rainbow stickers."

"Naturally."

"It's fine. I mean, I don't love the unicorn arse, and just now, seeing it through your eyes, it's a bit humiliating but—"

"I love it."

He winces. "Really?"

"Really," I say, charmed by this kid who is so self-unaware. I clear my throat, remembering I need to get to work soon. "So, you want to collaborate?"

"Yeah." He peers out through his frames, his cheeks still splotchy, and I wonder if I make him nervous. It's probably just the cold. "Is that okay?"

It is now. "Oh, sure," I say, trying to play it cool.

His face visibly relaxes, and it's fascinating. "Brilliant."

"I don't really know how to go about this," I start. "I've never collaborated before, and I don't really dance."

"I thought you moved marvelously," he says, and I feel *my* face burn despite the icy wind funneling around the corner of the building.

"Thanks."

He cringes, and this time *he's* the one babbling. "I meant that in a completely not creepy way. I just . . . You seem to really feel the music, and that's how I tend to write, so I thought we might be a good match. But I totally get it if you prefer to work solo. You probably already have a song picked out. You're like this musical savant, and I'm still learning, but I'd like to try." He seems relieved as he finishes, even capping it off with a little affirmative nod as if congratulating himself. Smooth, we are not.

"I'm willing to give it a shot if you are. When do you want to meet?"

His face is alight with relief, and I bite back a wistful sigh. "Sunday, before you work?" he suggests. "We could meet at the library. Or the mall. Someplace we can listen to music together."

"How about the club? I have keys. Phil won't mind me coming in early. That way, we'll have a quiet space to work."

"What time?"

"One thirty?"

"Perfect."

"Speaking of work," I say, regretful *and* grateful I need to leave, "I have to go. But I'll see you then?"

He beams, nudging his frames so I'm gifted a clear shot of his gray-blue eyes. "See you then."

It's not a date or anything, this arrangement Luke and I have to meet up at the Loud Lizard. Alone. Or whatever. But it feels strangely loaded. Not as loaded as it might if we met at one of our houses, but I still feel the need to show up fifteen minutes early and, like, clean or something. Which is ridiculous because the club is covered in decades of grime that, according to Phil, speaks to the character of the place.

I peel open the blinds that face the back of the building to allow light in and turn on the real lights, the ones we rarely use since no one wants a brightly lit bar. If you want to see your date in halogen lighting, Phil says, take them to Walmart. We don't do that shit here. We're in the business of dark corners.

When I ask him in my cheekiest tone what happens in dark corners, he likes to ruffle my hair and tells me to ask my mom.

I glance at my phone. Twelve minutes. I jump behind the bar and pull a couple of glasses out of the dishwasher, placing them on a rubber mat, faceup. I dig around in the fridge and remove the cling wrap from a container of cherries left over from last night, still marinating in their pink maraschino juice, and scoop out a generous handful. I dump them in my cup before filling it with lemonade and dropping in a decorative sword.

Ten minutes.

I wish I knew what Luke likes. I could have it ready for him. Maybe I can guess based on what I know, though it's admittedly not much. Punk-rock dad and composition class and gay twin brother. That feels a lot like things I know *around* him and not *about* him.

"Car Radio" song, though, I think, *and Flora Cash.* That alone tells me so much. I fill a glass with ice and water and throw in a lemon slice before moving to the modernized jukebox in the corner. I plug it in and tap around the screen looking for something in particular. As the front door opens, sending a miniature cold front into the air, I hit Play on Oasis's "Wonderwall." An oldie, but I think any respectable Brit would recognize the gesture.

Luke doesn't disappoint. His face lights up, and he bobs his head a little. He clears his throat. "There are two kinds of Brits: team Noel and everyone who's wrong."

I blush. "When I was younger, I had a crush on Liam."

He raises his pale brows.

"It's not my fault! My mom was a massive fan. She poisoned my mind against Noel and his unibrow."

He shakes his head, pretending to reconsider coming in, and I choke out a giggle. It's unsettling; I haven't giggled in a decade. He sits down at the bar in front of the water, pulling out a notebook and pen.

"Wow, are you really going to compose in front of me?"

"Definitely not. I've never done this with someone else. Actually, if you could not tell Cullen about this, that would be great. My family doesn't exactly know I'm still writing music."

That gives me pause. I sit down next to him, pulling my cup of cherries close.

"Still?"

He busies himself with his notebook, flipping pages until he finds a clean one. "Yeah. It's . . . complicated. My dad would love nothing more than for me to follow in his footsteps, and I would love nothing less."

"Not a fan of punk music?"

He pulls a face. "Not exactly. I like some. My dad was brilliant. I'm just not one for putting something out there for the world to judge."

"A purist?"

"Something like that." He grimaces. "That makes me sound stuck-up. I don't mean that, necessarily. It's like, all of a sudden, something you've worked so hard on becomes cheap. It turns into a judgment of *you* rather than the words. You had a crush on Liam Gallagher, for example. Was it his songwriting or his vocals or—"

"Definitely thought he was cute," I say.

"Right," he says, uncomfortable. "Look, I sound like a prick. I know that. I used to sing. Like at family parties and stuff. My dad would set me up on the piano in the backyard, and it was like this source of pride for him. He has loads of contacts in the industry, and they were all ready to sign me and put me in front of a camera. Then they start talking about how I needed to get contacts and could my jeans be a little more expensive and have I ever thought about a gym membership and have they taken me to a dermatologist for that acne and feeding me pop songs that were already written and I couldn't bear it."

"They wanted to make you a star."

He nods sheepishly.

I think on that. How it might have felt. To be tinkering around on your piano just for you. Feeling proud of something you've created only to have it spoiled.

"And you don't want to be a star," I clarify.

His small smile is grim. "Not at all."

Huh. Definitely not what I'd expected. It's clear to anyone who meets the Greenlys that Luke is quieter than Cullen, but I'd always assumed it was relative. "Can I ask why? Stage fright? Too shy?"

He doodles in the corner of a page. "Not really. It's not that I'm afraid to play or even that I don't like people. I just want to write songs. I happen to be a good singer, but I love to write the music. I don't need the rest."

"You're right," I say, with a teasing grin. "That does make you sound like a prick."

He grimaces again. "Exactly."

I'm still smiling, though, and I meet his eyes, willing him to feel my lack of censure. After a long moment of him fiddling with his notebook, I realize perhaps I suck at body language. I clear my throat, feigning boldness. "I understand, though. The heart wants what it wants and all."

He shrugs, sipping his lemon water, not bothering with a straw.

I try again. "I used to dance classically," I say. "And I wasn't terrible. When I was around twelve, I was offered the chance to audition for a high-stakes academy in Detroit. But I walked."

I trace the side of my cup, making squiggles in the condensation. "My dad threw a fit. I think he was hoping for scholarships or whatever. But"—I lift a shoulder—"I didn't want it. Moving to someone else's choreography, performing their vision, it wasn't my thing."

I raise my eyes to meet his, and he's smiling. The kind of smile where you don't even realize you're doing it. I feel my lips pulling to match, and I look away, feeling warm.

"So, back to the present, Mr. Purist. Are you sure you're okay writing for the showcase? You do realize this requires a performance on your part."

"Technically," he points out, "this requires a performance on your part. And yes. I knew about the showcase going into the semester, but my need for instruction won out over my misgivings. He continues lightly, "Besides, no one in my family knows I'm in the class."

"Same," I admit. "So, that works out."

His white-blond brows scrunch together behind his frames. "No one knows you're dancing again?"

It's my turn to feel on the spot. "Nah. I don't want to give anyone ideas. Now it's just this creative outlet for me. It's like, um, therapeutic. At any rate, that I need an outlet will make my mom feel guilty and sad. I'd rather avoid that."

"Is this the dad thing?"

I clear my throat, stabbing at a cherry and not meeting his eyes. "Probably."

He presses his lips together, understanding my "probably" to be a "definitely." I hear a car door slamming outside and glance at my phone. "Damn, it's already two."

Luke looks surprised but doesn't move from his chair. He closes his nearly blank notebook, and I apologize for the lack of productivity.

He shakes his head. "Not at all. This is exactly what we needed. If we're going to work together, we need to know what makes each other tick."

"Daddy problems?" I ask, feigning lightness.

His lips quirk in a half grin. "Among other things. It

seems we both have our secrets, and I'm honored to be in on one of yours, Vada."

That's a really sweet thing to say, and suddenly I find myself surprised at how not awkward this has been. "Ditto, Greenly. Should we do this again?"

"I have a better idea," he says, looking sly. "What are your thoughts on over-the-top weird art installations that require audience participation?"

Forget it. Awkward quotient just multiplied. "You mean like a flash mob?"

Another half grin topped off with rosy cheeks and eyes that hold a hint of a dare. He's clearly recovered from his initial hesitation. The back door opens, and Kazi comes in with the cold, holding a case of fruit from the outside freezer. I don't get up.

"Sort of, but less showy. Ever hear of a silent disco?"

"I've heard of a mobile concert. There's a park in Detroit that would put one on every year. You wear headphones and stuff?"

Luke nods. "No one would be watching us, because they'd all be in their own worlds."

"You want me to dance with a bunch of strangers? In a silent rave? In public?"

He grins, tapping his fingers. "Sort of. It's too cold for parks. There's a concert Tuesday night at the Filmore, but it's experimental. Everyone is being issued headphones at the door, and you get to play deejay. But the effect is out of this world. I went to one back in London. It's about as intimate a setting as you can get. And yeah, you have to dance, but no one is really watching. Well, I might watch. A little. But you could watch me, too. Fair is fair."

This could either be the coolest thing ever or super

awkward and weird. Luke must read this on my face because he backpedals.

"Yeah. Okay. It's stupid, and now you think I'm super weird. Which, admittedly, I am—"

I cut him off. "Hold on. Yes," I admit, "it's an unusual idea. But I'm also a little embarrassed I've never tried anything like it before. I mean, for all my bluster, if I can't hang with an experimental concert, who am I even?"

"Really?"

"I think so?" I straighten. "No, I *know* so. Yes. Count me in. Before I can change my mind," I finish with a nervous laugh.

His entire face lights up. "That's brilliant. I'll see if I can borrow Cullen's car and pick you up at 5:00? The show starts at 6:00, and maybe after we can get a bite to eat. I have an 11:00 p.m. curfew on school nights."

"Same," I say. "If you can't drive, I can ask my mom for her car."

He shakes his head. "No way. This is all on me." He starts gathering up his things as more people start arriving for the afternoon shift, including Phil, who definitely notices who I'm sitting with, and it's just as well since I need to intervene before Kazi cuts all the limes into fancy shapes again. Ain't no one got time for that sort of high-class fruffery.

I scrawl my number on a napkin. "Here," I say, passing it over. "Text me yours. That way we can make arrangements."

He takes the napkin and folds it carefully before tucking it into his jeans pocket. "Excellent." He flings his backpack over both shoulders and picks up his board at the door. "I'll talk to you soon, Vada."

"Bye, Luke."

I feel eyes on me as I watch Luke walk out the front door, and I busy myself with cleaning up our cups.

"What?" I bite out after a minute.

"Not a thing," Phil says mildly. "Not a single thing."

Later that night, I'm at Meg's. My mom was cooking dinner for Phil, and while they didn't explicitly tell me to make other plans, my mom's recently jumped on the Whole 30 bandwagon. Phil might have to put up with no cheese, grains, or sugar out of love and adoration, but I sure as heck don't.

"So, Vada, Megan tells us you got into UCLA? That's ambitious. I bet Mary's already crying over you moving across the country," Mrs. Hennessey says. I swallow my alfredo. Everyone calls my mom *Mary,* and I can't bring myself to call the Hennesseys anything other than *Mr. and Mrs. Hennessey.* They just feel like a Mr. and Mrs. kind of family.

"If she is, I don't hear it," I reply, keeping my tone light. "I'm sure she'll be sad—it's always been the two of us—but she's really excited for me." This is my staple response, and I've gotten good at it. Reviews are a mixed bag when it comes to my college choice. Marcus is against anything that's not free, Grandma Connie sniffs and wonders aloud why I need a career, and most everyone else acts like I am purposely trying to rip out my mom's heart.

The only one not against my choice is my mom, who is maybe a little wistful but extremely supportive and enthusiastic. I think Phil helps in that he's not going anywhere and is certain of my impending success. But also, my mom is just a stellar human being. Seriously the best.

"Mom, I told you, Vada's got California in her blood. She's going to rock their world out there." Meg's eyes meet mine, and we share conspiratorial grins.

She's all in, too. Meg's a year younger than I am, but in homeschool years, she graduated over the holidays. She hasn't told her parents yet, but she fully intends to join me out west; she wants to do a gap year.

Meg is . . . well . . . exactly the kind of kid who takes a gap year. She's tiny and effervescent. Her hair is multicolored, her nails are glitter, and she accessorizes with fairy wings. She teaches Sunday school, sings in the youth group worship band, and is a former competitive figure skating junior champion.

And somehow, she picked me to be her best friend. I have no idea why. I'm like the Grumpy Cat to her Hello Kitty.

"Still, we mother hens like our chicks close to the nest."

Meg shovels more food in her mouth, and I follow her lead, tearing a big piece off some extra buttery garlic bread. Poor Phil. Maybe I can smuggle some home for him.

"That's true," I say finally. I've learned it's best to not disagree with Meg's mom. She had Meg super young and has basically made raising her daughter her life's work. It's admirable, and she's done a bang-up job; Meg's delightful, obviously. But I sometimes wonder if now that Meg is grown, it's backfired on her. Like, what will she do when Meg moves away?

Of course she doesn't *know* Meg wants to move away,

so there's that. Instead, she gets to project her fears onto me and *my* mom, and Meg gets to watch. Which I bet freaks the hell out of my best friend.

I'd hide behind my fairy wings, too.

"Done?" Meg asks, and I'm already on my feet, even though I'm not sure where we're going. She turns to her mom. "Vada and I have to run." She flutters over to kiss her parents on the cheek, and her dad looks up from where he's been immersed in his reading on his tablet, surprised. Surprised dinner is over? Surprised to see us here? Who knows. In my fourteen years of friendship with Meg, I can count on one hand the number of times I've heard her dad speak.

"Thanks for dinner, Mr. and Mrs. Hennessy!" I say as Meg tugs me by the arm. We pull on our coats and are out the door.

I let her into my car and turn on the heat, giving it a chance to warm up. I turn to her, my expression amused. "And where are we running to?"

Meg rolls her eyes, the sunset catching the glitter on her lids, making her look like something out of a Tolkien novel.

"I needed out. Sorry."

I sink back into my seat. "Haven't told them yet?"

"I can't!" she moans. "She'll take it as a personal slight! I'm not trying to escape, I just want to see the world!"

"As you should," I agree, noticing, not for the first time, that she says *she* and not *they*.

"But she's terrified I will see too much and decide I want to embrace a life of sin."

I press my lips together, trying not to laugh. It's not funny, exactly, but pure-as-snow, won't-even-wear-spaghetti straps, and hasn't-seen-an-R-rated-movie Meg is the fur-thest thing from sinful.

"Shuddup," she says, her lips twitching.

"You have to tell her eventually. You can't just leave." I pull out of the driveway, figuring we can cruise around for a bit.

Meg nods, resolute. "And I will. But not yet. Movie?"

"Can't. I have to be home early since I'll be out late tomorrow." Ergh. I didn't mean to say that.

"What's tomorrow? Did you grab another shift?"

I hedge, taking my time fiddling with the satellite ra-dio. I put on some new wave. "Ah, no. I'm headed down-town. For a show. Of sorts. With Luke Greenly?" I finish like it's a question, and Meg is silent for a full minute. When I pull up to a light, I peek at her.

"Luke Greenly?" she asks.

"Y-yeah. Why do you say it like that?"

"Why did *you* say it like that?"

"I didn't!" I insist.

"Neither did I."

I roll my eyes, accelerating when the light turns green.

"Is it a date?" she asks.

"No!" I practically shout. "It's for an assignment."

"Luke Greenly."

"Yeah. What?"

She shrugs. "Fine. I'll say it. Luke Greenly? *The* Luke Greenly? The one you've had a massive crush on since freshman year?"

"What? What are you talking about? I have not!" My face burns, and I loosen my scarf, tossing it at her, and stab the Off switch on the heated seats.

"Oh, so you don't fall asleep to the sweet, soulful sounds of his voice?"

Wow, do I regret telling her that. "It's a soothing podcast."

"Okay, sure," she says knowingly, wrapping my scarf around her neck and checking her reflection in the mirror. "Let's get some Starbucks. I don't want to come back empty-handed."

"You can't avoid your mom forever," I say. I head toward the farthest Starbucks in town, giving us a little more time.

"And you can't avoid your feelings for Luke. But I'm glad you're hanging out. Even if it's only homework," she says, a too-knowing tone in her wording. "It's about time you figure out what he's really like."

I don't say anything. She's right even if I'm not ready to admit it.

7

LUKE

Glancing at the clock for the hundredth time—*Now I'm only fifteen minutes early*—I finally turn off the car engine and check my phone compulsively before dropping it into the center console and rubbing my sweaty hands down my pant legs. *This is only a homework assignment. Be cool, Luke.* I walk up Vada's driveway and rap a knuckle on the door before shoving my hands in my pockets. An older version of Vada answers the door. Youthful looking, but softer, as though through a slightly off-focus lens, and with wavy dark hair half pulled up off her smiling face.

"Welcome, Luke! Come in!" She opens the door the rest of the way and reveals Vada behind her.

"Hey, you're early."

"Yeah," I say. "Mum's rule. Show up early and always introduce yourself to parents." I turn to Vada's mom. "I'm Luke Greenly. Nice to meet you, Mrs.—uh—shite. Shoot. Carsewell?" I finish.

"You started off well," Vada quips, eyes dancing.

"You are too cute," her mom says, and my face is officially on fire. "Call me Mary. Everyone does. For the record, though, I go by Carsewell. Just easier."

"Right. Of course."

"It's nice to meet you, Luke. I've heard a lot about you."

"You have?" I ask, surprised.

"Of course, Vada's always—"

"Mom," Vada interrupts. "We should go. Traffic."

"Another time," Mary says with a wink. "Drive safe, Luke."

"Of course," I say. "We'll be back before eleven."

"Yes, you will," she agrees mildly.

Vada grabs a long scarf off a hook and winds it around her neck before settling a small bag across her body and flashing me a giddy grin.

"Ready?"

"Definitely." We walk out into the cool, damp night. It's been steadily staying lighter as the spring days grow longer, and the sun is coloring everything in an orange glow.

I cross to the passenger side and hold open the door. Vada presses her lips together but doesn't say anything. We get in the car, and I pass her my phone. "You can, um, play deejay, but it has to be from my playlist."

"Ooooh," she teases. "You don't trust me?"

I tighten my hands on the wheel so she doesn't see them shaking and attempt to casually exhale a slow breath before saying, in a (hopefully) offhand way, "More like my phone is hooked up to the Bluetooth. I'm afraid the most I can offer is whatever I already have."

Vada immediately starts scrolling, and the only sound over my speakers as we wind through the streets and out of her neighborhood is the clicking of her browsing. Soon enough, she chooses some Barns Courtney and lowers her window a quarter of an inch.

"Too warm?"

"Not really," she says, rolling her head to face me. "I just really love the smell of spring. I don't know what you call it . . . unfrosting? It's so clean and . . . wet."

"Melting?"

"No. That feels mushy. I like unfrosting better."

I pry each finger off the wheel one at a time and try to flex them into relaxing. "I'm definitely not laughing at you—inside, of course—so as to be polite, because that makes no sense."

She slugs my arm and turns up the music. I hide my grin. Contact. *Yes.*

We don't say a whole lot after that, but it's not uncomfortable. Vada's content to choose music, and though I've relaxed my grip, I've got both hands on the wheel, driving exactly two over the suggested speed limit in the far-right lane the entire forty-five-minute ride into the city. I'm so focused, I barely notice she smells like citrus and how it makes my mouth water. Or how the early-evening sun sets her hair on fire.

"Is it weird to drive on this side of the road?" Vada asks idly after choosing some Max Frost and fiddling with the bass before turning it down to a conversation level. The girl is goddamn meticulous when it comes to our travel soundtrack. Even if we can't fully hear every song, she makes sure it's played to the best of its ability.

I shake my head. "Um, n-not really. Not for Cull and me, at any rate. We learned in America. In London, we mostly used public transport."

"But your parents?"

I consider. "Maybe for my dad. My mum has dual citizenship. She's half-and-half, born in California, raised in England. My grandparents are academics, so she spent a lot of her life traveling between the States and Britain. My dad, though, he was a fish out of water for a long time. Still can't drink cold lager—says it hurts his sensitive Kingdom gums."

Vada snorts. "That's funny. Phil thinks anything less than frozen is stale."

"Not fit for a pub life, then."

"I imagine not. Have you been to many pubs?"

I lift a shoulder, careful to keep the wheel steady. "As a kid, yeah. My dad used to do some low-key touring when we were really little. Then, as his record label grew, he started taking us along sometimes to the more hole-in-the-wall venues. Especially if Mum was traveling."

"I've always wanted to travel," Vada says dreamily. "Like, out of the States. I bought a passport with my first paycheck, but so far the farthest I've gotten is Windsor, right over the border."

"I've never been to Canada," I offer.

She grins. "It's a lot like Detroit. But the money is prettier on the other side of the tunnel."

"I'll have to check it out. So, what does your mum—uh, Mary—do?"

Vada picks another song by lovelytheband, clearly feeling alternative tonight. "She's a principal."

"Really?"

"Yeah, elementary."

"I can see that. She's probably everyone's favorite."

Vada's smile widens. "She is. She's always late getting home from work because of former students who like to drop by. It's maddening and awesome. She loves it. She's been offered other positions in the superintendent's office, but she won't ever leave her kids. Actually, a position is opening up for a third-grade teacher at her school, and I think if it weren't for me, she'd be tempted to take the demotion and have a classroom again."

"Don't you want her to have a classroom?"

Vada nods. "More than anything. But we need the money. Or I do anyway. For college."

"Ah. Is that, um, why you were meeting with your dad?"

"Yeah. He's got a solid job in insurance. But I turned eighteen last fall, and he couldn't wait to stop paying child support. My mom has an account set aside for me. Education is, like, so important to her, obviously, and if I went in-state, it would be fine, but the music industry is out west, so that's where I want to be. And California is massively expensive."

"Your dad's not helping?" I ask. I've guessed some of this from the things Vada's let slip while talking to Cullen, but it's nice to get the full scoop. To see what makes Vada tick.

"Marcus hates the idea of me working in music and doesn't feel like he should owe me more money."

"But he's still your dad," I say. I can't imagine my dad cutting me off at eighteen.

"Only when it's convenient," she says. "He'll literally say, 'I have two kids,' referring to my half sisters, and I'll be standing, like, right there. Oh, this is our exit coming up."

I flip on my blinker. "That's . . . extra shitty, Vada."

"Yeah. It's not great." She's quiet a beat, and then, "You're very cautious, Luke Greenly."

"What do you mean?" A semi in front of us eases on its brakes, and I slow back a few hundred yards.

"Is this why you prefer your longboard? Are you afraid of the road?"

"What?" I ask, distracted. "I'm not afraid of the road. I just like my board. Gives me time to think and some quiet away from Cullen."

"You drive more cautiously than my nan," she muses.

"Nans love me, I'll have you know."

"I have no doubt. We're gonna make a right off the exit. The venue is a little way down this road, so we should find some parking."

I fight the urge to laugh. "I know. You realize it was *I* who invited *you*, right?"

"I remember. I just get excited."

"I couldn't tell," I say.

"This is either going to be super weird or the coolest thing I've ever done."

"Both, I imagine." I chance a look in her direction, and she is glowing. She's so beautiful. I clear my throat. "Thanks for doing this. Even if it *is* super weird and you end up hating it, thanks for being willing to try. I've always wanted to give it another go, and I can't imagine anyone else being adventurous enough."

She blushes, hiding her face in her hair. "I doubt I'll hate it. Thanks for inviting me."

We pull into a paid lot where a guy waits outside a booth looking bored. "Ten for the night," he says.

I pass him a twenty and wait for change before pulling forward into a spot and cutting the engine.

"Ready for the weirdest, coolest night of your life?"

Vada flashes me a megawatt grin, vibrating with anticipation. "Absolutely. Bring on the awkwardness."

Twenty minutes later, we're milling around on a concrete floor, surrounded by hundreds of people holding giant headphones and making small talk. When the overhead lights dim and the giant red stage lights come on, we're supposed to plug in. We have these little dials with endless music to choose from.

"I feel like an air traffic controller," Vada says, testing out the headphones.

"You look like one, but cuter," I say without thinking, because I'm an idiot.

She blinks and pulls one of the sides away from her ear. "Sorry, what?"

"Nothing."

She leaves one side of the headphones hanging off and sticks the dial in her back pocket, appearing utterly natural in this setting. I say as much, and one side of her mouth lifts.

"Dim lighting, loud music, heavy crowds, concrete. It's very much my comfort zone."

I feel my lips curl to match. "Mine, too."

The lights dim, and I pull on my headphones, tugging out the dial and clicking through the options. There's something super freeing about this. Like, no one knows what is pumping through my speakers. It's the feeling of being all alone in a crowded room. I take a minute to look around. With the flashing lights, it's hard to make out much, and that was before the fog machines started. The tiny hairs on my arms stand on end, and something inside of me burns with anticipation.

I have no idea what I'm looking for until I find it. Something to match the giddy feeling of being here, in this place, with her. Never in a million years would I choose this song if anyone were looking, but no one can judge me here.

I let my eyes slip closed, and I can't be still; the backbeat is too strong. I'm on my toes before I decide to move, and I'm jumping. Like, *jumping*, jumping. Up and down with my hands at my sides and my head banging around and my hair flailing, and it's incredible. I don't even listen to the lyrics. I just jump and jerk and shake. My shoulders drop, my breath sharpens, my pulse flies away, and it's goddamn perfect. I've never felt so self-absorbed, and I can't make myself care.

It's three songs before I open my eyes, remembering I'm not alone. I knew—felt—the subtle brush of strangers against my skin, but if they apologized or wanted me to, I couldn't hear it. There's no room for common courtesy in this place.

As the song changes, I see her next to me.

And wonder if this was a massive miscalculation on my part.

Instead of an escape, the song blaring in my ear be-

comes my soundtrack. The voice is pleading, screaming for a girl to let him go—to have mercy and let him
be free—as the gorgeous girl in front of me is spinning,
whirling, sucking me in, and for what the fuck ever reason, doing it in inexplicable slow motion. The fog machines blur her features, but when she opens her eyes
finally, they pierce my own, and I'm frozen, struck dumb
and stupid.

She beams a smile and grabs my hand and tugs me
toward her. She does a slow spin under my arm, and my
other hand finds her waist, prompting her to turn and
draw out with our arms spread between us. She doesn't
let go, instead curling into me and fitting. The music in
my ears slows, and I slow to match. She doesn't object.
Her arms find their way around my neck, and I rock us
together. She closes her eyes, and her lashes flutter over
the tiniest, most perfect constellation of freckles spread
across her cheeks and the bridge of her nose.

Well.

That's it.

There's absolutely no coming back from this. Science has shown, once you start noticing constellations in
freckles, you're fucked. I need to put a stop to this before
I do something mental like press a kiss to her bare shoulder or spout the lyrics to "Anna Begins." (Which, *by the
way*, is the best of Adam Duritz's decades-long collection
of works.)

The song changes, and *thankyouchrist* it's something
with angry guitars and a twitchy backbeat. I pull back,
ever so casually and point to my headphones like *Oh, hey,
got to go where the music leads*, and hopefully not like *Sweet
bollocks, I want to make you scream my name.*

If only Zack could read my thoughts right now, he'd know I was the furthest thing from a monk.

Vada nods and starts another painfully slow groove on her own, and I slam my eyes shut for posterity because I know logically there is nothing overtly provocative about how she is moving or how we are dancing. It's three years of longing turning my stomach. I knew it would be like this if I ever got close enough to smell her scent and feel her soft skin.

I need to get my shit in order. This is a school project. I close my eyes, turning my headphones up louder and losing myself in the next few songs until I can feel myself slipping into that distracted, centered place. My head slips side to side on my neck, and my hands rise above me, mimicking the movement. I turn before opening my eyes, taking in everything fresh. The view through my glasses is jarring. So clear and focused instead of the molded, colored shapes on the back of my lids.

Groups of people are in circles, taking turns in the spotlight, almost like you would see at a wedding. A lot of people dance alone, eyes shut and bodies feeling the music. Couples are making out. No surprise there. The music blocking everything out makes you feel like you're invisible. It's a false sense of privacy, but I get it and can't bring myself to be annoyed by those taking advantage.

Slowly, I spin to where Vada was last. This time I'm prepared. I brought her here to do something weird and experimental, but also to study her. Allow myself to be inspired by her. The song I am listening to ends, and I pull out my toggle, muting the music but keeping on the noise-cancelling headphones so the rustles of bodies and smacks of kissing don't interfere. I watch her and listen to my mind.

I've always been able to do it—compose. Create. I assumed everyone could until I was ten and realized Cullen couldn't. I'd always thought Cullen and I could do everything the same. Until I didn't. Until I could make songs in my brain and he couldn't find a girl attractive.

Turns out sharing 50 percent of our DNA doesn't mean much.

Vada sees me, and I nod. She seems to understand and scrolls through her stations, finding one that works for her, and turns her back to me.

It's not as voyeuristic as you might think, I swear. I'm past that. I can compartmentalize like a painter working with a nude model.

God, don't think of her nude.

It starts with a backbeat. I work mostly with piano, but like a rapper or spoken-word artist, I need something concrete to hit against. (I don't know *why*, I just *do*.) It's not long before I find myself moving along with her. Not touching. Not even close. My eyes are already closing, and I'm humming, but no one can hear me. I can imagine what is moving her, and I want to write *that*. I want to be the one who moves her. There are words, but self-preservation takes over, and I only have the energy to create the melody.

One day, the words will come. Hopefully, I'll be ready for them.

8

VADA

This feels like home. Well, okay, if I'm being really honest with myself (and I *am* only because no one can see or hear me and therefore this place feels like a magical portal), home was when Luke Greenly held me between his long, pale, strangely muscular arms.

But the rest of the night is close enough. I found a station specializing in jam bands, and there are songs on here I haven't heard since my mom used to play Dispatch while she cleaned our scuzzy bathroom in that tiny studio apartment right after the divorce. Phil would love it. The man seriously digs Guster. He told me once he tried to grow dreads but instead ended up shaving his head when he couldn't handle the smell of beeswax.

Heaven, that's what this is.

Luke is watching me dance. I can *feel* his eyes on me, and it feels fucking fantastic. Behind those serious black frames, his eyes glint with something I've never seen before, and it makes me feel stupid powerful and sexy. It also makes me feel like I want to feel him up in the bathroom—or let him feel me up, but I already gave that particular thought a firm *no*. This is a project. For school.

But I am so very tempted. Why are his lips so perfect? And his shoulders so broad? And why do I love glasses so much? It's not like a Clark Kent thing, is it? Do I have a nerd fetish? I don't even know. I just know all I want to do right now is kiss him, spring showcase and Madame whatever-her-name-is be damned.

Before I'm ready, because I don't think I will ever be ready, the lights come up and the music stops, and the night is over.

"Hungry?" Luke asks as we shuffle toward the exit to turn in our headphones.

"Starving," I say, realizing I am.

He grins. "If you're up for a bit of a walk, there's a diner near here that makes the best grilled cheese on the planet."

We head back out into the cold, but since my blood is still buzzing with the feel of Luke's gaze, I'm not uncomfortable. I leave my scarf loose around my neck, and the wind carries the ends, twining them with Luke's fingers and dancing them across his chest in a way that makes me jealous.

Be cool, hormones.

Within a few minutes, we're entering a brightly lit classic dive of a diner where the servers go by *waitress* and still wear aprons over their frocks.

"This okay?"

I take in a lungful of grease and nod. "This is perfect."

We sit down, and Luke flips his mug up for coffee like a grown-up. I bite my lip, feeling flighty and adult.

I skim the menu but already know I'm getting whatever grilled cheese they have because ever since Luke mentioned it, it's all my taste buds want. Well, that and, "I'll have an Oreo shake, please," I add when the server comes for our drink order.

"They're big," she says skeptically, eyeing me up and down.

"Excellent," I say.

We order after the drinks arrive, and I groan when the ice cream hits my lips. "So fucking good."

Luke smirks over his steaming cup of black coffee.

"So," I start. "Did you like it? Do you feel the creative juices flowing or whatever? Or just weird?"

He shakes his head. "Zero weirdness. Opposite of weirdness, actually. Totally inspiring. How about for you, though? I had to, uh, watch you. Was that rude? Or weird? Exhibitionist? Do I need to apologize?"

I snort, dipping my straw in the shake. "Um, no. You don't. It was cool. I could lose myself in the music and ignore it most of the time. A little awkward because I feel like I dance like a dork, but"—I shrug, flushing a little—"you picked me, so that's on you."

His teeth flash. "I did. And you don't dance like a dork. It's very . . . erm . . . not dorky."

"Good."

"Is there any genre of music you can't stand? Anything I need to steer clear of?"

I slowly shake my head. "I mean, not really. I'm pretty eclectic in my tastes. Unless you're a closet Stevie Nicks fan."

He makes a face. "Not really, no. She sounds like my grandma after smoking for a hundred years."

"Cheers, Luke," I say around a mouthful of whipped cream. "I think we're gonna get along marvelously."

"Nothing else?" he prompts.

"You're really worried about this, huh? Seriously." I shrug, stirring the last dredges of whipped cream into my shake. "I've never done anything like this before, and likely never will again. I have no experience to work from here, so follow your heart or whatever, and we'll be good."

"Follow my heart? Aren't you a little worried I might make a mess of things and you'll be left dancing to something resembling the Bee Gees?"

I swallow wrong and spend the next thirty seconds hacking until my eyes are streaming and I need to blow my nose on the condensation-shredded napkins. *Way to play it cool, Vada.* "Okay, fine," I concede when I can breathe. "I'd prefer to avoid disco." I start to tick off on my fingers. "See also: '90s hip-hop, stadium hits, and ska."

He slumps back on his seat, theatrically screwing up his face behind his lenses, which unfortunately does nothing to make him less stupid-good-looking. "Ah, no, there I have to draw the line. No ska? *No ska?*" He raises his voice, and I shush him, giggling. Where is this impulse to giggle all the time coming from?

"I'm sorry. I can't handle it. It's the horns."

"You don't like horns?"

"In moderation, I love them. But there's something about ska that makes everything feel greasy and dirty."

He raises a brow. "Do tell."

"It's like . . . day-old, tepid pizza slices and flat pop."

"Interesting. Do you do this word association thing with all music?"

I grin. "Honestly, I have no idea. Try me."

"Opera."

"Blue velvet and icicles. Hot chocolate. Lace cuffs. Fillet."

"Okay, too easy. Singers and songwriters of the '70s."

I press my lips together. "Scrambled eggs, moccasins, and espresso."

"Two thousands' screamo."

"Black licorice, bondage pants, the smell of Sharpies, and broken glass."

He settles back, his arms folding across his chest. "Bluegrass."

"Dusty denim, carrot cake, strawberry Kool-Aid, and sunshine yellow."

"Eighties hip-hop."

For a minute, I'm stumped. "Gold chains . . ." He smirks, and I hold up a finger. "Silence, peasant." I close my eyes, milking it, and roll my neck on my shoulders. "Gold chains, Dr. Pepper, miniskirt, Adidas."

"Get the fuck out of here," he says, smiling. "How is it possible you are right?"

I spread my hands in an "I just am" gesture and pretend to flip my hair, even though it's in a knot on the top of my head.

The server returns with our food just in time to distract me from the things that Luke's sparkling eyes are doing to my insides.

"Okay, extra credit," he says, swallowing a bite of cheeseburger. "Grilled cheese is what genre?"

"Psh," I say. "Sixties beach party, obviously."

"You think they ate grilled cheese on the beach?"

I shake my head, swallowing the melty deliciousness that is buttered Texas toast and American cheese. "Of course not. That's not how it works. The actual paraphernalia is irrelevant. It's the feeling you get, Greenly. Like, the aesthetic or whatever. It's not rocket science. Just your gut. Try one."

"Fine. Give it to me."

I feel the smile pulling on my lips. "Punk rock."

He groans. "I walked into that one, didn't I?" He takes a sip of coffee, wipes his hands on his napkin, and straightens. "Punk rock, to me," he clarifies, and I wave him to go on, "is blackout curtains, sawdust, worn trainer bottoms, warm beer, and cold concrete."

I narrow my eyes, tilting my head to the side. "Is that punk rock or your dad?" I immediately move to apologize, but he surprises me.

"Both. Naturally. Can't have one without the other, I'm afraid."

"Fair enough."

"Did I pass the test?"

"With flying colors," I say, feeling unsettled. I hadn't expected Luke to reveal so much. Maybe he didn't mean to, but he has.

"Now," he says, picking up his burger, "if we were talking about my brother, we'd have to go with his all-time favorite glam rock and call it: rainbow, glitter, nachos, and Zack."

"Too easy," I agree. "Was Zack your friend first or Cullen's—?"

"Soul mate?" he offers.

I feel my cheeks heat, but I don't know why. "Sure."

"Mine first. By like two months."

"And how's that?"

"Sharing my best friend with my twin?"

I nod.

He releases a long sigh. "Usually a nonissue. Zack is good at compartmentalizing. When he's with me, he's my best friend. When he's with Cullen, he's my best friend. He's just also in love with my brother. Thank God it was returned, or it would have been very uncomfortable."

"Do you ever worry about that?"

"About them breaking up?" He shrugs. "Not really. I can't see a world where they wouldn't be together, honestly."

"So, it's not odd for you at all, ever?"

"Oh, it's definitely odd at times—like when they, uh, you know." He coughs. "Consummated things."

I snort. "I forget you're British until you say something like 'consummate' instead of 'sex.'"

"Yeah. Well. That got weird. Not that they meant it to, but they both wanted to talk about it to me since I am both the twin *and* the best friend."

"Together?" I gasp.

"No! God, no. Not at the same time. I don't think they even know they did it, which is sort of the issue. They confide in me and live in denial that they both might be doing it."

"Maybe they need to find a new person."

"Probably," he agrees, dragging a french fry through ketchup. "I imagine they will next year when I leave for college."

"Who do you confide in?"

He screws up his face, making his glasses bob on the bridge of his nose. He nudges them with a knuckle. "Yeah. That's the issue. Zack. I mean, it's not like I have a whole lot of secrets." His ears turn pink at the tops, and he clears his throat. "But if I do, I have to tell someone not in my family because it usually has something to do with them, and that means Zack. And Zack doesn't like to keep secrets from Cull since they have this whole 'always tell the truth' policy."

"Yikes."

"Right."

"So . . ."

"So, I guess I'm the odd one out, and maybe I should make some new friends, but I'm eighteen and moving away, and honestly"—he scratches at his hair, ruffling it and pulling it behind his ear—"I'm a bit of an introvert. God," he says, looking at the ceiling. "I sound pathetic, don't I? I'm a third wheel."

"Not totally," I say. "I mean. If you're an introvert, you're a high-functioning one who danced in front of hundreds of strangers. Besides, I get it. Alone in a crowd, remember?"

"Yes! Exactly that," he insists excitedly. "I don't need to be locked up away from everyone, but I don't need to talk to them."

"But you're talking to me just fine," I offer.

"Well, you're different."

"How so?" I should stop prying, but I can't seem to help myself. I'm not usually this nosy. I leave that to Meg.

"You're . . . Vada," he says simply.

"It's true."

"I don't know." He laughs, and the sound makes me want to cuddle into my jacket. It's coaxing and rich. "I've never felt different around you. Maybe it's the hair. I'm predisposed to favor gingers."

Goodness, I've never been so happy to have red hair.

The server chooses that moment to interrupt and drops off our check. I glance at my phone, and I grow a little sad. It's getting late. "We should head home."

"Yeah. Let me take this on our way out."

Luke pays, patently ignoring the bills I'm holding out to him, and I tuck them back into my pocket, vowing to buy him something when the mood strikes. We're quiet on the way home. Which feels right.

He passes me his phone, and I play music from his collection of playlists and try to not think too much about how much every song makes me hyperaware of his warm body near mine, or the way his soothing voice croons under his breath, or how his long fingers tap on the steering wheel.

Or how very much I want to kiss him. Still. Even after leaving the club and sitting under the harsh halogen lights of the diner. Even when the magic of Other fades, I'm still vibrating with interest in the cool light of reality.

I'm taut as a bow by the time he pulls into my drive, minutes early. I can see my mom's shadow as she peeks out from behind the curtains and know she's watching, so before my limbs get any ideas and try to wrap themselves around every inch of Luke or anything, I reach for the handle.

"Thanks for coming tonight, Vada," he says.

I settle back into my seat for a moment to look at him. "I had a blast. Thanks for thinking of me."

"Always," he says, then shakes his head. "Er, I mean, anytime."

I huff out a nervous laugh and immediately lunge out of the car, trotting up to the door. When I make it, I spin and give a wave. He waves back, his lips moving, but I can't make out what he's saying in the dim light. And then he reverses, headed home.

I'm suddenly wrung out and haven't forgotten it's a school night, so I kiss my mom good night and head upstairs to my room. It's so quiet after the loud ringing of music, my ears feel almost tender. My feet sinking into the soft carpet, the old floors beneath creaking ever so slightly, is extra soothing. I pull on warm pajamas, brush my teeth, and wipe away my makeup. I fold myself into bed and pick up my phone. Before I can change my mind, I shoot off a text. It's probably too much, but I'm feeling a lot and, well, fuck it. It's just a song.

Of course, nothing is ever "just a song" with me, and

I get the feeling nothing is ever "just a song" for him either, but, whatever. Too late.

VADA

<u>YouTube: Led Zeppelin "Thank You"</u>

When I wake up the next morning, his single-line response is there.

LUKE

"There would still be you and me."

Are you there, God? It's me, Smitten.

9

LUKE

The morning after the silent dance party is a drudge to get through. It wouldn't have been so terrible, but I stayed awake thinking about Vada's text long after the rest of my house rumbled with my dad's leaf blower snores. I knew the song she referenced without even listening to it, though I can't tell you when I last heard it. Zeppelin isn't played with any real regularity around our house, but my dad taught us to pay due respect to the legends.

Still, my memory didn't do it justice. If it were anyone other than Vada, I'd assume she'd chosen it for the title. Obvious enough. She was grateful for the night out. But it *was* Vada, and admittedly, we only had our first *real* conversation recently, but I've been reading her blog for years, and I know she knows exactly what she sent me.

What I don't rightly know is how to take it. There's how I *want* to take it, and how I *need* to take it, and I was awake a long, long time trying to decide which one was going to win out come morning.

Spoiler alert: Neither. Or both.

I'm fucked.

But also a little bit happy?

By the time I reach my lunch hour, I've completely missed my morning classes. I was there, and I took notes, but it would go like this:

American Lit Teacher: What are your thoughts on the symbolism of the color red in *The Scarlet Letter*?

Me: Maybe Hester Prynne was a ginger. Like Vada.

Geo Trig Teacher: Solve for B in this quadrilateral equation.

Me: Why don't you solve this relational equation?

PE Teacher: Suit up for dodgeball!

Me: I hate gym.

Okay, so not the last one, but you get the idea. It's been useless. I slide my tray down the line and choose a breaded chicken sandwich, plopping a bunch of extra sandwich pickles in a small cup and grabbing two mayo packets, distractedly.

"Hey, stranger."

I swallow. "Hey, Lindsay. How're you?"

I feel, more than see, her long, pale hair flash over her shoulder in a rush of great-smelling shampoo. That's one thing I'll say for Lindsay, she always smells good. Though I've yet to find a girl who doesn't smell awesome all the time, so it's hardly a point in her favor.

"Not bad. We missed you last night," she says conversationally, ladling a healthy scoop of fake cheese sauce on her french fries.

I slide a little farther, picking up an empty cup for water. "What was last night?"

"Basketball game?" she says. "Zack was awesome. There's talk about the state championship."

"Ah," I say, inwardly cringing. Shite. I forgot about the game. Not that I make it to all Zack's games, or even most of them, but I pride myself in at least knowing what's happening in his Sportball world. "I had plans."

We're halted at the checkout, and I shift my stance, trying to appear open but focused on my tray. Lindsay deftly maneuvers around to face me, blocking my view of the rest of the cafeteria.

"That's too bad. Maybe next time. Anyway, I was wondering what your plans were for the prom?"

I clear my throat. "Prom? Isn't that in May?"

She shrugs. "It's eight weeks away. Lots of people have dates already, though. I thought maybe we could go?"

I try to keep the confused look off my face, but I don't think I pull it off. I nudge at my frames with my shoulder, nearly upsetting my sandwich, and I move up in line. "Wouldn't you rather go with someone who didn't break up with you?"

Her face falls. "Well, sure," she says, a blunt edge to her voice. Somehow, we're side by side now. "But we're still friends." She says it like she's willing it to be true, but I'm not convinced we were friends to start with. Sure, we've hung out in the same group before, but we barely know each other. Maybe if she had known me better, she wouldn't have posted videos of us kissing on social media.

Or maybe if I had known her better, it wouldn't have gotten that far in the first place.

To be fair, I did say we'd "stay friends." That one time. When I broke up with her. (I'm rubbish at boundaries.)

We make it to the checkout, and I hand my student ID over to be scanned. When she does the same, I break away, but Lindsay is fast on my tail as I fill my cup from the water dispenser.

"Yeah, you're right," I say, answering her. "But I'm not sure I'm even going to the prom, and anyway, I'll bet there're loads of guys who want to go with you."

"Your brother was homecoming king," she says. "Of course you're going."

I narrow my eyes as I try to make sense of *that* statement, skimming the room for Zack. "I didn't go to homecoming either. It's not really my scene. Much more his."

"So, you're telling me you're still on the fence. Okay. But if you decide to go?"

She's not interested in hearing anything other than yes. I wasn't with Lindsay long, but that personality trait was abundantly clear from the beginning. Our breakup is still raw, though, and I imagine, given time, she'll find a better option.

"If I decide to go, and I won't, but if I do, you'll be the first to know."

She beams, her cheeks flushing. "Great. I'm planning to go in turquoise this year, so keep that in mind."

I can't help it; my jaw drops. Oh, to possess even a

tenth of her gall. Before I can argue, she's off toward a table of her friends, who all wave at me as I join Zack and a bunch of his teammates at another spot.

I slide my lunch onto the table, and Zack raises his heavy brows over what is likely his third PB&J.

"I think I was offered a prom date? Or I was offered to *be* a prom date?"

He chews thoughtfully. "She asked you to the prom?"

I unwrap my sandwich and tear open a mayo packet. "More like she asked if I would take her, and when I said I wasn't going, she suggested I could take her when I changed my mind."

He shrugs this off. "Did you agree?"

"Not in so many words, but I'm not sure that would hold up in court."

"She's slippery."

"She is," I agree. "But that's okay. I have zero interest in the prom."

"Even with a different date?" he asks, meaning pressed into every word.

I glare at him before covering the chicken patty in pickles and replacing the bun, taking a bite.

"I'm just saying, you might regret it later."

"I won't."

"But what about—"

I cut him off with a look.

"How was last night?" he asks, his eyes gleaming.

"What the fuck, man? What's with the eye twinkle all of a sudden? It's like you're channeling Dumbledore."

"Rude."

I sigh. "It was good," I say, my voice low. I toss a glance at the rest of the guys at the table, but they're busy strategizing or something. That Zack is super gay would be an issue in most towns, and he's faced his share of grief, but never from the team. I might not fit in with those guys, but he does. Turns out, they care more about winning than who he spends his free time with. Part of that is Ann Arbor. Part of that is Zack and Cullen. You can't help but root for them.

"Only good?"

"I'm not sure." If I can't tell Zack, who can I tell? And I *need* to tell someone. The conversation with Vada at the diner, still fresh in my mind, I pull out my phone. After a quick look around, I open my text from Vada and pass it to him.

After a moment, he passes it back. "Okay. I'm assuming there's more to it from the look on your face, but I don't know Zeppelin."

I slump back into my chair, stifling a groan. "Never mind, the bell's about to ring anyway."

Zack sighs, rolling his eyes in an overexaggerated way and pulling out his phone, before, in a very pointed voice, saying, "Siri, what are the lyrics to 'Thank You' by Led Zeppelin?"

As Siri works her magic, he mumbles under his breath, "And I thought Cull was the dramatic one." His eyes dart back and forth, and his thumb scrolls through the sparse lyrics. I watch as his eyes grow wider.

He looks at me, stunned, and I instantly feel better.

"What does this mean?" he asks.

"Thank you?"

"Okay, I'll try again. Are you freaking out?"

"Not necessarily," I lie.

He grins.

"What does this mean?" I ask, turning it around on him.

He shakes his head right as the bell rings. We gather up our trash and walk over to the bin, tossing everything in. "I don't know. You and Carsewell are on a different level from mere mortals. There is one thing, though . . ."

"Yeah?" I ask as we file out through the double doors.

"You should have been clearer to Lindsay about the prom thing. Sounds like you might have plans."

It took me until the end of Wednesday to decide I didn't care what the song meant. Or, rather, *of course* I did, but I didn't have the stones to ask Vada to clarify, so I needed to leave it alone.

Instead, I decided two could play that game. I desperately wanted to get inside her brain, and the best way I could think to do it was texting.

It's easy to be bold when texting.

LUKE

Worst home improvement
show?

VADA

Is this hypothetical?

LUKE

No. This is current events.

VADA

FLIP OR FLOP.

LUKE
Oooooh. What is it you don't like? The awkward divorcees or the fake tans?

VADA
It's all painful. The overblown dramatics are vomit-inducing. They are always just shy of missing their financial/time/creative budget.

VADA
Also, every house ends up looking the same. Too many bathrooms and taupe everywhere. And chevron pillows. And gross backyards that need sod.

LUKE
Wow. Don't hold back.

VADA
Why do you ask?

LUKE
My dad's on a This Old House kick. He hasn't left the basement couch in three days. My mum just keeps bringing him meals.

LUKE
He's taking notes, Vada. I'm worried he's plotting a giant reno.

VADA

snicker I have so many questions.
Is he handy? Do you live in an old
home?

> LUKE
>
> Sort of. He's far handier with
> a guitar, but he gets around
> a small project all right. And
> yeah, we live near Burns. Big,
> creaky old house, rickety
> garage, and a patch of grass.

VADA

Plenty to get into trouble with, is
what you're saying.

> LUKE
>
> Halp.

VADA

He needs a hobby.

> LUKE
>
> He needs a job.

VADA

What does a punk rocker do when
he retires?

> LUKE
>
> I suggested he work at Trader
> Joe's.

VADA

HAPPIEST PEOPLE EVER.

> LUKE
>
> ikr?

> LUKE
>
> He declined. He's bored but
> a bit crusty. I can't see him
> having a whole lot of patience
> for the clientele.

VADA

Maybe not.

> LUKE
>
> He keeps threatening to buy a
> club, but it's been years and
> Ann Arbor's not exactly lacking
> in sports bars.

VADA

Definitely not. At least twice a shift
Phil grumbles about the "goddamn
Bee Dubs conspiracy"

> LUKE
>
> Do I even want to know?

VADA

Not really. It's tied into some
"corporate conflagration of
patriarchy and government funding"
or something like that.

LUKE

That . . . doesn't sound like a
real thing. But Cull needs me.
Gotta run anyway.

LUKE

YouTube: "Wish You Were
Here" Pink Floyd

VADA

:) Me too.

10

VADA

I'm not a runner, but I can stroll for ages. Give me miles
of quiet path and the newest Welshly Arms album and I
won't need to stop for hours. Particularly when the temperature is around freezing and most particularly after a
phone call from my dad.

The man could motivate a marathon runner with his guilt trips and narcissism. But knowing that doesn't help. Why do I even answer my phone when I see his number? It's never good. It's never "Hey, kiddo, just checking in."

I was sitting at the library with Meg when his name lit up my screen. I could tell *she* could tell by my face it was him.

"Maybe it's about missing dinner," she offered. I packed up my things, promising to call her later, and was out the door before the librarians could get annoyed with my ringing phone.

Instead, it was a lot of "I miss you, you never come over" interspersed with a healthy serving of "one hundred facts about how having small children is harder than he could have ever imagined, and I couldn't possibly understand." Never mind that he has me, a person who was once a small child. That belonged to him.

My mom thinks he just doesn't see me that way. I'm not his daughter. I'm his sometimes-parent, sometimes-babysitter, sometimes-conscience. But never his kid and *never* his responsibility.

I should have let him go to voicemail. (But that's a whole other thing, because then I have to *call him back*.)

He wanted tickets. His wife, Jane, is burned out from the kiddos. So, he wanted to take her out and was thinking I might have a hookup through work, and also could I watch the babies?

Fucker. And what am I supposed to do? Be petty and go, "Sorry, Dad, but if you don't have money for my tuition, I don't have free tickets for you."

Instead, I told him *I didn't know*. I had to pick up more

shifts for work to save for school. Which is true. And felt petty, until he said, "Oh. Great! That's very responsible. Let me know when you find some tickets!"

That right there is how you *know* he's not going to lend me one damn cent, because he rarely encourages me to work *more* at Phil's club.

It's fine. It's just my life's ambition, my one shot away from this place and him and a childhood of almost-but-not-quite. If only he would move away. If he's not going to be my dad, he may as well leave. Cut out the complicated emotional roller coaster. Why doesn't he have to answer for *anything* and I have to answer *for everything*? Why does he get to be my father when I'm not his daughter? He teases the idea of moving south—to warmer climates—but never does. He says it's because of me, but as we all know, one, it's never about me, and two, he means I would be too far away to babysit.

That's some bullshit, if you ask me.

I turn up AJR's "Sober Up" and tuck my earbuds carefully under my stocking hat. My feet pound the sidewalk with the increasing beat, but I draw my breaths in long and deep. Inhale through my nose and exhale through my mouth, pursing my lips.

The wind picks up, cooling my flushed face and the wetness on my cheeks. I swipe my tears away, determined not to give him a second more of my time.

I repeat my five-year plan like a mantra cycling in my brain. Work for Phil. Take over *Behind the Music*. Acceptance into UCLA's prestigious music journalism program. Check, check, and check.

My next step is the most vital.

It's been years in the making. Every summer, Ann Arbor holds a free lunchtime weekly concert series that has an enormous local following. Phil is like some kind of psychic wizard when it comes to predicting talent, and I've been studying under him for years, spending hours talking radio and music and genres, and I'm ready for more responsibility at the club.

This is it.

Athletes spend hours training their bodies to withstand competition. Scholars spend their days with their noses in books, absorbing knowledge in their chosen field. I've done the same in my own way. Music is my obsession, my life's blood. It runs through my veins, coloring my skin. My natural inclination is to rock, but that's not enough if I want to make music my career.

I listen to the greats, the not-so-greats, the once-had-potential-to-be-greats, and the will-be-greats. I memorize lyrics, listen to podcasts, read biographies, and correct Wikipedia pages.

Every waking minute I'm not doing stuff for school, I'm at the Loud Lizard absorbing it all. It's better than any internship. It's the real life down and literally dirty. It doesn't matter if my dad gives me money for school. The experience is what they want.

No, the dad part is just for me. Phil says to give him a chance, and I'm working up to it. It's like this dance of simultaneously hoping he won't fuck this up and knowing he probably will and that it's going to hurt like hell when he does.

But I have to know. I can't leave here not knowing. Which is stupid because logically, he should be the one having this constant inner pep talk, and he's not.

My mom's church was having this whole series on forgiveness, and I tried to follow it. For her. Turn the other cheek and all that. Except I'm turning my cheek so much,

I'm set to spin. How do you forgive someone who doesn't think they've done anything wrong?

After school the next day, I get to work on the next part of my plan, the one that ends with me flying solo on Liberty Live. I talked my mom's ear off over dinner at our favorite Ethiopian place, hashing and rehashing all the details, and we agreed everything starts with Phil (boss Phil, not her boyfriend, who happens to be my boss, Phil).

At exactly 4:00 p.m., I knock on Phil's office door.

"Vada," he says, peering at me over his smudged bifocals. "You don't need to knock. You texted two minutes ago from the parking lot."

I pull out the chair opposite his desk. Mustard-yellow stuffing is spewing out the cracked fake leather, and the metal is so rusted the wheels creak when you move it—like someone used it for an office chair beach race years ago. Knowing Phil, they did. I perch on the edge, straightening my mom's button-down. My mom said it gave me a professional edge. I think it makes me look like an exasperated server in a Tide commercial, but whatever. Phil removes his frames, his eyebrows twitching as he takes me in.

"What can I help you with, Vada?"

My hands feel weird. Like, what even are arms? What do I do with them? I settle them in my lap. I want to check my phone for no practical reason.

Phil's expression straight-up says he thinks I'm having a stroke.

I clear my throat. "Here's the thing," I say. "I've been working at the Loud Lizard for two years."

He nods for me to continue.

"Well, you should give me a closing shift. As a manager. To, you know, manage."

He leans back, resting his hands across his well-earned belly. He's wearing his favorite gas station shirt today. The one that reads *Phil's 550* and has Bud Light and Marlboro patches on the pocket. "Go on."

I exhale. "Okay, so I was thinking. I've been at every show for the last year, but you're always here, too. Which is great because I've learned so much from you. Obviously. Like, everything. But what if you took a night off?"

Phil tilts his head, scratching at his beard. "I'm listening."

"I mean. I wouldn't be alone." I start ticking off on my fingers. "On our average night, there are at least two bartenders, two security (one of them stationed at the door), and one hostess. That's not even mentioning the front-loaded waitstaff on Saturdays." He raises his brows, and I rush on, "Not that I would presume to cover a Saturday night, but like, what about Sunday?"

"Sunday?"

"Er, right. Or anytime. I'm wide open. Except when I'm in school, obviously."

"And why should I give you, a wet-behind-the-ears eighteen-year-old, a management shift? The whole weight of *my* club resting on your shoulders. The day-to-day operations of managing a bar and concert venue?"

I blink. "Why the fuck not me?"

He laughs, full-bellied, and presses his hands to the desk. "Thank Christ, you had me nervous there for a second. There she is. Where did you get that shirt?"

"My mom," I mutter.

"Right," Phil says, his eyes lifting to the ceiling. "I thought it looked familiar." As my mom tells it, she was a bit on the nerdy side, and Phil was this extra cool metalhead back in high school. They haven't changed much.

"So . . ."

"Yes, you can have the job," he says gruffly. "I've been thinking about taking a night off. Or at least leaving early. Sunday is a good *trial*."

"Okay." I'm not disappointed in his cautious tone. I'm *not*. I have to earn my opportunities.

"That's not to say you couldn't handle more," he says, no doubt taking in my expression. "But *Mary*," he emphasizes my mom's name, "might kill me if I let you close any other night. You still have to graduate, kid."

I meet his eyes. "Thank you."

"You've more than earned it."

"I won't let you down. I'll even help you find someone to replace me as second bartender on Sundays."

He laughs. "Vada. Easy, girl. I trust you. You, uh, know this comes with a pay raise."

I press my lips together. "I wondered, but I'd take it either way. I want the experience."

Phil's expression is stern. "What have I told you?"

"Never work for free. But I'm not! The experience is invalu—"

"Never. Work. For. Free," he says, tapping his desk with two fingers to accentuate each syllable. "If you don't value your time, no one else will. I'm hiring you for your ridiculous brain and enthusiasm. I am the one winning out here. Now ask me for a raise."

He leans back, and I cave in around my stomach, feeling stupid. "Can I have a raise?"

"No."

"What? But you just said—"

"Ask again."

I roll my eyes with a huff. "Mr. Josephs, my time is valuable, and I know my shit. I've worked at this club for two years. I've paid my dues. I would like a five-dollar-an-hour raise."

Phil's brows jump, and I almost waver. But I don't.

"The raise is two dollars."

"Four fifty."

"Three, and that's my final offer. I'm not made of money. *Fucking Bee-Dubs*," he grumbles before holding out his meaty hand. "Pleasure to have you aboard." I shake it.

"Thank you so much!"

"You're welcome. Now get out of here and change your shirt. You're making me want to buy detergent."

I lied before. I don't think Ben and his lumber sexy beard are attractive. Right this minute, the way he's wheedling his way out of his Sunday-night shift because he has to *study for midterms* . . . flannel is overrated, and so is he.

"I can't believe this. It's my first night," I mumble into my hands.

"Look, Vada. I'm sorry. I forgot Phil wouldn't be here, but it's not like you need him. Or me. You could run this place in your sleep."

I glare at Ben, cursing his twisty beard with my eyeballs.

"And who is supposed to pour drinks while I'm running the place, Ben?"

"Kazi?" he offers. "I'm really sorry, Vada. I feel like a dick. But I can't stay."

I rub at my temples, feeling a thousand years old. "Kazi,

if he shows, won't be here until nine. The headliner won't even get onstage until then. And I can't close alone, Ben. I promised my mom!"

"You're not alone; you have the security dudes, and you know his girlfriend, Tess, always shows up attached at the hip."

I glare at Ben. "Again. *If* Kazi shows up."

"Call Phil?" he says before hurriedly changing direction to, "I'll call Phil."

"*Fuck.* Hold on." I say, holding up my hand and thinking fast. I can do this. Can I do this? I need two hands to cover the bar. Sundays are generally light, but local favorite Salvador Retriever is playing. If I push two-dollar drafts, that'll cut down on mixed drinks. So, two bartenders, but really only one, with another on standby. Security dudes can handle crowd control, and I can assign one of them to the door. This is fine. Don't panic. "Don't call Phil. He's in Ohio with his sick mom."

I can't do this. I start to feel dizzy and stupid, and hot tears surge into the corners of my eyes and *don't cry, don't cry, don't cry.*

"I can stay."

I whirl around, and Luke is standing there, holding his longboard.

"Sorry. I overheard you were . . . um, Cull just left, and I wanted to let you know we're all wrapped up in the sound booth . . . but, I can stay. Er . . . I don't technically work here, but I can help keep an eye on things if you're pouring drinks. I'm good at following directions."

I consider half a second. I mean. I literally have no other options. It's 8:00 p.m. on a Sunday night. "Have you ever mixed a drink?"

He grins. "Grew up around pubs, remember?" Right. Famous punk musician. The Greenly boys have been mixing drinks since the womb.

"Are you eighteen?" The Loud Lizard is technically "all ages" unless we specify an over-twenty-one show, and even then, you only have to be eighteen to serve alcohol in Michigan. Trust me, I've been studying the loopholes for two years. Nevertheless, I can't have anyone under eighteen behind the bar.

"Last month."

"Oh thank God," I say, impulsively hugging him before stepping back awkwardly. "You're hired."

His eyes widen, and I rush to correct myself. "I mean, for tonight. Unless you, um, want the job? Either way, I owe you."

"I'll let you know. But tonight, I'm yours. Or whatever. I'm here for you," he says earnestly, shoving at his glasses before dropping his board with a clatter. "Shite."

"Here," I say. "You can lock up your stuff in Phil's office."

"So, I can leave?" Ben asks. I seriously forgot he was there.

"I thought you didn't have a choice?" I remind him acidly.

"I don't."

I wave him away, pulling out my keys. "Stay here until we're back, okay?" As I unlock Phil's door, I whisper under my breath, "And then you can fuck the fuck off."

Luke snickers.

"Sorry," I say. "This is my first night closing the club alone. I practically had to beg Phil for this shift and promised I could handle the extra pressure even though he was leaving town, and now I'm short staffed."

"It's fine. Really. I'll text my mom to let her know."

"I can drive you home later," I offer.

"That would be great."

"I'm not kidding, Luke," I say, smiling for real. "I owe you. You're saving my life here."

"Happy to help. So, what time do the doors open for the show?"

I glance at my watch. "We have five minutes." I take a deep, cleansing breath like my mom taught me. In my nose, out my mouth. "Five minutes. I can do this, I can do this, I can do this."

"Vada," Luke says. I've noticed when he says my name, it comes out like *Vay-der* rather than *Vay-duh*. I like it.

"Hm?" I say, exhaling again.

"We can do this. It's like my granddad the car salesman always says—under promise, over deliver. This is a dive bar, not Saint Andrew's Hall. So, play it cool, and if we happen to remember water bottles in their dressing room, we'll come off looking extra classy."

"Water bottles?" I ask, panicking.

"You have any?" he asks.

"Sure."

"Great. You have no idea how magical a couple of water bottles in the mini fridge can be. Have any lemons?"

"Behind the bar," I say, bemused.

He nods once, his blond hair flopping around his ears. He tucks one side back and moves to the door. "Perfect. A couple of lemons with the water and all of a sudden you're not only prepared, you're high class as fuck."

I snort, following him.

"What?" he asks as I close Phil's office door and lock it behind me.

"I don't think I've heard you say *fuck* before. It sounded odd. Like, you're too posh to say *fuck*."

"Well, that's fucking ridiculous," he grouses, jumping behind the bar like he owns the place. I wave Ben out as Luke pulls out a handful of water bottles and fills a glass with lemon slices. He considers for a second. "What kind of band are they?"

I tip my head. "New alternative. Sorta electronic."

He pulls out the Jägermeister and a few shot glasses, arranging it all on a tray. "Dressing room?"

"Well, more like backstage. There are a couple of rooms past Phil's office. I'm sending them to the one farthest back."

"I'm on it. You do what you need to do out here to get those doors open, and I'll make sure the opening act is taken care of next."

I want to cry out of pure gratitude. I want to know more about this super-capable version of Luke. Fumbling Luke was cute, Secure Luke is . . . hot? Superhot. Instead, I rush to the doors where there's already a line and square away security with Dave and Mike before throwing the doors open to the crowd.

A moment later, Kazi rushes in, dreads flapping.

"You're on bar," I say. "Two-dollar drafts. There should be a sign under the register."

He salutes and hops behind the bar, grinning affably. I might not love Kazi, but at least he takes orders well and showed up tonight. Which is more than I can say for Bearded Ben and his, um, beard.

Luke returns and stands alongside me, watching the club as it fills up. The opening band is tuning up, and for now, everything is working out. I join Kazi behind the bar and drag Luke with me.

"How about I show you around back here while it's still moderately quiet?"

Luke grabs a bottle and tosses it in the air, twirling it.

My eyes widen. "Or not?"

"I'm surprised I caught it. That was a stupid move. I was trying to look cool, but I could have dropped it. Sorry about that," he mumbles sheepishly.

I bite my lip, trying not to laugh at his chagrinned expression. Fumbling Luke is plenty hot, too, I guess. "Well, good thing you did. But we're sticking to cheap drafts tonight. On the off chance anyone's too fancy for beer, you can push it off to Kazi or me. Ever work a register?" I ask.

"No, sorry," he says, and he sounds so contrite, I have to fight off another smile.

"It's totally fine. Kazi," I ask the dirty hippie, "if Luke writes it all—"

"How about he deals in cash? You good at math?" he asks.

Luke shrugs noncommittally, and Kazi says, "Can you count up? You can cash out if you count up." Kazi pulls out a few bills. "So, like, the total is $5.25, and they give you a ten? First, always hold on to what they gave you and put it right here." He plops it on the top of the register. "That way, no fucker can be all, 'Oh, I gave you a fifty.'" He pops open the register and counts singles. "Six, seven, eight, nine twenty-five," and he moves to quarters, deftly pulling them out. "Fifty, seventy-five, ten dollars. Done." He flashes his pretend ten. "Give them their change, and then put your money in the register."

"So no fucker can say I gave them a fifty."

Kazi lights up. "Exactly. Point for the Brit."

"Good," I say, motioning to Kazi to take care of three frat guys flashing their bills. "It shouldn't be overwhelming tonight, and if it is, I can hop back here as soon as the show starts and help out during intermission."

11

LUKE

Two hours later and I'm dead on my feet, and I don't even know how Vada is still standing. We're hunched behind the bar, and she's snacking on a cupful of maraschino cherries, her head bobbing along to the music.

The band is decent. They play mostly originals but threw in a few Something Corporate covers that featured their keyboardist. I could really dig that. It gave them an emo sound without delving too far back into the early 2000s. They also pulled out a remix on "Vienna" by Billy Joel that would have made my dad weep into his beer. As it was, I could barely keep myself from singing along.

With my eyes closed.

Correction. I can't stop myself.

Vada's head tilts onto my shoulder tiredly, and she says, "You have a pretty voice, Luke."

Before I can get all embarrassed and dig up an entire

childhood's worth of drama and think too much about her leaning so close, she says, "You know how you know a song is really exceptional? The secret's in the eyes. If you can't possibly feel the lyrics with your eyes open—if it's just too much to contain—that's when you know it's good. *Really* good."

"I've never thought of it like that. Is that how you write your reviews?"

"Oh no," she says. "I'm veeeery professional and calculated when I blog."

"Oh. Sorry, I didn't mean to imply—"

"One eye-closer gets a mention," she interrupts, grinning and holding up one finger. "Two eye-closers and I'm forever your girl."

I laugh. "That *is* awful scientific."

"Am I wrong, though?" she asks, her brown eyes twinkling in the flashing lights of the stage.

"No," I admit. "You're not. That's accurate."

"So, I don't think I've ever asked . . . I'm assuming you play an instrument?"

"Piano since I was little. But once I decided I wouldn't be pursuing music, I stopped taking lessons. My dad was not thrilled."

"Ohhhh," she says, grinning wickedly. "I bet you broke his heart."

"You'd think," I say lightly. "Consequently, he sort of hates the podcast."

"Really?"

I affect my dad's rough Cockney accent. "If'n yer not gonna use yer gift, don't be fuckin' with the podcast jes ter rub it in yer dad's mug."

Vada's eyes widen. "But you're with Cullen!"

"True, but Cullen can't carry a tune. Believe me, if he could . . ."

"Oh, I believe you," Vada says, her eyes crinkling.

"So"—I hold out a hand and let it fall to my side—"I will always disappoint my father, who is left saying things like, 'I love both of my sons equally, but Cullen a little more.'"

Vada gasps. *"He does not."*

"He does!" I insist. "He's mostly kidding. I think. If it wasn't for my mum's insistence that I'm her best chance at blond grandbabies, I'd be sunk. Saved by the gonads."

"Saved by the gonads," she repeats gleefully. "That should be on a T-shirt."

"I have one," I deadpan. "Etsy."

"You don't!"

"I don't."

"You know, Cullen could always find a blond surrogate one day. Your gonads aren't as precious as you think."

"Well," I consider. "That's . . . true. Damn it, Carsewell."

"Sorry."

"Such a ballbuster."

Her eyes widen, and she giggles. I'm not usually very funny. Is it possible someone can *make* you funny?

The band wraps up their set, and Vada yells for last call before they can return for a three-song encore.

We won't technically shoo anyone out after the show, but it's after 11:00 when Vada asks Kazi to raise the house lights to nudge people toward the doors. Kazi's girlfriend, Tess, shows up to drive him home, and she helps wipe down tables and clean up trash off the floor while Vada and I straighten the bar and run the dishwashers so everything is ready to go in the morning. The band came up afterward, and Vada paid them and thanked them for coming, and I went to clear out the backstage area. The waters and Jägermeister were definitely appreciated.

Not bad for a couple of teenagers.

We leave everything in a reasonable state. Vada says Phil will be in tomorrow before opening with a janitorial crew to mop the floors and clean the bathrooms. She divvies the tips between the three of us and locks everything else in a safe in Phil's office.

Kazi and Tess take off, and so does a security guard, leaving us with the other. He doesn't speak, hasn't all night, but as we're walking out, Vada says, "Night, Mike! Thanks for the escort." And he waves. He waits in his car until we pull out, so Vada doesn't tarry, even though her car is freezing.

"Sorry, Mike's got little ones at home. I don't like making him stay out any later than usual. When Phil closes, he leaves at the end of the show. He only stayed for me. Or, well, us."

"No worries," I say. "Warmer than boarding."

Vada huffs into her fingers before reaching into the console. "I think my mom keeps a pair of her driving gloves in here . . ." She pulls out a pair of skinny pleather gloves and tugs them on, flexing her fingers at the stoplight. "Not much better, to be honest."

I reach into my bag. "Here, try these." I pass her a couple of knit mittens with fleecy lining.

"Oh my gosh," she murmurs. "These are the warmest ever."

"I know. My mum found them. They're a bit . . . colorful . . . but I don't care."

Vada rubs her hands together, holding the mittens to

her face. "Totally miraculous. Thank you. I need to get some of these."

"I'm on the west side," I say.

"Hm?"

"I live on the west side, off Huron."

"Oh! God. Sorry. I wasn't even . . . I was just going home. Autopilot."

We sit in companionable silence. I'm exhausted, and my feet kind of hurt from standing so long, and I feel like I could sink into the heated seat of her mum's car and fall asleep forever.

"I was serious about the job. I mean, I have to check with Phil, but we talked about hiring someone to replace me at the bar. Plus, Kazi has been working more and more at Whole Paycheck."

I snort. "Whole Paycheck?"

"Oh, you know where."

"I do." I let my head roll to the side and take in Vada's profile. Her auburn hair looks black in the dark. "If Phil wants me, I'll take it."

"Really? That's fantastic. You did great tonight. I was suffocating, but you really saved the day with that water stuff."

I shrug, but I'm pleased. "Who would have thought a lifetime of Charlie could prepare me for a career in anything useful?"

"Seriously," she agrees.

I direct her into my drive, and the motion light clicks on. "Thank you again and again, Luke. You're my hero. Oh!" She goes to remove the mittens.

"Keep them. For tonight," I say. "I'll get them from you next time I see you."

"Thank you."

"Good night, Vada."

"Night, Luke."

She waits for me to get inside, and I wave her away, locking the door behind me. I creep upstairs to my room and fall into bed without bothering to brush my teeth. My phone lights up with a text, and I almost drop it in my haste to pick it up.

VADA

Made it home. Thanks again!

LUKE

Happy to do it.

VADA

YouTube: Awolnation "Handyman"

"How is it that you're so freakishly strong? Were you bitten by a radioactive spider as a child?"

I groan out a breath, pressing the bar up from the center of my chest, and look up Zack's nose. I readjust my grip, and he holds the bar until I nod and lower it again for five more reps. With a final exhale, the bar clinks back into place, and I slowly rise to sitting, wiping my hands on my basketball shorts. Zack hands me one of the gym towels and gives me a look like I'm some ill-mannered plebian. Whenever we have a day off school, Zack and I hit up the gym, using his dad's day passes. The equipment is way better than the stuff in our school's basement, and there's a hot tub.

I wipe my face with the towel. "Cull got the perfect eyesight and straight teeth. I got braces, contacts, and a pull-up bar."

"He does have nice teeth, doesn't he?"

"Your turn," I say.

Zack lowers himself onto the bench, and I stand over him, spotting. He starts off strong, and I check his form in the mirror. He's arching his back. Lifting more weight, out to prove something. The next rep, when he shoves the bar up, I grab it from him.

"Hey!"

"Hey, yourself." I remove five pounds from each side.

He narrows his eyes but doesn't argue. This time, his back stays flat. I catch someone familiar in the mirror and curse.

"Who?" Zack asks under his breath.

"Karly Lawton, six o'clock."

"The podcast groupie?"

I nod. I met Karly last month at a StarBust show we were promoting for the Loud Lizard, and she's since showed up at two other places. By "accident."

Zack shakes his head with a low chuckle. "For someone who doesn't like the limelight, you sure do attract a lot of attention."

"Maybe she's coming for you."

Zack looks down at his rainbow-striped knee socks.

"Hey, Luke! I thought that was you!" Karly is all sunshine and sweetness, but I just can't today.

"Heeeeey, Karly."

"What is this, like the third time this month? What are the odds? Do you work out here?"

"Ah, not often, no."

Karly beams. "Well, then, this is fate."

Zack stands and extends a hand. "More like teachers' in-service day. I'm Zack, Luke's best—"

"Man. He's . . . my man." I finish, feeling hot. He's gonna murder me. And then Cullen will murder me. And make fun of me forever. "This is Karly. She's a, um, loyal listener."

"I thought Cullen was dating Zack," Karly says. Because she *is,* in fact, a loyal listener and my brother has mentioned Zack in every conversation we've had for two years.

"He is," I say, wincing. "Sorry, I don't know why I said it like that. Zack's my best friend. And you have an excellent memory."

Zack raises a brow and opens his mouth, but Karly interrupts. "Oh my gosh, were you pretending you were gay?"

"Er . . ."

Karly's face flushes a bright red. "Wow. That's . . . that's super humiliating. I was only saying hi, Luke. Don't flatter yourself." Karly spins on her heel and marches back across the gym to where a few other girls are looking at us strangely, and I turn to Zack.

"So, my turn?"

He shoves me at the bench, replacing the weight and adding some. "That was pathetic, Greenly."

"I choked."

"You could politely decline her advances."

"I did. In a way." I lift off the press bar and grunt. Zack raises a brow but doesn't say anything. Fuck, this is heavy.

"Nah. You didn't."

I replace the bar after five, lowering my arms and letting the blood rush back into my fingers.

"Do you think she meant she was humiliated, or I should be?"

"Definitely both."

"I'm sorry. I didn't mean to use you."

He raises his brow again.

"Fine, I absolutely meant to use you. I'm sorry I purposely used you."

"Better," he says. "But since it backfired, it's fine. You owe me Iris's turtle brownies."

I grimace, though my mum makes brownies for Zack every week anyway, so it's not like it's a big deal. "You came up with that fast. Almost like you've been waiting for me to owe you. Basketball?" I ask. I need to get out of view of the fitness floor.

"Basketball," he agrees.

After he soundly trounces me on the court, we head to Chipotle, and I check my phone while we wait for our orders. Cullen posted our latest podcast link this morning, and we have the usual three first commenters: Phil, Zack, and Vada.

Phil Josephs @PHILtoCHILL
The only Teen Wolf worth talking about is the Michael J. Fox version. I'm ashamed to know you.
9:07 AM

Zack Granger @ZackAttack
I'm way hotter than Derek. No contest.
10:11 AM

Vada Carsewell @Vader18
Yeah but who keeps someone else's
@bestbuy order? Stand your ground,
Luke!
10:15 AM

I snicker and tap to respond.

Luke Greenly @TheLukeGreenly
nods THANK YOU. It's sacrilege. What are
we living, The Purge?
12:31 PM

I look up to see that Zack had grabbed our food. "What are you smiling about?"

I dig in, not bothering to wait. "Vada."

He pauses, burrito halfway to his mouth, and I swallow. "I mean, something she tweeted at the podcast. She agrees that I can't just stream *Teen Wolf* and forget my missing orders."

"That's stupid, for the record."

"It's not. It's the bloody principle."

"That no one cares about but you!"

"And Vada. That's two. We're practically starting a revolution."

Zack smirks. "And while you have your little two-person revolution against the United States Postal Service, someone else is watching your DVDs, and you could have already streamed the episodes five times over."

I ignore him, standing to fill my drink.

When I get back, my phone lights up with another notification. "No way!" I say after scanning it. "Vada tagged

Best Buy in her comment, and they are in my DMs asking what happened!"

I forget my lunch as I type out a message to them. "That's amazing," I say, picking up my fork. I drop it again. "I need to tell her."

I type out a quick text message.

> LUKE
>
> I owe you! Thanks for tagging Best Buy! They are resending my TW order!

I set it down and pick it up.

> LUKE
>
> *TeenWolf gif*

I pause, smiling to myself.

> LUKE
>
> YouTube: Duran Duran "Hungry Like the Wolf"

"Okay," I say, dropping my phone at last. "Now I can eat."

Zack blinks at me, his burrito gone.

"What?"

"Nothing." He shakes his head.

"Okay." My phone lights up with Vada's reply, and I forget my lunch again.

12

VADA

The following Thursday, I'm sitting in Red Robin waiting for my dad. I glance at my phone to check the time, and Luke's last message pops up. He's working the bar with Kazi tonight and cracking me up. Apparently, Kazi has to leave early *again* because of his shift at Whole Foods, and we've been hypothesizing for the last two hours about what he does there. After another glance around, I type:

> VADA
> Whole Foods called, Kazi, and they've got an opening in soy candles.

Gray dots, then . . .

> LUKE
> Gluten Digestives is looking for a tester, Kazi, and we think you're our man!

I snort. Luke hasn't worked there long enough to know, but Kazi honestly calls off at least once a month due to gluten contamination. But for real, Celiac is a mother effer. My mom went gluten free once and I had to eat at Meg's every night for a whole week.

VADA

We need someone to trim
our organic herb gardens on
Saturday afternoons from 1–4.
We pay in dried pomegranate
bookmarks.

LUKE

But you can only wear 100% locally
sourced cotton or that's an auto fire.

VADA

But for the love of Whole
Paycheck, don't cut your
glorious dreads. Your scalp is
our aesthetic.

LUKE

We offer room for job advancement.
If you don't suck, we can promote
you to wine and cheese pairings.
But only at the farmers' market.

VADA

We offer valet to elderly rich
people who have nothing to do
but grocery shop every day.
Would that interest you? You'd
need a hairnet.

LUKE

YouTube: Rusted Root "Send Me On
My Way"

VADA

**HOLY SHIT GREENLY YOU
LYRICAL GANGSTER.**

I pull up my YouTube app, scrolling for something perfect. Rusted Root. *Damn.* He's good. But I'm better. I grin, hitting Send.

VADA

YouTube: Grateful Dead
"Touch of Grey"

"Sorry we're late." I glance up, startled. My dad's snuck up on me, and he's not alone. He's brought my stepmom, Jane, and the twins, Haven and Margo, who are barely a year old.

I'm furious, and I can't show it because it's not their fault he's an asshole who hides behind his sweet family.

My dad walks over, leaning down to hug me, and I pat his back before standing to hug Jane. Margo raises her chubby hands at me, and I pull her into my lap, scooting back into the booth. I love my sisters. Growing up, I hated being an only child. I always wanted to be a part of a big family. Margo bangs the silverware on the table in front of us. I easily pry it from her fingers and smack a kiss on her soft cheek. She reaches for my hair, playing with it and babbling mostly nonsense words. My red hair is a constant source of entertainment for the twins.

Jane orders an iced tea, shifting Haven to another arm, and smiles kindly at me. "How's life, Vada?" Jane's lovely. Sweet tempered and patient and pretty and blond. Jane even remembers my birthday, which is amazing. A lot of people dislike their stepparents. I'd trade my dad to keep mine.

"Fine," I answer over Margo's babbling. "Just . . . fine."

She shifts again as Haven starts to fuss, and the server asks if we're ready to order. We always get the same thing, so in no time, the server leaves, and Jane is trying again.

"How's the club?"

"Great," I say. "Phil's letting me close on Sunday nights."

"That's wonderful!"

"Does it come with a raise?" my dad interjects.

"Yeah. A little one," I hedge, even though Phil's probably paying me too much. No need to tell Marcus that. He'll either, one, think Phil is showing off, or two, use it as an excuse to make me pay for dinner and learn "responsibility."

"Good."

Margo grabs for the silverware again, and I deftly manage move all of it except for the spoon, which she scoops up and immediately starts to smack on the table. Which, whatever. Me too, kid.

Our food comes, and I place Margo into a high chair and start to break up her food so Jane can still eat while she feeds Haven. My dad doesn't move to help. I honestly don't know how she lives with him.

"How's the college search going?" Jane asks between bites, focusing on me earnestly. "Still looking at UCLA?"

My eyes flicker to my dad. *Of course* he didn't tell her. "Yeah. I got into the music journalism program there, which is an amazing opportunity. I'm looking into funding now."

"I wish I could've gone to college in California," my dad grumbles around his burger. "Must be nice."

"Well, I mean, it's the best in the country for what I want to do."

"You want to write for *Rolling Stone,* right?" Jane offers with a smile.

"Or something similar. Yeah."

"That's amazing, Vada. So driven," she says. "Particularly for your age."

"Thanks—"

"Find any scholarships?"

My eyes cut to my dad. "I'm applying for several, yeah. And filling out my FAFSA." I swallow hard, my food forgotten in front of me. "I'll need you to fill one out, too, *Dad.*"

His eyes narrow, and he stops chewing. "You do?"

"Well, yeah. You and Mom both have to. It's how they base my financial aid."

"Listen, Vada, I have two kids and—"

"*Three,*" I remind him. "You have three kids."

He puts down his napkin. "Right. But it's not like I have extra money lying around. I'm sorry, but babies are—"

"Expensive. I know. But so is college, Dad."

Jane gets up, adjusting a squirming Margo and the diaper bag. "I'm gonna go change her. Marcus, I'm leaving Haven."

He waves her off. "Vada. I'm sorry, but I thought you and your mom had this all worked out. I've been very clear. I'm done paying."

"What about the child support? Can't you—" I take a deep breath, feeling desperate. "Can't you keep sending that while I'm at school? Like, for food and stuff?"

He's shaking his head. "That money's spoken for.

As soon as you turned eighteen and I didn't have to pay it anymore, I joined a country club. Dues are expensive."

"A country club," I repeat dully.

"For work. It's good networking. Maybe you need to think of someplace closer. Community college, even. California is expensive."

"I can't! It's . . . I can't. Phil says if I'm serious about music—"

"Oh, well, if *Phil* says." My dad's tone drips with sarcasm. "How's that college degree working out for my old friend Phil? He brokering record deals? Producing? It's a wonder he keeps that dumpster of a club afloat, if you ask me."

My vision suddenly blurs, and I'm so flustered I can't think. He's making me sound like I'm spoiled and that's so . . . *like him*. I push my food away. "I have to go."

"You haven't eaten, and Jane is still in the bathroom."

"I forgot. I have to work," I lie. "And you were late."

I scoot out of the booth right as Jane returns with Margo. I kiss Margo and hug Jane before pressing a soft kiss to Haven's sleeping face. Pulling my purse across my shoulders, I reach into my wallet and toss a ten on the table. "For the tip," I say. "I'll see you around, *Marcus*."

I get in the car and pull out before I can accidentally see them leaving. But I don't go far. Instead, I pull into the mall parking lot and hide in a sea of minivans.

I have a million great reasons why my dad should help me with college and why I'm not selfish but goal-oriented, and fuuuuuuck, it doesn't matter because he's not going to listen. I feel hysteria clawing at the back of my throat because what if I can't afford college and what if I need to go to junior college? It's not the worst thing. People do it all the time.

But it's not even school that bothers me. It's the *not leaving here*. It's still living in the same town with him and coming in second or even third place for the rest of my life.

I can't. I can't be only that. I've worked too hard. I have to get out.

My phone buzzes, and I swipe at my eyes, pulling it out to see a random email notification and the response Luke must have sent earlier.

LUKE
I'm not worthy! The Grateful Dead.
Are you serious?

Despite myself, I grin. It's stupid how happy that stupid text makes me.

VADA
Sorry, I was at dinner with my dad.

LUKE
Rescheduled from a few weeks ago?

VADA
Yeah. Good memory!

LUKE
Phil might've mentioned it.

VADA

Riiiiiight. He's worse than my mom.

LUKE

I've been meaning to ask you about that . . .

VADA

Yeah. Decades of pining + "Netflix and chill"

VADA

Don't tell Phil what it really means. They think it means watching Netflix and falling asleep on the couch. What did he say? Boyfriend Phil is sort of adorkable.

LUKE

Nothing really, he just looked sort of fond?

I laugh to myself, settling deeper into my seat.

VADA

Fond? And how does one look fond, exactly?

LUKE

. . .

LUKE

. . .

LUKE

Besotted?

VADA

What.

LUKE

I DON'T KNOW, OKAY!

LUKE

He just gets this look on his face.
Sort of like . . .

LUKE

I mean, it was obvious he feels strongly
about your mom. And then he said you
were going to dinner with your, uh, dad.

VADA

Yeah. It wasn't great.

LUKE

Wanna talk about it?

VADA

Not really, but . . .

VADA

Maybe this. YouTube: Snow
Patrol "Life on Earth"

LUKE
brb

I check my Snapchat while I wait for him to listen, but I'm distracted and vulnerable.

LUKE
. . .

LUKE
Sorry. That song is meant to be
heard on headphones or not at all.

VADA
Accurate. You need to hear it
in your throat.

LUKE
Yeah. I'm sorry, Vada. He's a fucker.

I snort. That's succinct and so perfectly fits my thoughts.

VADA
Thank you. He is. Anyway, I
need to drive home.

LUKE
Hold on.

LUKE
Something for the ride. YouTube: Mt.
Joy "Silver Lining"

I'm still smiling as I pull into my driveway.

Meg must've heard about my dad through our moms because on my way home, I got a text that she was on her way with Ben & Jerry's and a couple of Redbox movies.

The doorbell rings, so I dash down the stairs. Meg flutters in wearing her ever-present fairy wings and pink extensions. She's really like one of those pixie dream girls John Green characters are always following across the country, but unironically so.

She hugs my mom. "Aunt Mary! You look divine. Have you been drinking more water? Your skin is fabulous. Like a baby's butt. Seriously."

My mom grins, flipping her hair over a shoulder. "I'm glad someone noticed," she says. "I have, thanks. A gallon a day."

"You look radiant." And she does. I haven't been paying attention, too consumed in my own drama, but my mom looks really, really good. Fresh-faced and happy. Huh. Maybe she *does* know what "Netflix and chill" means.

"And Vada!" Meg throws her arms around me, squeezing tightly. "I brought ice cream and a little something extra. When childish sperm donors strike, we must retaliate with something rebellious." She holds up a bag of temporary tattoos and propels me up the stairs.

We enter my room, and she plops me down on my bed before sitting crisscrossed facing me.

"What the actual frickery?" she starts.

I fall back onto my comforter and stare at the ceiling. "I don't know. *Am* I being selfish? Like, am I asking too much and propelling myself into a debt-laden adulthood?"

"The truth?"

I shut my eyes with trepidation. "Yes. Always."

"No." She's emphatic. "So stop. Remember that time I was supposed to come to your NHS ceremony last year and your dad brought that rando coworker along instead and used up the last ticket and I had to walk home in the rain?"

"Yes."

"Remember the time your dad showed up to your dance recital late and missed your performance and didn't even realize it?"

I close my eyes more tightly. "Yes."

"Remember the time you went to the Dirty Harries concert with that kid from my youth group, and your dad showed up reeking of pot and drilled him about safe sex?"

"Jesus, yes. It was only like six months ago. Peter still won't talk to me."

"He's not right, and you're not selfish, Vada. It's okay to aim high. *You got in.* That's amazing. The money will come. Or it won't, and you'll take out loans and pay them back when you start writing for *Rolling Stone.*"

"Okay. You're right."

"Good. I can tell you aren't convinced, but that's eighteen years of Marcus's wackadoo absentee fatherisms talking." She raises her hands, plastic bangles clattering toward her bony elbows, and shakes them, banishing the negativity or whatever. "So, Five Below had a BOGO sale on tats." She reaches into her bag. "I love you, but I'm claiming the Hello Kitty ones."

I nod grimly. "Of course."

"But you can have the Pokémon ones."

"How about we just eat ice cream? I'm not feeling particularly rebellious tonight."

Meg deflates, but quickly recovers. "Okay. But you have to start talking." She passes me a pint and a spoon.

I tear it open and dig my spoon in, giddy that it's a little melty. "About what? I already told you about the dinner that wasn't."

"Not about your *dad*," she says impishly, scooping a bite of Cherry Garcia and crunching on a chocolate chunk. "About *Luke Greenly*."

"What, why?"

She holds up my phone. "Because I accidentally sat on your phone, and he's been sending you mad messages."

I rip it away from her and tuck my phone away without glancing at it, even though it kills me. I pick up my spoon. "Make yourself useful and put in that movie, will you?"

When she turns away, I can't help but let a smile slip.

13

LUKE

I don't technically *need* an after-school job. My parents make decent money and have always told us education comes first. They didn't want us to stress out about spending money. Since the sixth grade, we've gotten a weekly allowance so long as we've stayed on the honor roll and completed all our chores.

That I've willingly taken on a part-time job at a bar of all places is apparently beyond comprehension for my parents. You'd think they'd be complimentary about their eighteen-year-old son taking on a little extra responsibility. Instead, they're wearing matching expressions of bewilderment.

"It's just a part-time job, Dad."

"I thought you hated interacting in public."

"I don't hate it. I just don't love it. This is a good exercise for me. For personal growth."

"Personal growth?" my mum repeats.

I can practically hear my twin's eyes roll. "Jaysus, guys, let it go. Why does everything we do have to be rooted in psychological pathology? Why can't he just want to work in a bar?"

"I don't see why you'd toil away in a dive bar when you could be onstage making ten times as much." It's as though the man can't help himself.

"I'm not even going to answer that, Dad."

My mum shrugs, but my dad still looks puzzled. Fact is, I don't really know why I want to work at the Loud Lizard so badly. Before I heard Vada freaking out at Ben, I didn't. I don't need the money. I don't have a ton of spare time. But I wasn't lying when I said I liked it for personal growth. My shyness is crippling some days, but when I'm there, I feel fine. It's like wearing a hoodie the third day in a row. It's comfortable and smells like last night's dinner and reminds you of a time you fit in.

Whatever that means.

Eventually, my dad picks up his slice of homemade lasagna and takes a bite, dragging the mozzarella from his lips where a bit smudges up in his salt-and-pepper goatee. I sink into my chair and pick up my fork, relieved. I hadn't counted on the third degree. I wondered if they would object to the late hours, but I'm eighteen. They can't technically tell me no. (Well, they could. I live under their roof. But they wouldn't.)

My fingers itch to text Vada and let her know I'm good to work. *More. Work more.* Truthfully, I'm already on the schedule.

Off the record, Vada Carswell might be a bit of the reason why. Not (just) because I have, like, deep-seated, years-long feelings for her or anything but because she's cool. Interesting. Down-to-earth and not at all like anyone else I spend my time with. I hadn't realized how little I see of her at school. Our paths rarely cross, and that seems wrong. We have a near constant text stream going, but I couldn't tell you what her favorite shirt is.

Which is definitely something you would know if you were *interested* interested in someone, right?

She's practically a pen pal when you get down to it.

Of course, I could just ask her about her favorite shirt. And then I'd know.

"You'll need to get a ride from Cullen to work tomorrow, unless you plan to board," my mum interrupts my thoughts.

I glance outside, which is pointless since it's dark. "Would you mind?" I ask my brother.

"Nope. I can drop you off on my way to Zack's. But can you get a ride home?"

"I think so."

"From who?" my dad asks.

"Vada, probably," Cullen says. "Right?"

I nod, quickly taking another bite of pasta.

"Vada a bird?"

"A girl," I say after I swallow.

"A woman," my mum corrects automatically.

"That," I agree.

"She cute?" my dad asks.

"Ginger," my brother replies.

"Really?" My mum perks up and sips at her glass of red wine.

I don't bother responding.

"You've always had a bit of a thing for gingers," my mum says, sly as a game show host.

"Have not!"

"Ginny Weasley."

"Bonnie Wright is brilliant."

"That bird from *Pitch Perfect*," my dad offers.

"First of all, it's *woman*, and in my defense, that shower scene was eye-opening for twelve-year-old me."

"Fine, Mandi Simonson." Cullen's gleam is triumphant, and I snort.

"Whatever. She was my first kiss. And I have a feeling you arranged that so *you* didn't have to kiss her and out yourself."

"Like it was a secret. And you were super into her."

"Freshman year, I was super into Bonnie Wright. Mandi was a fair candidate."

"Fair candidate? Who are you? The crown prince?"

"So I like gingers! You people are maddening. That means nothing. I don't even know if Vada is working tomorrow night."

"Ten to one, she's working, and she'll drive you home, and twenty to one, you are texting her under the table right now."

"Ha! I don't even have my phone at the table. Manners, little brother."

"By two and a half minutes, and that's only because you left it in your room."

"Boys," Mum interrupts drolly. "Enough. You know I don't tolerate bickering on a single glass of wine."

Dad refills her glass.

"Two and I lose my inhibitions, Mr. Greenly."

"That's the plan, luv." My dad winks in an overtly cheeseball way, and Cullen shoves away from the table.

"On that note, I have homework to do."

I grab another slice to go. "Me, too."

My brother is halfway up the stairs before he shouts, "Remember, dick pics are forever!"

My mum chokes on her sip. "He's not serious."

I gather up my plate and glass and grumble, "He would know."

"Lukas Aaron Greenly."

"Kidding, Mum."

The next night, I'm behind the bar with a rugged-looking University of Michigan student named Ben. He's the one I'd overheard backing out of his shift the first night I worked. I've never really talked to him before, but he's pretty cool. Rolls his sleeves a lot. And keeps reapplying this beard balm stuff he carries in his back pocket.

Which is a bit weird, but we all have our quirks. I bite my nails, which is objectively more disgusting than smoothing essential oils in my facial hair. Not that I have any facial hair.

I watch as Ben carries on with a couple of college girls,

friends of his from the look of things. One seems more smitten than the other, touching Ben's arm across the bar and licking her lips like she'd like to taste him—and get a mouthful of beard balm, presumably—while her friend keeps scrolling through her phone, sipping at a generic lite beer, and looking bored.

"Kami and Liz," a voice says next to me. I startle to see Vada leaning back against the freezer chest.

"Who's who?"

"Kami's the one devouring him with her eyeballs, and Liz is her wing girl who prefers EDM and body paint."

I consider. "That doesn't sound like Ben's jam."

Vada grins, her teeth flashing in the neon. "Not in the slightest. I have to imagine Kami returns the favor, but I don't know when. They're here every single one of his shifts."

"He's not interested? She seems nice."

She gives a small shake of her head. "I don't think he has a clue."

I turn to face her, eyes wide. "You're not serious."

"Completely. I've even tried to help her out, but he's a lost cause."

"He's fixed his beard a hundred times. He's got to be interested."

Vada nods, tucking a chunk of auburn behind her ear and revealing the multiple simple stud piercings outlining the delicate shell of her ear. Someone motions for a drink, and I jerk my gaze away from Vada.

"Two gin and tonics."

I fix the drinks and slide them across the bar, accepting the payment.

"Have you tried to tell him?" I ask.

"Duh. But we're our harshest critics, right? When Ben

first started here, one of our customers was all over him. Totally dug the beard. She would wait for the end of his shift and try to talk to him at his car. Turned out she had a boyfriend, and the guy showed up to pick a fight with Ben, who, despite the sizable forearms, is more of a pacifist. Phil had to call the police and everything. Ben thought he was toast. More trouble than his two weeks of experience warranted."

"But he's still here?"

Vada nods her head. "Phil doesn't fire anyone. Like, ever. I get the impression Phil was a bit of a fuckup as a kid, so he likes to offer grace whenever possible. Ben can't help that he's pretty."

"You think he's pretty?" Not that I care. I don't. Mostly. Why can't I grow facial hair?!

"I mean." She squints and tilts her head as if she's trying to be objective. "Sort of. If you're into beards, which I'm not." *Thank God.* "He looks like he belongs on paper towel packaging. Or starring in one of those Hallmark movies where the hero is this mountain man shut-in after his fiancée dies, and then some spunky elementary school teacher gets lost in a snowstorm and ends up marooned at his cabin, and he lends her dry clothes that are way too big for her, and they have hot chocolate by the fire and fall in love despite his jaded views and her besotted innocence. Then, her know-it-all sister-in-law turns up three days later in a giant snowplow and brings the minister with her because she had a dream that was assuredly gifted from their dead grandparents, who fell in love in the same cabin seventy years before."

My mouth is hanging open.

She turns pink, her hair falling over her ears. "Or you know. Something like that."

"Did you actually script a Hallmark movie about Ben just now?"

It's dark, but I think she's cringing, and it's kind of adorable to see her flustered.

"They have a very clear formula to those movies," she says, her tone defensive.

"You don't say. How many have you watched?"

"Listen, I have a low tolerance for murder shows. And anyway, am I wrong?"

I regard Ben. He's pouring a couple of Moscow Mules into brass mugs for an older couple reliving their alumni experience. I *could* see it, actually.

"Fine. You're not wrong. Possibly missing your career as a TV drama writer, but not wrong."

"Hallmark wouldn't know what to do with me."

I take in her profile, the piercings, the oversized Pixies tee knotted in the back, the *fuuuuuuck* scribbled on the back of her hand in blue pen. "No. Probably not." I shove off the chest, smirking, and grab a shaker off the shelf in front of me. "I have an idea."

I pull together a couple of pink drinks, and when Ben turns to help another customer, I carry them over to the ladies.

"On the house. This one's for Kami, and this one's for Liz."

"Thanks!" Kami says, immediately taking a sip. "What's this called?"

"I like to call it *caught in a storm*, and that one's *wing-man*. Or woman, as it might be. Consider it a bit of liquid courage and ask the lumberjack out. He's shy, but he's been primping all night long."

Kami's eyes widen as she takes in my words, and she throws back the entire drink, eyeing up Ben. "On it."

I walk back to Vada, and we watch Ben's face flame behind his beard as Kami holds out a hand. He passes her his phone with zero hesitation, and she types in her number with a gooey smile before hopping off her stool and strutting away. Ben watches her before reaching for his phone and asking us for a minute away.

Vada waves him off, her lips twitching, as Kami's friend Liz walks back in. She pulls a twenty out of her wallet and holds it up in front of me.

"This is for you. Thank you. Finally! Now maybe I can stop sitting here every Sunday afternoon while they lust."

I accept it with a sheepish grin. "Glad to help."

Liz leaves, and I pocket my bill before settling back against the chest. Vada shakes her head. "You are full of surprises, Greenly."

"Hey, you dreamed up the thing. I just moved it along."

"We make a decent team," she says, nudging my shoulder.

I bite down on the inside of my cheek to keep from grinning. I want to say something smooth like, "We should team up more often. Like, on Friday night. On a date. Where we make out." But then I remember I'm not smooth, and what if I am reading this all wrong and she meant *team* only as a super-platonic team metaphor and then I'll feel like an idiot, so instead I say, "I guess we do."

"Speaking of, I heard you might be coming to class to observe us dancing again this week for the showcase." Vada frowns, wrinkling up her nose so her freckles scrunch together.

"We are. But if you'd rather I not come, I don't have to. I have plenty of material."

"Material?" she asks lightly, her freckles spreading.

"You know what I mean."

She nods. "It's not that I don't want you to watch, obviously, but dance class is sort of sacred to me. It's where I go to work out my issues."

"Fair."

"Are you sure?" she checks.

"Absolutely."

"I like you, Luke."

I bite my tongue, chasing away a thousand responses before settling on a casual, "Likewise, Vada."

14

LUKE

YouTube: Nirvana "Heart-Shaped
Box"

VADA

Ugh. We're fighting.

LUKE

What? Why? You can't censor me.

VADA

Kurt Cobain? Really? Where's
the creativity?

LUKE

Oh, so sending a link for a song
that's over twenty-five years old is
"lacking creativity"?

VADA

Nirvana is the pits, man. (With
the exception of David Grohl,
OBVIOUSLY.)

LUKE

Cobain was the pits. Nirvana holds up.

VADA

YouTube: Pearl Jam "Better
Man"

LUKE

Pearl Jam is just as old and grungy,
Vada.

VADA

Yet Eddie Vedder is still
kicking it.

LUKE

Ah. So, that's your issue.

VADA

Maybe.

LUKE

Interesting.

VADA

I can feel you psychoanalyzing
me from across the room,
Greenly.

LUKE

So, sit still, ffs. When you move
around, you mess with my brain
wave-reader.

VADA

Hilarious.

LUKE

Gotta go. Michigan leading at
halftime means a whole lot of "shots
all around" are about to happen.

VADA

YouTube: Bastille "World Gone
Mad"

LUKE

. . .

LUKE

. . .

LUKE

Well played.

One of the very best perks of my job is when Phil is all,
"Hey Vada, there's this new band named (Not) Warren

coming to town, and you need to check them out," and he sends me for free.

And I get to write about it as if anyone cares what I think.

But according to the *Behind the Music* stats, a few thousand people *do* care. It's mind-blowing.

Tonight, he sent Luke with me. I'm very, very chill about this, obviously. I had kind of hoped by working with Luke, and, by default, texting him, I would decide he was weird. That happens, you know? Like, you could low-key crush on a guy from afar because he has a hot accent and ruddy cheeks, but you get to know him and he doesn't even know who the Smiths are or hasn't heard of Amy Shark and then, magically, you couldn't care less about how he looks like Christmas morning after carrying in a box of limes from the shed out behind the bar you both work at.

But Luke *does* know who the Smiths are and even sent me a link to "Please, Please, Please, Let Me Get What I Want" the other night, causing me to swoon on the spot, startling Meg, who afterward kept checking me for a fever.

And he's so damn likable. Ridiculously considerate and smart and always humming under his breath and, well, the Christmas cheeks thing and . . . I'm sunk.

(I haven't asked him about Amy Shark. He's probably president of her fan club, and I'd have to straight-up propose to him, and we're too young for that nonsense.) (Also, college.)

So, here we are. So close to each other we're rubbing elbows, and I can somehow feel his body heat through the sleeve of my hoodie, and he smells like Tide PODS.

To the band's credit, they are killer. So much so that

I hardly notice the delicious way my coworker smells. We're in that weird fake-ending spot right before the band comes back on for an encore, and I wonder idly whose idea this whole pretense was in the first place? Like, "We're all done, folks. Have a good night!" and three and a half minutes later, "Just kidding, we thought of two more original songs and a super-long cover to play for you guys, so thank God we didn't turn all the lights back on."

"I wonder who the first band was to do the delayed encore?" Luke asks, his voice slightly raised over the murmur of the crowd. "It's not like we don't all expect it now."

Jesus Harold Christ.

He looks at me; his eyes practically glow in the dim blue light of the stage. "Like, what are they doing back there? Counting to one hundred four times?"

"Microwaving a Hot Pocket?" I suggest.

"Retying all their shoes, double knotted?"

"Checking their Instagram feeds."

"Checking your review blog, more like," he says, and I feel my face grow hot.

"I doubt they even know," I say.

He holds a fake mic to my face. "Ms. Carsewell, just how many eye-closers did tonight's performance warrant?"

I'm tempted to bite his hand. To taste it or fend him off, I can't tell.

"Honestly, at least three. They were excellent."

He nods, pulling his hand back and stuffing it in his pocket. "They were really good. And history has shown the best is still to come," he says as the stage lights come on once more and the crowd roars its approval.

The lead singer plucks at his electric guitar as the secondary vocalist takes center stage. She has an incredible indie Meg Myers sound going for her, and I almost wonder if she'd be better served as the main vocalist.

She could pull it off, if this pop-y electronic track is any indication. She drapes over the mic sensually, and I watch the guitarist watch her.

"Wonder if they're sexing it up?" Luke's breath is in my ear, and I jump. "Sorry!" he says.

My eyes are wide. "I was thinking the same thing!"

After that, I'm totally distracted. If they aren't sleeping together, they ooze chemistry. Sex appeal can boost a band from great sound to great show.

It can also disintegrate a band faster than Spider-Man facing Thanos.

For their final song, they do a duet, during which I forget my own name or where I am or what day it is. The lyrics are soft and achingly powerful. I wish I had written them. I haven't ever been in love, but I feel it in the song and their voices, and it *fucking sucks to be in love.* My heart is quiet, and my breath stops in my lungs. I'm so still that I can feel my bones creak when I come to life once more. *That* is the best fucking feeling in the world. The lights come on, and my throat hurts from screaming and my hands itch from clapping, and Luke turns to me, brushing a tear from my cheek with his thumb.

"Five eye-closers," he says. "Easily."

"Holy shit," I reply. "What just happened?"

"I think we saw history being made."

We stare at each other, the room erupting around us,

but don't move. I'm afraid to. At last I close my eyes, taking a picture in my mind.

I want to live in this moment forever, and maybe I'd like it okay if Luke were here, too.

15

LUKE

The night after I see that band with Vada, I finally have the house to myself. My parents went to see the latest Marvel movie, and Cullen is out to dinner, and it's awesome. I'm a high-functioning introvert in a houseful of raging extroverts.

I've pulled my keyboard out of my closet and set it on its stand. After switching it on, it glows at the touch as though it's been waiting for me. I lightly press a few of the keys, caressing them, and immediately feel stupid. *It's only a cheap keyboard. Get your shit together, Luke.*

Pulling aside my curtains, I reassure myself the driveway is empty before returning to sit at the keys. I play a melody that's been itching to get out. Once. Twice. Changing it a little and humming under my breath. Changing it again. Then I close my eyes and let go.

I've had the song in my head for a while, but it wasn't until that class, and then at the silent disco—until I saw the way Vada moved, her shape backlit by the streaming, pulsing lights—that everything clicked into place.

I can't get the picture out of my brain.

(I suspect I will die with it on my eyelids.)

Something inside of me came alive that first day in the studio, and it's been growing and stretching free ever since. Every time I happen across Vada in the hallway at school. Every shift we work together, when she laughs at my inane jokes. Every song she sends, revealing tiny pieces of her that I'm not sure anyone else gets to see.

I hadn't realized how much she'd gotten to me until the words began pouring out, my stomach clenching more and more with each line. This can't be good. This is exactly why I've been okay with reading blogs and friendly smiles from a safe distance. This, whatever it is inside of me, is—is *a lot*.

That's the thing about music; it's the absolute maddening truth. It's what makes the good songs so powerful. The more agonizing the truth, the better. I'm not ready to bare my soul like that. You can be damn sure *this* song isn't going into the showcase. I scratch out a line, frustrated. I need something more casual . . . generic . . .

"Who're you singing about?"

I jump with a crash of the keys, stumbling off the back of my stool.

"Fuck me, *Cullen*, don't you knock?"

Cullen huffs out a laugh, bouncing once on my bed. "I did. You were lost in the moment, so I let myself in."

"How long have you been sitting there?"

He shrugs. "Long enough."

It's full-on dark out. I glance at my watch. Nine thirty. I've been playing for two hours.

"So, who were you singing about?"

I rub at my neck, feeling how hot it is. "No one. It was just a song."

"That you wrote."

"Yeah, well. It's been a while. Wanted to see if I still could."

"That was really excellent, Luke. Why'd you give it up?"

I glare at him, incredulous. "You know why."

He waves the thought away like a gnat. "That was before the podcast. Loads of people listen to you every single week."

"Not live."

"Everyone's a little shy in front of crowds. You'd get used to it."

"I like my privacy, thanks. I'm not like you guys."

Cullen's expression darkens. "What's that supposed to mean?"

My eyes dart around, grasping for a way to make him understand. "You and Dad and Mum, you're all brilliant at commanding a crowd. You live for the attention. I don't want anything to do with it. On the podcast, I can pretend it's you and me talking. I don't see the others. They aren't real to me. I don't want to sing for crowds. I don't want anyone trying to guess who I'm singing about or picking the lyrics apart. It's not for them."

"But it *is* for someone," he insists.

I shake my head.

"Bollocks. Fine. You're too afraid to live up to your potential or whatever. Classic Luke. But you're cheating whoever that was about from hearing it."

I exhale sharply, dropping into my desk chair. "How d'you even know it was about anyone? Why can't it be about no one?"

He pauses like he wants to say something else and has reconsidered, instead saying, "Because those weren't imaginary feelings. That was some deep shit, and it was really good, Luke. And *whoever she is*"—he emphasizes the words—"*she* deserves to know someone feels that way about her."

"Luke! I didn't expect to see you tonight." Phil slides behind the bar to where I'm leaning on a counter, my head bobbing to the low thrum of music playing over the speakers. It's early yet, but the game-night crowd should be making its way in soon. It's March Madness season, after all.

"Ben asked if I wouldn't mind filling in. He had a date."

Phil's grizzled cheek twitches under his wire frames. "Ah yes. I hear you're to blame for that."

I lift a shoulder. "Perhaps. I was looking for more hours."

"Well, you got 'em." Phil pulls out a glass, shovels in enough ice to hit the rim, and fills in the spaces with iced tea. "How are you liking things so far?"

"I love it," I say honestly. "It feels homey."

Phil nods as if I didn't just compare his bar to a log cabin in the woods.

"I mean," I try again, "I'm comfortable."

"There are two kinds of people in the world," Phil says, taking a pull from his tea. "The kind who listen to music and the kind who live inside it. The kind who listen to it come to my bar, have a drink or five, and leave with a friend. The kind who live in it never really leave."

"Well, I'm only on until ten," I joke.

"And I'll probably kick you out before then. It's a school night." Phil slips his drink onto a storage shelf under the counter and pulls a rag out of the bleach bucket to wipe down the bar top. I should be the one doing that, but he waves me off before I can protest. "But that's not what I mean. Even when you walk out of here, finish school, drive across the country for college or whatever, you'll carry the music with you. It's in your bloodstream. I can tell."

I nod because he's right. I don't know how, but he is.

"So, tell me something. How'd Charlie Greenly's son end up here? I thought your dad was overseas making a fortune producing."

"Eh," I say, turning the hard liquor bottles so the labels face outward. "He was, but he . . . lost interest? I don't know. Mum was offered a position at U of M, and they decided to give her dreams a shot for a bit. They're ridiculously in love. He sold off his portion of the label and moved here, barely batting an eye."

"Taking their twin sons with," he concludes for me.

"Well, they could hardly leave us behind. It was fine, though. We were always moving around as kids."

"You interested in following in your dad's footsteps?"

"Not really, no."

"Not a punk fan?"

"More like a not-performing fan."

Phil points to a photo behind the bar. "Me neither. I hid behind my drums, but when the rest of the band branched out, I decided behind the bar was more to my liking."

"I didn't know you played."

"And sang, believe it or not. We were more Alkaline

Trio to your dad's Bad Apples, but we did all right for a garage band."

I stare at the photo, taking in an action shot of a younger, thinner, hairier Phil behind a gleaming drum kit with the name *Loud Lizard* emblazoned on the front. "You were the original Phil Collins, dual singer and drummer," I say.

"Eh, Phil Collins is the original Phil Collins, but I did all right."

"Where's the rest of your band now?"

"Insurance agent, high school teacher, mortician."

"You're not serious."

Phil grins. "Completely."

"You're the only one who stuck with music? That's sort of depressing."

"Depends how you look at it. Objectively, they're making more money. Well, not the teacher, but that's not his fault."

"Music is a fickle arsehole," I say without thinking.

Phil laughs. "Indeed. Though it served Charlie well. I'm glad. Did he ever tell you he played here? Had to be around '92. Bad Apples were a fine group of randy gents." I grimace at the mere picture of my father as "randy," and Phil whoops. "You look like him, you know?"

"Yeah."

"Not so much your brother," he says. "He must take after your mom?"

"He got all the Greek."

"Can he sing, too?"

"How'd you know I sang?" I ask, because that's what he's really asking.

"You hum to yourself." He taps his ear. "It's a gift."

I shake my head. "Nah, he wishes. It'd be better if he did. It's wasted on me."

"Says who?"

"Guess." I sound sullen, and I bite my tongue before I can say more.

Phil lets out a breath, his eyes skimming over the still-quiet bar. I move to the dishwasher and start to empty it in preparation, careful to not meet his eye.

"There's more to music than singing, you know."

"I like to write," I say.

Phil helps me with the dishes, removing one that's still covered in condensation and drying it with a clean rag.

"Do you play anything?"

"Piano."

"You any good?"

I shrug.

"So, yes. Is this a stage fright thing or a general wish to play behind the scenes?"

"The second one."

"Fair enough. And Charlie doesn't love it?"

"Hates it."

He leans forward on his forearms. "Sure he does. It's hard to understand when you live for the crowds, and Charlie Greenly sure as hell worked a crowd in his day. Have you ever seen it?" he asks suddenly.

"Footage of my dad? Not in years, actually. Though I've seen him in the kitchen, so I can imagine."

Phil is already shaking his head. "Nah. It's not the same, I guarantee it. He was like a fucking firecracker up there. I thought for sure he was on speed, but he said he avoided the hard stuff."

I turn red. "He says heroin messes with your pecker."

Phil barks out a laugh. "I'm sure I have footage some-where. I'll dig around for it. It's worth watching."

The crowds start to filter in, and Phil and I cover the bar in equal parts. I watch him interact. Even though I'm available, most people wait to catch Phil's eye. He's the legend. They came for him as much as they came for the beer and Big Ten basketball.

And I can see why. He's easy like his bar. Comfortable. Genuine as fuck. It's the most unsettling-slash-settling thing I've ever encountered.

I wonder what the footage he has of my dad performing will look like. I honestly can't imagine it. My dad stopped being a punk rocker long before we came along. The Charlie Greenly I know wears his seat belt and goes to wine tastings and plays Mario Kart. I've heard some of his music, and it's good. Really good. Raw and edgy and heartfelt.

I inherited more than my blond hair from him. The pressure of what *could be* weighs on my chest so heavily, I feel short of breath. It's not that I don't *want* to create music. I do. I just can't perform it live. It's too personal. Cullen interrupting my songwriting the other night felt like a straight-up violation.

No. I couldn't do it. Play my own words in front of an audience? I can't think of anything I'd hate more.

16

VADA

It's unseasonably warm when Phil shoos me out of work early Saturday night. I'm not on the schedule anyway, and I suspect he's feeling extra generous after I hooked him up with Luke. Luke's so diligent, he's putting the rest of us to shame. The first time they worked together, Luke kept calling Phil "Mr. Josephs" to all our great amusement. Phil let him for a good hour and a half before I intervened.

"Go." Phil swats in my direction. "Get into trouble. Be a kid."

I wipe my hands on a clean rag. "Really?" I ask even as I'm untying my apron strings.

"Really. But don't get arrested. Mary would definitely blame me."

I reach for the tip jar and dump it out behind the bar, counting out my share and shoving it in my back pocket before I reach for my phone and tap out a text to Meg.

> VADA
> Off early. Where are you?

> MEG
> Around the corner. Fly Fishing doc
> at Michigan Theater. *eyeroll*

Yikes. Meg's social life is even worse than mine.

VADA

Can you escape?

MEG

Be there in five.

"Night, Phil!"

"Text your mom!" he shouts back, and in response, I wave over my head and shove through the back door, nearly smacking Luke in the face.

"Gah! Sorry!"

He laughs, surprised. "My fault. I wasn't watching."

He's wearing a jean jacket, and the denim does ridiculous things to his gray-blue eyes, making them pop, even behind his frames. "Are you working?"

He shakes his head. "Nah, I'm picking up my check. And tips from last night. I forgot to grab my share, and Phil saved it from Kazi."

"Ah," I say, leaning a hip against the door. "Yeah, you gotta watch him. His dreads hide secrets." I turn to see Cullen and Zack standing behind Luke. "Coming in for a job, too? I'm on a roll for recruitment these days."

Cullen shakes his head. "I don't do manual labor. Germs make me nervous."

Zack rolls his eyes and reaches out his hand. "I don't think we've officially met. Zack Granger."

I shake his giant hand and tilt my head, looking up at him. "You're even more enormous in real life." Zack is handsome in a classic way. Tall, tanned skin, prominent Adam's apple, well built. And yeah, really tall. Zack appears stretched out and about three years older than the rest of us.

"I get that a lot."

"It's a compliment. You carry it well."

"He does, doesn't he? Not an inch wasted," Cullen says, looking his boyfriend up and down. Zack beams at the attention. It's adorable. I don't know when Zack came out as gay. It's like one day he was there, holding Cullen's hand in the hallway and kissing him after school and it just looked right. What he was wasn't definitive. He was just Cullen's, and Cullen was his.

"Anyway," Luke says, clearing his throat. "D'you just get off? I mean, did you finish? With work? Are you done with your shift?"

Cullen mutters something under his breath, and Luke turns red, shoving him away.

I decide not to comment on the slipup, even as my own face grows hot. "Yeah. Phil let me off early. I was actually just meeting—"

"Me! She was meeting me!" Meg says in a harried voice, stripping off her jacket as she jogs up. "Lord, it's warm out."

"Well, it *is* fly-fishing season," I say glibly. She snorts, and I turn to everyone else. "This is Meg. Meg, this is Zack, Cullen, and Luke. Luke Greenly," I say and bite the inside of my cheek when I see her eyes light up. "Luke and Cullen Greenly, I mean. They're twins." Jesus, Vada, just *stop*.

She immediately holds out a hand to Luke, who's staring at her rainbow fairy wings with interest. "Pleasure to meet you."

"I'm Luke," he says.

"And I'm Cullen," his brother interjects. "Love your wings."

Meg curtsies. "Thank you. I feel they add a bit of whimsy, don't you?"

"Absolutely," says Zack, straight-faced. "Not just any-one can pull off wings."

I press my lips together, watching Luke take in my best friend. Because this is sort of a deal breaker for me. Meg's important, and we're a package deal. Not that any-thing is, like, *happening* with Luke. But just in case. Best to know ahead of time.

"Do you listen to Lorde at all?" Luke asks after a beat.

Meg's smile is megawatt. "Heck yeah, I do."

Luke squints. "You remind me of the 'Green Light' video. Have you seen it?"

"Oh my gosh, yes!" I agree excitedly. "Oh my god, Meg. Totally. Lorde dances down the street alone in her dress and sneakers, and it's so adorable and whimsical as fuck. It's perfectly you."

Meg is already pulling up the video on her phone as we move off to the side to allow people into the club. A few seconds later, she's twirling under Zack's arm and sing-ing along. For a giant basketball star, Zack is remarkably graceful.

I glance at Luke, and out of the corner of my mouth, I whisper, "You got all that from fairy wings?"

His eyes brighten. "It's a gift. Sort of like that whole genre-aesthetic thing you do. She feels like Lorde danc-ing down the boulevard in the middle of the night to me."

"Incredible," I say. I'm tempted to ask what song makes him think of me, but I squash the thought quickly.

His full lips lift in a small smile as if he can read my mind, and he shakes his head. "I'm still working on you. Some people jump right out at you. Meg and Cullen, for instance. Cull's clearly Panic! at the Disco—"

I hold up a hand. "Wait! Let me think." I watch Cullen

with Zack and Meg. All three are dancing, Meg the pixie belle of the ball. Zack, stalwart and warm, steady as they come. But Cullen? He's like this brilliant technicolor. I think of every Panic! at the Disco song I've ever heard. So many come to mind, but . . . "'Dancing's Not a Crime,'" I say.

Luke raises his brows under his blond waves. "Are you sure?"

"One hundred percent."

He nods, looking at his twin. "It's like it was written for him. Even Zack agrees."

"It could be his life's motto."

"I'm pretty sure he's been advocating to make it the prom theme."

"If anyone could do it . . ."

Luke agrees. "If he could channel just an ounce of that superpower into philanthropy, he'd be able to fix global warming."

Lorde wraps up, and we're starting to get stares from people walking into the bar. "Where're you three headed?" Meg asks, tucking her phone in her back pocket.

Cullen points across the street. "Only the best place in the universe. Pinball Pete's."

"The arcade?" I ask. "I've never been."

Zack blinks. "You work across the street."

"But I always enter and leave out the back. It's not really on my radar."

"Well, today is your lucky day," Cullen says, taking my arm. "Inside those Day-Glo doors is a mood ring with your name on it."

"Cullen. We would need to pool *all* our tickets for a mood ring! It's like seven hundred tickets for something that will inevitably turn my finger green. It's not even real science."

"Hush," he says over the loud tinkling and chiming of the zillions of games.

This place is like a fever dream. Blinking strobe lights, loud music echoing from the row of driving games, and the clatter of change machines spewing more chances.

Also, super fun. Way more fun than I'd expected when we first descended the stairs into this dungeon of an arcade. Turns out, we all suck at pinball, despite my lifelong assumption I would be great at it. But we've found our hot spots. Zack is murdering Luke in Skee-Ball, and Meg won't leave the moving shelf game. She's got a stack of quarters, and she's determined to win the jackpot.

"How many do you have so far?" I ask Cullen, nodding at the stash of paper tickets dangling from his back pocket.

"Plenty," he says. "And I've come prepared with a secret weapon."

"Which is?"

"My winning smile."

I roll my eyes with a groan. "We're doomed. I'm just gonna cash in for some Dubble Bubble."

"Stop!" he says, jumping in front of me and grabbing my hands in his. "We can't give up! There are certain machines that give out more tickets. Meg's on quarters. She's bound to strike it rich. And Zack is a Skee-Ball prodigy. It's his hands," he offers with a sly smile, leaning close. "Magic hands."

I remove my hands from his grip, smacking his shoulder with a grin and glancing around for something to spend my last four quarters on. "Are those Dance Dance Revolution?" Before Cullen can say anything else about

Zack's magic anything, I make a beeline for the vacant machines.

I squat down, looking for the amount needed, and it's a dollar. Perfect.

"Dance off?" Luke suggests, holding his last dollar out. He must have gotten tired of losing to Zack.

"'99 Luftballons'?"

"Done," he says.

"Have you done this before?"

His lips quirk. "Maybe. Are you scared?"

I straighten. "Not a chance. If I win, I get all your tickets. There's a mood ring with my name on it."

He shakes my hand. "Your funeral."

I bend down to retie my Chucks and remove my long-sleeved work T-shirt, passing it to Zack to hold. Luke pretends to stretch his lats, and when he does, I notice he's removed his jean jacket and is wearing a solid white T-shirt. A fitted one that stretches taut across his chest.

So, that's not fair.

I shake off my thoughts and spit on my palms, rubbing at the soles of my shoes.

"Ew, Vada." Meg snickers. I ignore her. This is serious.

We hit Start and step onto the arrows. At first, it's slow. Step forward, step back. Together, apart. Luke's with me step-by-step, and I can't help but mouth along with the singer. I love this song.

About a minute in, it starts to pick up, but I'm here for it. I don't glance at Luke, but I can feel him keeping time beside me. I slip into the beat, and I'm in the zone. Getting a little cocky, I take my hands off the bars. I can hear voices behind us but won't let myself concentrate on anything but the beat blaring around our heads. My calves are burning, and my face feels warm. I swipe at sweat on my upper lip, but I'm smiling so hard, my cheeks hurt. This is the most fun I've had probably ever.

"Getting tired yet, Carsewell?" Luke asks, not sounding at all tired.

I don't respond. I just keep dancing on this ancient machine. Step touch. Step touch. Jump apart, jump together. Jump diagonal. The song is clearly winding down because it shifts into hyper speed, and I gulp. I can do this. I put my hands back on the bars, but that throws me. Damn it.

I get off beat, and my screen lights up with misses. I try to catch up, but I can't. Before I can recuperate, the song clicks off, and Luke's victorious. I can't be mad, though. He looks so damn cute with his hair sticking up off his forehead, slicked with sweat, and his T-shirt clinging to his abs.

Nope. I'm not even a little mad.

I pass over my tickets. "Fair and square," I say, giving a fake bow. "I'm not worthy."

He shoves my tickets into his pocket. "It's okay. How could you possibly know I was the seventh-grade DDR champion back in London?"

"No!" I say, choking on my laugh.

"Hell yes. I'm not too proud. I beat out Cullen for the title."

"He did?" I confirm.

Cullen shrugs easily. "I'm heavy on my feet."

I follow Meg back to her quarter shelf. "I've been thinking about this," I say. "What if you put in more than one at a time?"

She holds out the three she has left. "Worth a shot." One by one, they plop in, and the entire continent of change shoves off the shelf, the winning chime ringing out.

"Holy smokes!" she cheers, collecting the still-streaming tickets and winding them around her fist.

"Yikes," I say with a grin a minute later as she feeds tickets into the redemption machine. "Your parents will never forgive me for starting your gambling habit."

"It's true," she says happily, her wings bouncing. "There's no coming back from this den of iniquities." She pulls her receipt out and reads the total with a squeal. "I'm full-on corrupt."

I follow her to the counter, and she decides to cash in all five hundred of her tickets for a plastic pirate sword. All those quarters. For a prop. Which she's using to stab Luke in the back, making him laugh in the best way as we head back up into the early-spring sunset. The air feels fresher up here, and the sounds are muted. I thought working in a bar was an assault on my eardrums, but that was something else. Another hour and I'd have gained an eye twitch, for sure.

I glance at my watch. "It's late, Meg. I should take you home."

"We need to go, too," Zack says. "My sister wanted the car tonight."

"Actually, looks like my mom and dad are leaving the theater," Meg says, glancing ahead and waving her sword above her head. "I'll head home with them."

I give her a quick hug, and she dances off. Zack and Cullen cross the street ahead of Luke and me to where a red Jeep is parked in front of the Loud Lizard.

"You headed back in?" he asks.

"Nah. But my car is out back."

Luke and I linger. I don't know why we don't cross the street except that when we do, this is over.

He reaches in his pocket. "I got you something."

"More quarters?" I guess. He holds out his hand, his fingers wrapped around something small.

I hold out my hand under his, the heat from his skin infusing mine. He presses something sharp in my palm.

"A mood ring! This must have cost all your tickets!"

"All *our* tickets," he says. "Sadly, it's too small for my fingers."

"It's adjustable, you nerd."

His face is innocent. "Ah well."

"Thank you," I say. Feeling weirdly touched. It's a cheap toy, for crying out loud. It's totally gonna turn my finger green. (Because I'll never take it off.) We cross the street, and Cullen and Zack are already in the car. Watching us. So, I wave, flashing my mood ring, and cut through the alley to the back of the building. I'm glancing at my ring again when I hear a groan, and my stomach sinks.

Asshole Marcus is slumped against my car.

I curse under my breath and glance at the back door to the bar. "Does Phil know you're still here?" I hold out a hand. "Never mind. Don't answer." I hesitate half a second before the image of my poor stepmom having to load up the sleeping babies to come and get Marcus has me unlocking my door with a beep. "Get in the car. I'll drive you home."

I get him buckled in and pass him a plastic bag that I find after a cursory search of the back seat. "Don't you dare puke in Mom's car."

He crumples the bag in his fist and looks at me, irritable. "Watch the tone."

I stab at the radio and turn it loud, ignoring *that* stupid statement.

Before I've had the chance to back all the way out of my spot, he's turning down the music. "Who is it?"

I bite the inside of my cheek. We've been playing the radio game since I was born. My dad slaps his hand over the lit display. "No cheating."

I huff, desperately wanting to ignore him and knowing I won't. "The local college station doesn't have names anyway, Marcus." I listen for a second before I say, "Too easy. Social Distortion."

"Song?" he quizzes.

That takes me longer, but I know it as soon as the first lyric comes on. "'Ball and Chain.'"

"Lead singer? And at least two facts."

I recite blandly, "Mike Ness. Social D was often called the punk version of the Rolling Stones, though I disagree. And Mike had a heroin addiction."

"Probably not the only one," he concedes. "Why don't you think the Rolling Stones comparison is accurate?"

He's not curious. He's quizzing me still. Marcus doesn't want to talk. He wants to teach.

"Because he's not fucking Mick Jagger, that's why."

"Mick Jagger is overrated," he says predictably. Marcus hates the Rolling Stones. For a long time, I thought I did, too. Until I realized I only hated them because I never gave them a chance. I'd inherited my dad's opinion like it was canon. "And watch your language," he continues. I scowl into the darkness.

When I get to the next light, I turn in my seat to face him. In the shadows, his face looks haggard. He's still in his suit jacket from work, which means he hit up Phil the second he got off. Probably right after Phil kicked me out. Did Phil guess he would show? Has my dad been coming in a lot lately? I need to have another talk with my boss. He's protecting me again.

"Why aren't you home with your wife and kids?"

"I'm with my kid," he says easily. Like he's not breaking my heart. "Who is it?"

The light changes, and I slam on the accelerator with a bit too much force, slamming us both back in our seats. He curses under his breath and clutches his bag tighter.

"Jimmy Eat World. 'The Middle.' Came on to the emocore scene in the late '90s. Their best song is 'Hear You Me.'"

"That's not a fact," he says.

"Actually. It *is*. After Grandma Carsewell died, I played it until your CD disintegrated."

"I always wondered what happened to it." He's quiet as I turn in to the upper-middle-class neighborhood he and Jane call home. It's full of townhomes, the really nice kind. With high association fees and home security systems.

"Clearly, the student deejay is feeling their grunge tonight. Pearl Jam, 'Daughter,'" I say as I put the car into park in his drive. Sometimes the radio game really gets to the heart of the matter. Marcus sits, staring at his hands as the opening strings of the electric guitar confirm my answer.

"Don't think I'm too drunk to notice what you're implying."

"Oh, please. This is your game, Marcus. You taught me this trick."

"If you're going to wield lyrics that way, you'd better know what you're talking about."

"And if you're gonna start lecturing me on music or life, you'd better know what *you're* talking about. It's the name of the song. That's it. You taught me facts. Just facts. *Know the facts.* I know them. Thanks. Your job is done here."

Marcus doesn't bother saying thanks for the ride. He opens the car door, staggers up his front stoop and into his house without a glance back at me.

Which is for the best. That fucker doesn't get to see me cry. I know "Daughter" isn't about me. It's about a child with a learning disability whose parents beat her for struggling. The story is awful, and I can't relate to it. But sometimes it's the feeling of a song you relate to. Marcus doesn't understand that kind of nuance. He doesn't get feelings. If he did, maybe we wouldn't be in this place. His knowing I'm his kid and my not ever getting to feel like it.

17

LUKE

"The world would like you to believe that love is like an Ed Sheeran song. All bare feet in the grass, kissing in the dark, growing old together," I say into my mic. "But it's not. I mean. Look at Eddie. The man barely has it together, from the look of it. He's a poor man's Rupert Grint who gets revenge on his exes with breakup anthems worthy of TSwift."

Cullen stares at me, his eyes wide. He opens his mouth to respond but shakes his head. Finally, he says, "Poor man's Rupert Grint? I think the lad does better than that. What does Rupert have, millions of pounds and an ice cream truck to his name? I'm pretty sure Ed Sheeran has a lady in every district. Perhaps a fella, too, if he's into that kind of thing, which I sincerely hope he is."

"He's married, but that's not the point."

"Allegedly," he scoffs.

"The point is, love's not like any of that. It's not some prefabricated song meant for weddings, and it's not a lay in every city. It's deeper than that, and I resent the implication that males, regardless of their preferences, aren't capable of being aware of the difference."

Cullen leans back in his seat, pulling his mic to him. "So, you're saying the flowers and the candles and the Hallmark holidays and fancy expensive restaurants aren't romantic?"

"No, I mean, yeah. Okay. Those *can* be romantic," I say, frustrated. "I guess I'm saying it's not the actions themselves so much as the intention. Just because good ole Eddie sings those sappy songs and looks like he hasn't showered, everyone thinks he's so bloody sincere. But he's not."

"Okay. I'll bite. What *does* make real, sincere love?"

I scrub my hand down my face, thinking. It's not a hard question. It's all there, boiling beneath the surface like one of my songs. "Love is . . . it's bringing an umbrella when rain is forecasted, but, like, not for you." I think of our parents. "It's serenading someone off-key in the kitchen while they chop red peppers lengthwise because they know you like them better that way. It's pulling the car in backward at night because your partner gets edgy when they have to back into morning traffic. It's buying overpriced moisturizer in bulk because one time they mentioned they liked the scent." Cullen's lips spread into a slow smile, and I keep going.

"It's noticing things. Seeing parts of them even they might not know exist because you've been studying them since the moment you first laid eyes on them. It's memorizing their phone number even if you have it programmed because God forbid you ever lost your contacts. It's reading their mood by the song blaring through their headphones. It's experiencing something so extraordinary you can't tell if it was just that mind-blowing or if it's only because they were there with you that you were so affected. Like they make everything better. It's an eighteen-year-old bloke spewing terrible poetry at his twin that we will most assuredly have to cut out because he's clearly out of his head," I finish.

"No way," Cullen says quickly. "Not a chance, that's all staying."

"I don't even know what I'm talking about," I grumble. "I broke up with my last girlfriend over Instagram."

"Having regrets?" Cullen asks shrewdly.

I wave a hand. "No, no, of course not."

"So that"—he waves his hand in a flourish—"wasn't about your ex?"

"What? No! That wasn't about . . . I wasn't talking about anyone real—"

Cullen's expression is skeptical. "That sure sounded like *someone*."

"It wasn't," I insist, sweat breaking out on my neck as I replay all the things I'd said.

Cullen leans forward, pressing his hand on either side of his mic. "All right. It wasn't about anyone. But if it was, what would you want to say to that person? Hypothetically? Maybe like your future love?"

I scrunch my eyes closed against the flash of freckles and swallow. "Purely hypothetically, since that wasn't about anyone real, I would say . . ." I straighten. "I would say I'm not the best guy. There are definitely better, taller, smarter guys who can grow facial hair and have big muscles and a car . . . but I would be the best guy for you. We'd fit, and I wouldn't try to change you because that would mean we wouldn't fit. And I would only ever want the best for you because that's what love is. Love is the lyrics to someone else's melody."

I cringe and clear my throat. "That definitely has to get cut."

Cullen shakes his head, amusement painting his features. "Get real. This is golden."

"This is *pathetic*. I sound moony-eyed."

"You might be," he agrees. "But listeners will eat it up."

I flip the switch on my mic and scoot away from the table. "I need some air."

Cullen narrows his eyes before nodding. "Why don't you head out? I'll stick around to clean up the tape and be home soon."

"Do you have enough to salvage?"

"I'll manage. You have your board?"

I nod, already packing my Mac away. Two minutes later, I shove out the front doors into the dark night and drop my longboard to the ground with a sharp clatter, clicking my backpack straps together across my chest. I forgo music—my head is too full to hear anything—and push off, coasting the giant hill that leads from downtown out to the neighborhoods. I take the long way, winding up and down a few streets, letting the icy air whistle past my ears until the ache is too much. I turn onto my block and pick up my board, carrying it the last few feet up our drive. The lights from our house give off a warm glow, and inside, I see a near replica of the image I'd ranted about tonight. My dad, dancing around the kitchen with his wooden spoon and singing to my mum, who's playing sous chef and chopping ingredients. I push open the door, the hot air making my cheeks tingle, and remove my coat, hanging it on a hook before kicking off my shoes.

I cover my ears and walk into the kitchen, teasing, "What is this?"

My dad grins. "This, m'boy, as you well know, is Goldfinger."

"It's torture," I say, grabbing a carrot from the cutting board and popping it in my mouth.

"Your ma liked it well enough back in the day."

"Yeah, well . . ."

My mum shoves another carrot in my mouth. "You don't know. Their cover of 'Just Like Heaven' made me swoon in my Doc Martens."

"Good for you, Mum." I roll my eyes, but she knows I don't mean it, even though I have to swerve to avoid Dad, who's still twitching and spinning around the island.

"Cull back?" she asks me.

"Nah. I boarded home. He was finishing up some things." I slouch into the living room, flipping on the TV and turning it up to hear it over my dad's rendition of

"Here In Your Bedroom." I find a rerun of *Brooklyn Nine-Nine* and lean back into the couch, resolving not to think about anything else tonight.

VADA

My blog post about our concert is up *bites lip*

LUKE

Are you hinting that I should read it right away?

VADA

Maybe. Idk why I'm so nervous about this one. It was just so incredible, I'm feeling inadequate.

LUKE

Full disclosure, I have a Google alert for when your blog updates.

VADA

YOU DO NOT.

LUKE

I comment on every single one. I'm obsessed. With the blog, I mean.

VADA

Shut up.

LUKE

You shut up. Ever hear of
L8RSK8R?

VADA

That's you?! Now I want to read
back!

LUKE

groan Don't judge me.

VADA

. . .

VADA

. . .

VADA

This goes back two years. I'm
tearing up, Luke.

LUKE

Because I'm creepy and you're
scared?

LUKE

Please not that.

VADA

YouTube: Greg Laswell "And Then
You"

LUKE

Oh. Well, then. I'm glad.

The following morning, I make a decision. Maybe Vada and her plans have rubbed off on me. The thing is, like Vada, I applied to school in California. Berkeley, to be exact. My mum's an alum, so that helped me score early admission, but mostly, I wanted to be far away from my family. I need some space. I want the freedom to be who I want to be without my dad standing over my shoulder and making his own, overlapping plans. Berkeley also happens to have one of the most prestigious musical composition programs in the United States, and I sort of hoped the genius might rub off on me.

I thought I might apply down the line. Like, next year, or after I got my gen eds out of the way, but I'm starting to think there's no real reason to wait.

I take a deep breath and click on the application icon on their website.

Worst they can say is no.

18

VADA

Behind the Music

by Vada Carsewell

The Beatles on *The Ed Sullivan Show.*

Nirvana on *MTV Unplugged in New York.*

Carrie Underwood's audition of "I Can't Make You Love Me" on *American Idol.*

There are moments when the musical world stops turning for a split second and listens. Just listens. As if the entire population, all the damn genres, stand up as one and recognize a shift in the culture.

Recently, friends, I felt a shift. A mother-loving seismic imbalance that unseated me completely and threw me across the room before I could even think about finding a doorway. That shift is called (Not) Warren, and they were incredible. Five eye-closers for real, and y'all know I don't give those freely.

The reason for the fanfare comes down to the magical pairing of Carl Andrews and Maureen

McCarthy. I was smitten from the first jaunty, electronic mix, but by the end, I was ready to cry my eyes out. Experiencing the way their aching vocals intertwined. Like burning alive, but somehow worth it.

I'm afraid I can't do them justice, but I can do this: get thee to your favorite (legal) streaming platform and check them out for yourself.
In this very precise order, or I can't be held responsible:

"All the Words"

"Kingdom of Now"

"Fallen In Like"

"What You Don't Say"

Then take two Motrin for your inevitable heartache and comment in the morning.

—Vada

Sunday is easily becoming my favorite day of the week. After the rocky start, my Sunday crew has gotten our shift down to a science. Particularly when we're all here. Things were busy early on for March Madness, but the game ended well before our usual 10:00 p.m. close, and since it's the last day of spring break, I don't have homework. Now it's 11:00 p.m., and we're sweeping the floor and the jukebox is blaring. We pooled our tips and set the machine to random and are playing a game of "Name That Tune." Whoever says it first gets a dollar. I'm up, but barely. Top 40 isn't really my forte. Luke is close behind, and Kazi is surprising us all in third. Ben is straggling neck and neck with Kazi's girlfriend, Tessa, and our bouncer, Mike, refuses to compete because he's a ride-or-die Journey fan. And *only* Journey.

I collect a dollar as I win another round and do a little twirl with the broom. "I think we need to sweeten the pot."

"That's because you're winning," Kazi grumbles good-naturedly.

I ignore him. "What if the loser has to empty the bathrooms' garbage?"

"Not clean toilets or anything?" Luke asks, dipping a rag in solution before slopping it back on a stool.

"Nah, we have a crew for that. But we have to take the garbage out before—The Neighbourhood!" I shout, cutting myself off and swerving my hips, while holding on to my broom as a mic and belting the first lyrics.

Ben shakes his head. "Not fair! I was listening to you!"

I ignore him. This song is my jam. Tessa starts in on the chorus of "Sweater Weather," holding the ends of her rag over her head and spinning in a circle in her high-heeled black boots. I swerve around to face Luke and Ben, belting it out while Kazi twirls Tessa in a circle. They can be really cute when I'm in a good mood, and the end of this song swings into the sweetest bridge, *always* putting me in a good mood.

"Sorry," I say breathlessly once it's over. "As I was saying, we have to take the trashes out or they can start to smell."

Luke's eyes are doing their twinkle thing sucking me in and I can't look away. He doesn't seem to mind. "Right." A new song clicks over on the box, and before I can open my mouth, he says, "'You'd Be Mine,' Annie Mathers," in a smooth voice.

"The Brit knows country?" I ask as Tessa squeals and moves to make it louder.

"Some. I like Cash and Chris Stapleton okay. Mathers snuck up on me, but you've got to admit, she's got soul."

"I like 'Coattails' a little more," I admit. "When Marcus pisses me off, which is always, I like to crank it up."

He grins. "I could see that. I might need to borrow that idea."

"'*Beat It*'!" Kazi yells, jarring Luke and me from our weird version of a staring contest.

I groan, shaking off the flutters in my stomach. "Damn it, lost focus."

"Michael Jackson, may he rest in peace," Ben says, making the sign of the cross. I snicker at his antics.

Everyone knows the lyrics to this one, and Luke does a surprisingly strong moonwalk. Kazi's patchouli dreads swing all over the place, and Ben hops up on a chair, moving in a way that reminds me of a dad at his daughter's wedding reception. I've got tears streaming down my face, and my stomach hurts from laughing so hard at this stupid crew.

The music slows and turns melodic, and before I can skip ahead to something else, Luke elbows me. I follow his eyes to where Kazi and Tessa are slow dancing, wrapped around each other. Damn. They're gross. Also, adorable.

Ben starts to gather up his coat. "Kodaline," he says, taking his stack of dollars. "See you, guys."

Kazi and Tessa move as one for the exit, and I lock the front door behind them. Before I can turn off the music, Luke tugs at my hand. "It would be a shame to waste it. Paid a dollar of hard-earned tips." Even at his tug, it's a question. If I didn't want to, we wouldn't.

Oh, I want to. Desperately so.

I pinch my lips together to keep them from smiling off my face. He spins me once and pulls me in. We're sticky and smell like disinfectant and sweat, but his hand is dry and cool as it takes mine. His other hand is at my waist, and he's singing under his breath and not hiding it from me.

It warms me down to my toes.

I cock my head to the side. "You knew this one."

He shakes his blond hair out of his eyes, and his grin is only a little sheepish. "I was distracted."

He releases my hip and spins me out gently, and my breath catches at the sweetness in the old-fashioned gesture.

"I did, too," I admit.

"I figured." We sway in silence for a beat. My chest is tight, but in a happy way. I'm not nervous around Luke anymore. We seem to have moved past that part and are ever so slowly creeping toward something new.

But the level of intentionality in this—our movements in sync and our faces, at times, only inches apart—it's rife with expectation. I've never had this with anyone. Luke crept up on me. I was comfortable in my crush.

But it's as if Luke wants something to happen, and I'd never thought about having my feelings reciprocated. I'm not sure how to proceed.

The song ends, and I release his hands to turn off the machine. Our shoes echo on the concrete floor. I check that Phil's office is locked and turn off the lights so only the dim Exit lights are lit.

"Vada?" I can hardly make him out, and his voice is barely above a whisper. He grabs my hand, stopping me from opening the door, but not cornering me.

My skin is on fire where he's touching me. So stupid hyperaware of every single one of the atoms that make him. "Yeah?"

It comes out in an exhale. "I don't know what I'm doing around you."

My heart squeezes. His profile is painted in gray, his glasses reflecting the parking lot lights, so I can't see his eyes. I watch the rise and fall of his chest, the nearly imperceptible constriction of his throat.

"Me neither."

His laugh comes out in a soft huff, and he raises a shaking hand to fidget with his frames and brush his hair back. I grab his fingers, pulling them between mine, and say, "I've never held hands with someone. Is this okay?" I'm so grateful for the darkness because I've never felt so ridiculous and vulnerable.

He wraps his longer fingers over mine and squeezes them in a way that is an instant balm to my nerves. "Like this," he says.

"See?" I say. "Easy-peasy."

With my free hand, I pull open the door, and we step out into the light. Mike is there, sitting on the hood of his car, waiting, and I wave him away. Luke's got Cullen's car, but it's parked next to mine. He has to let go, and already I miss the feeling of his hand. Reluctantly, I reach in, turning on my car to get the heat going. Luke does the same and looks over the top of his car to smile at me. We stand there smiling like idiots for probably too long.

I should feel self-conscious, but for some reason, I don't anymore.

"Good night, Luke."

"Night, Vada."

We get in our cars and pull out into the night. A few minutes after I've made it back home and am getting ready for bed, my phone chimes.

LUKE
YouTube: Kodaline "What It Is"

I'm finishing responding to comments on my blog to distract myself from swooning over Luke when I decide to check my email before bed. I nearly auto-delete the first, assuming it's spam, but thank goodness my eyes are faster than my shaking fingers. This can't be real. No frigging way this is real life.

Ms. Carsewell,

We're thrilled to offer you the opportunity to apply for a place on our newly developed, on-the-ground teen music review team at *Rolling Stone* online. Everything will be done remotely, but we would like to commission teens to attend shows and report back on performances for our website. The tickets will be paid for in advance, but payment per review only comes upon acceptance.

Should you choose to apply for the position, we are asking you to submit a sample of your writing that is

appropriate to the position (i.e., music related) as well
as a letter of recommendation from a source within the
music industry.

The attachment outlines the pay scale per article and
the potential timeline of events. The scheduling is flexi-
ble since this is a team comprised of college students. I'd
have a handler of sorts within *Rolling Stone* who would
coordinate my scheduling.

I click through the document looking for the lie. This
can't be real. But everything checks out. They claim to
have found me through *Behind the Music*. I'm to expect a
follow-up phone call if I'm interested.

If I'm interested. Like. What?

I immediately email back because I'm not an idiot and
then take time to calm my breathing because this can't
be real even though it definitely sounds real. I check my
email again, hoping for a response, but it's only an auto-
mated confirmation (on *Rolling Stone* letterhead, no less)
that they've gotten my response and will be in touch
soon.

Fair. It's close to midnight.

I open up my *Behind the Music* drafts and scroll through
for a sample to use, but if they've already seen my blog,
should I use something new? I need to go to another show
immediately, if so. But this week sucks, and next week
isn't much better. I could always review an album, but
it's not the same. My gig is live music. It's what makes me
stand apart from the rest. *Relax, Vada. The deadline isn't
for a few months*, I think. I can definitely see a show and
write up a review in that time.

What I really need is Liberty Live. It runs all summer,

but the first show is only five weeks away. Immediately following graduation. Interviewing a band and reviewing a show that I helped manage from start to finish? That would be enormous. How many other eighteen-year-olds could say that on their applications?

Just in case, I refresh. Nothing. *Fine.* I close my laptop with a click and settle back against my pillows and grab my phone instead. Looks like Cullen loaded *The Grass Is Greenly* early this week, maybe since it's the end of spring break. I reach for my earbuds, plugging them in and turning off the light while the podcast downloads. I sink into my pillow and let Luke's soft voice wash over me.

Oh. My. *Gosh.*

19

LUKE

Something has definitely changed. I'm not Mr. Popularity by any stretch, but I'm liked well enough. A hazard of being Cullen's twin. Everyone likes him, so they like me by default. And despite what my brother might imply, I *have* dated around a little.

But this morning, I feel like every girl I ever dated is trying to kill me with her eyes. And that's not . . . normal. I'm usually on good terms with my exes.

My fingers work the familiar combination on my locker in the senior hallway, and I raise the latch with a click. I like to keep my locker neat, so I find my book quickly and shove it into my backpack. Another group of girls walks by, openly glaring at me.

"Morning, ladies," I say experimentally. They walk on. I swipe at my face. "What in bloody hell—?"

"I think they're mad at you." I turn to Zack, who's leaning against the bay of lockers with a smirk, his thumbs stuck in the straps of a backpack.

"Right. I guessed that. But why?"

Zack straightens. "Well, you did break up with Lindsay, so she has reason enough. And didn't you dump Rachel before that?"

"I guess. But I talked to Lindsay, remember? She was fine. A bit delusional about the whole prom thing, but otherwise okay."

I follow Zack's eyes, and Lindsay and her best friend, Mary Anne, are in a huddle of girls at the end of the hallway. They turn at once to shoot daggers at me, and I look away.

"Yeah, I don't think she's going to hold you to that, man."

"Probably not," I concede, closing my locker with a click. "No real loss. I could honestly not care less, unlike a pair of homecoming kings I know. More of a relief, to be honest. She was pretty insistent on the turquoise."

Zack ignores the jab. "Did you hear the podcast last night, by chance?"

His tone is offhand, and I start walking toward English, him at my heels. "Not the final version. I went to bed before Cull got home." Not that I slept. I couldn't stop my brain from replaying the way it felt having Vada's body pressed against mine, interspersed with the fact that we'd held hands. That meant something. At least that's the conclusion I'd settled on around 2:00 a.m. Then I'd downloaded the entire Kodaline album and listened to it twice through, finally drifting off sometime before my alarm woke me. "Thought he was out with you, actually."

Zack's cheeks flame, and he suppresses a grin.

"That's what I thought," I say. I continue lightly, "I feel like I should be offended that my best friend prefers my brother."

Zack laughs, good-natured. "He kisses better."

"You can't know that."

Zack shakes his head as if dispelling the thought. "Okay, but back to my point. Did you hear what Cullen put out?"

"Nooooo . . ." I trail off slowly, things clicking into place. "Jesus. Did I say something about Lindsay?"

"Not exactly. Which is . . . sort of the point."

"We talked about celebrity couples and revenge breakup songs—" I start.

"Really?" cuts in Zack.

I pause. "Yeah, really." My stomach starts to knot up. "Why, what did you think we talked about?"

"Well, I mean, there was some of that, but you sort of went into this long rant about real love . . ."

"*No.*"

Zack grimaces apologetically. "That's what I figured."

I spin on my heels, tugging out my phone. "I need to find Cullen. The fucker was supposed to cut that stuff."

LUKE
Where are you?

CULLEN
Study hall, why?

"It was kind of nice. I mean, I could completely see your parents in it, and that bit about the lotion, well, I mean, I didn't know Cullen had done that for me."

"Holy . . . you could tell all that? I was just talking. I didn't even know what I was saying." I stop, starting to panic.

"Well, yeah." Zack interrupts my thoughts. "Anyone who's been around your parents knows how in love they are."

I'm nearly at study hall, English completely abandoned. I'll get a late pass from Mr. Fallon, but first I need to see my brother.

"I have to go to geo trig," Zack says. "And besides, this is between you two."

I wave him away. "I'll see you at lunch."

I walk straight up to Mr. Fallon and ask to see my brother. Something in my face must belie an emergency, because he motions for Cullen. I drag Cull out to the hall-way by his arm.

"What did you do?" I snarl.

"What are you on about?" he asks, ripping his arm back and adjusting his rolled sleeve. "Don't you have English?"

"Lindsay is furious. Won't even talk to me."

Cullen lifts his hands in a placating way. "You dumped her. That's nothing to do with me. I didn't think you wanted her back."

"I don't, but all her friends won't talk to me."

Cullen's expression is blank. "Again. Not my problem."

"Yes, but we *were friendly*. Then I record the podcast with you and it goes live, and she hates me. What. Did. You. Do?" I repeat.

Comprehension dawns. "Ah. That. I didn't do anything. You left, I cleaned the copy and posted it."

"I told you to cut the nonsensical bullshit."

Cullen narrows his eyes. "And I told you *not a chance*. That bullshit was the most genuine thing you've ever said."

I slump against the opposite wall, my head spinning. "I can't even remember what I said. I was definitely talking about Mum and Dad. There's no way that would upset Lindsay. I don't get it."

Cullen looks like he's holding something back.

"Well, let's rerecord. After school?" I pull out my phone, scrolling for Phil's number. "I'll see if the booth is free."

"It's already posted, Luke. Obviously."

Shite. Right. I'm all turned around and flustered. "So, that's it. It's out?"

He nods. I exhale slowly and let that sink in. So, Lindsay is mad. That's . . . expected. Almost. I mean, we did break up, and I did talk about love. I scrub at my gritty eyes. Okay. Strangers listening won't be a big deal. They don't even know me in real life. Besides, our listeners barely number in the hundreds. It's not like we're nationally syndicated or anything. It's fine. By this time tomorrow, it will be forgotten.

"Okay."

Cullen scratches at his short hair, causing it to stick up from the product he uses. "Okay?"

"Yeah. I mean, there's nothing I can do. Lindsay just threw me is all. She must have listened last night. I guess she cared more than she let on. It's fine."

Cullen looks like he wants to say more, but Mr. Fallon peeks his head out.

"Everything all right, boys?"

"Better, yeah. Thanks, Mr. Fallon. I should get to class."

He hands me a tiny white slip. "Already signed off. Just pass this to Mrs. Montemayor."

"Um, thanks," I say, taking the slip, surprised.

"I enjoyed your show last night. I'm a big fan," he says. "Back to your seat, Cullen."

I pocket the late pass and exchange confused looks with my brother before heading to class. Before I make it, I have another text.

CULLEN

Listen to the podcast and . . . don't
kill me, okay? I had my reasons.

I knew it.

I detour into a bathroom and log on to my podcast app, clicking on the link. It takes a minute to download, and I almost give up. When the green circle finally completes, I hit Play. There's our intro. I skip ahead. Celebrity cheating scandal. Okay. Dread is filling my stomach as I skip ahead again. There's my rant. I listen to the entire thing. I sound like an idiot, but it's not terrible. I wince at how that must have sounded to Lindsay or any other girl I'd dated. Clearly, I wasn't talking about them, but I also don't think anyone could have figured out who I'd meant. Not that I'd meant anyone.

All right, fine, Vada has seeped into my psyche. I didn't wax poetic about her freckles, so that's something, but barely. It's probably fine. I was recorded *before* the slow dancing and hand holding. Technically. I exhale, my breath shaky. Fuck, Cullen. I missed English for this? I'm about to close out the app, but my finger hovers on the line. It says there's five minutes left. I swallow hard.

The sound changes, and Cullen says something about a special message for an anonymous girl in my life. "Luke won't say who this is about, and to be honest, I don't even know if he realizes who he's singing for. But whoever this is meant for? They deserve to hear it. It's called 'Break for You.'"

And there's my voice. Singing the song that night in my bedroom, when I'd thought I was alone. *My* voice, the one I don't let anyone hear, and *my* song. The fucker recorded my song and posted it online. Not only that, but he'd named it. Without asking me.

And now *she'll* hear it. She'll hear it, and she'll know. *Fuck.*

20

VADA

LUKE

YouTube: Smashing Pumpkins
"Disarm"

> VADA
>
> I hate hate HATE these things.

LUKE

Me too. I'm shite in an active-
shooter drill. They told us to pick
up "everyday items" to arm
ourselves, and I grabbed a bin of
protractors.

> VADA
>
> Well . . . those have sharp
> corners, at least?

LUKE

Only if you manage to throw them
like boomerangs.

> VADA
>
> I'm in the "run for your lives"
> group.

VADA

I feel like this would be less traumatizing if we called it "Zombie Apocalypse Drill."

VADA

Like, same protocol, but less staring at your classmates and wondering, "How good is your aim with an assault rifle?" followed by "Why is this real life?"

LUKE

This is madness, for sure.

VADA

YouTube: Gary Jules "Mad World"

The active-shooter drill interrupts my lunch hour. I sit with the same kids I've known since eighth grade. We aren't super close or anything, but we're that kind of comfortable where we know one another's siblings' names and remember that one time freshman year when you had that allergic reaction to Red Dye 40 and blew up like a balloon.

That kind of thing. I've been sitting with Ja'Kai, Cate, Laura, Heather, and Ahmed every day for years. It's an automatic choice. All our last names start with *C* or *D*, and we've always been in the same homeroom and lunch.

All of this is to say, I barely think about it. I bring my lunch, I sit down at the same table, grimace as Cate sits on Ja'Kai's lap the whole time, and share commiserating looks with Heather before Ahmed and Laura interrupt with some ongoing argument about quantum physics or bioelectrical engineering or plausible genetics or some other fake-sounding branch of science.

Today, everyone arrived on cue, and I had just pulled out my plastic Tupperware containing a cold slice of pizza and my copy of *Les Misérables* when the alarm sounded and announced the lockdown drill.

The weirdest part of these drills is the silence. Even though it's only a drill, there's this eerie energy vibrating over students filing out or hunkering down, depending on the scenario. It's as if Principal Carlisle casts a *Silencio* curse over the student body. Or, more likely, the act of pretending you could be murdered at eighteen (or sixteen, or twelve, or seven) is innately damaging. There's not a single one of us who's not thinking morbid thoughts as we shuffle out the emergency exits and scatter to the woods behind our school toward our predesignated "safe place."

The uncomfortable implication being that school is *not* the safe place.

I tuck my phone in my back pocket and rub my hands up and down my arms to warm up. I regret leaving my cardigan in my locker after last period. There's still a chill in the breeze, and the leafless trees over our heads clack against each other.

"Uh-oh, Turton is pissed," Ja'kai is saying in a hushed tone, tucking his hands deep into the pockets of his hooded sweatshirt, and I watch as a cute Lindsay Turton huffs past us, still carrying her salad. My stomach growls. "You'd think someone ran over her puppy or something."

Laura perches on an overturned log, rolling her eyes as she picks the bean sprouts off her grab-and-go sandwich and readjusts the plastic container on her lap. "Seriously. Lindsay and Luke barely dated. They weren't even going to the prom."

I've never understood how the prom became this relationship-status identifier. Like, Achievement Unlocked, you have a prom date, so you obviously mean business. Until a month later, that is, when graduation rolls around and you decide to break up.

My eyes catch on a white-blond head bobbing through the masses, and it's as if my perception shifts ever so slightly. Like when you tweak the toggle on a microscope and everything sharpens even if you didn't realize it could get more defined. Except, instead of a slide of onion skins, it's Luke I'm magnifying. He's been let out of his hiding place. Kids are milling around, most pretending not to notice we can return, instead choosing sunshine and fresh air.

Hey, if you're going to evacuate us under threat of imminent death, the least you can do is be lax about when we return to our lunches.

Luke is standing with Zack and a few of the basketball guys in the middle of a grove of evergreens. He doesn't see me, and I don't try to catch his eye. Instead, he's intent on Lindsay, and he looks . . . bothered. The thing is, Sunday night was . . . amazing. The slow dancing, the hand holding, the giddy smiling. All of it. And then the song happened. And then it really, really happened when person after person shared the link . . .

"Don't tell *her* that," Cate is saying, still referring to Lindsay and the prom date that wasn't. "I saw her at the Nordstrom's at Briarwood a few weeks back." Cate stabs at her chili fries with a spork while sharing Laura's log. Some meat sauce drips on her Converse, and she brushes it off in the grass.

"I feel the need to remind you all that it's March," Ahmed says blandly, his fingers clicking across his phone screen.

Cate flicks her long, sandy layers over her shoulder and throws a glare at him. "You can't just buy a gown last minute, not if you don't want the same one every other girl is wearing."

Heather agrees. "I'm planning to check out Grand Rapids next weekend."

Jesus. Not that I've ever gone or ever planned to go, but still. Last year, instead of the junior prom, my mom took Meg and me to see Judah & the Lion in Detroit. They were fabulous.

"What about you, Vada?" Laura asks politely. That about sums up my friendship with these guys. Polite. Vaguely interested.

I shake my head. "I don't have a date."

"Well, it's still early. You can get the dress now and worry about a date later," Cate says.

"Easy for you to say," Heather says. "You've had a permanent date since sophomore year. I don't want to end up like Lindsay with an expensive dress and no one to see it."

"It was a breakup," Ahmed says. "Not the end of the world."

"Correction. A breakup followed by a very public, very viral, grand gesture about *another* girl."

"Brutal," Ja'kai agrees.

"You guys make it sound like Luke meant for the song to go viral," I say, working hard to keep the defensiveness from my voice. The internet is weird. It only takes the right pair of eyes—or, in this case, ears—at the right moment, and your life blows up. "I don't think he had any idea Cullen would post it." Not with the way he spoke about his rejection of his dad's plans for a career in performing. No way.

"Did you even listen to it? I mean, that shit was definitely intentional," Laura says. "It had to be a setup. Isn't their dad like extra famous in England?"

"He *was*. But Luke doesn't want anything to do with that."

Heather narrows her eyes at me, and I fiddle with the pages of *Les Mis*, deliberately not glancing in the direction of Luke and his friends. "How do you know?"

I shrug, trying to look disinterested, but I doubt I pull it off. I suck at pretense. "We work together. He told me. It's not his thing."

"Sure sounded like it was his thing."

I shrug again. Not that I would admit it—I'm mortified at how little self-control I have when it comes to Luke—but I've probably listened to his song at least a hundred times. It's the most beautiful thing I've ever heard, featuring the purest and most beautiful vocals from the throat of the most beautiful boy I've ever seen.

It's a holy trifecta of hot mess, and I can't be held accountable.

"Did you see what happened last night? Fucking Buzz-feed ran some article of the 'Most Romantic Gestures in Teen Rom-Coms,' and to finish it off with a real-life clip, they linked to the podcast. It's not going anywhere," Ja'Kai says.

Oh God. Now I feel even worse. No wonder Luke looks

so . . . well, objectively still good, but not like *good* good. He looks stunned, honestly.

Heather whistles low. "No wonder Lindsay's upset. She lives for that kind of thing." I feel my lips pucker in a grimace, but it can't be helped. *Lindsay* is upset? How selfish is she? Did she not know him at all?

"Isn't that why they split up?" I can't help but point out. "Didn't she try to Instagram their first kiss or something bananas like that?" She's the wooooooorst.

Ja'Kai snickers, dipping a handful of fries into ketchup. "Bet she wishes she'd held off on that."

I shudder. "That's super weird. So invasive."

"Says the chick with the big-time music blog," says Laura.

Oh, here we go.

"Yeah, but I don't post anything personal about the bands. I only critique what they put out there either in a public venue or an approved recording."

"I guess. But you still depend on the faceless masses to make your name famous."

"That's sort of the point of a review, though. Not to make my name famous but to share my opinion with the faceless masses."

Ahmed raises an eyebrow.

"Hey, Vada." Luke is walking toward us, trailed by Zack. I haven't technically spoken to him since the Song. I mean, we've texted, obviously, but I don't work Mondays or Tuesdays at the club now that I'm managing the Sunday shift. More to the point, I haven't seen him since we danced and I . . . haven't mentioned it. Neither of us have. I don't know how this all works. My fingers are itching to call Meg and beg her to tell me the protocol for when you finally hold hands with your crush and then his love song about Who Knows Who goes viral and all you really want to know is *was it about me?*

Please, God, let it have been about me.

But also, holy shit what if it was about me?!

Ja'Kai unintentionally helps me out, giving one of those guy nods and a "Hey, Luke, Zack."

Luke's smile is dimmer than usual, but his gaze finds mine, and I can't help but match it, my heart giving a tiny jolt at the sight of him. He's wearing an old-man cardigan over his white, fitted V-neck. His hair is all mussed up and tossing in the wind, and he raises a hand to attempt to smooth it out of the way of his glasses. "I didn't know you were still out here," he says.

"I should head back in, actually," I say. "I left my lunch at the table."

"Hey, Luke! Great song!" Heather says, and if she were closer, I'd kick her.

He looks away from me. "Thanks."

"Last I checked, it was up to ten thousand hits! That's amazing, bro," Ja'Kai says.

"Yeah," Luke says, clearing his throat. "Yeah, I saw that."

"Actually, *I* saw it," Zack interjects lightly. "I've appointed myself as Luke's social media analyst. Vada, how's it going?"

"I didn't fake die today, so there's that."

"Me neither," he says. "Thanks to this guy." He ruffles Luke's hair. "Saved by a bin of protractors. Did you know they're the ninja stars of the geometry wing?"

"I was thinking boomerangs."

Zack raises his brow and exchanges glances with Luke, who tries to look busy.

"Nice *ring,* Carsewell."

I don't bother to look. I haven't taken the mood ring off since Luke gave it to me. "Thanks."

"What's dark blue mean, I wonder?"

Luke interjects. "Hey, d'you need to get your lunch before next period?"

"Yeah. I should go." My stomach growls again.

"We can walk you. We have lunch next."

Laura and Ahmed start gathering up their things, and Laura asks, "Do you mind if we walk with you?"

They follow Zack, and Luke lingers for a minute. Something silent passes between them, and Zack nods slightly, leading the group in as if they were there for him. Amazingly, they follow like little ducks all in a row.

I shake my head, and Luke laughs under his breath. "Yeah. I call it the Zack Effect. People can't help but follow him. It's the height, I think."

"Or something. He's . . . comforting."

Luke agrees. "Yeah. Totally. My mum says he's like a walking hug." He looks at me. "How's *The Miserables?*" he asks, nodding at my paperback.

"Terrible. Utterly devastating and depressing on every page."

His face lifts. "It really needs Anne Hathaway to make it palatable."

"Indeed. Though her solo made me ugly cry in the theater."

"Cullen dragged me along, and I could barely sleep afterward. The part with the little revolutionary?"

"Oh yeah. I guess it's to be expected. It's not like they tricked us. They didn't call it *The Happiest* or anything like that."

"Not like *The Lovely Bones.* That was misleading, eh?"

"I never read or saw it," I admit. "Not about anything lovely, I suppose?"

He shudders. "Not even close. I had nightmares for a month after seeing that movie on TV." We're at the doors, and he pulls one open, allowing me through first. We take the back stairs up to the cafeteria, and when we get to the top, I see Lindsay watching us. Luke notices and looks uncomfortable.

I want to say something that will make him feel better, but I don't know what. I decide on honesty.

"I listened to your song."

He freezes.

"Like, a lot of times." I make a face. "A lot. God," I say, hiding my face in my hands. "This is embarrassing, but . . ."

He looks green. I hesitate, but I've gone this far.

"It's the most brilliant thing I've ever heard, Luke. Countless eye-closers, okay? But I know it's not what you wanted. The 'prick' I know couldn't possibly," I say, reminding him of our conversation way back when this all started. He'd called himself a "prick" for wasting his talent . . . but I don't agree. He's not wasting it. He's saving it. "It's not okay what Cullen did, and I'm sorry he violated your privacy. I can't even imagine. And I know it's causing you all sorts of grief, and I'm sorry for that, too."

His face is unreadable, and I feel mine grow boiling hot, and I'm feeling a bit sick now. "And . . . I am rambling and sound like a crazed superfan, so I'm going to shut up, and if you could just forget the last like hundred seconds—"

His hand covers my mouth, and he shakes his head.

"It *was* an enormous violation, and I'm still reeling over it, but I'm also *very* glad you liked it. That helps. I admire your taste and consider you a friend"—he clears his throat—"and so just shut up with your self-conscious prattling." My lips grin against his skin, and I have to stop myself from kissing his palm.

Which is, like, weird, right? Why would I do that? What is happening?

"Prattling?" I ask, my attention snagging on the realization he just called me a friend.

His lips quirk. "Yeah. Prattling. I hate that everyone else heard my song. But I hate it less that you have."

"Oh." *Oh.* "Well. Good." I think.

"Besides, I watched you dance that day in class. The one where you didn't know I was there? And while we haven't talked about it, it felt . . . like more than dance. Anyway, my point is, we're even. Okay?"

I'm a little stunned. Because he's right. It was more than dance that day, and I didn't mean for anyone to see it. "Guess it's all out there now, huh?"

"Guess so."

"Hey! I have an idea! We should partner up and do an embarrassing and revealing performance for a live audience!"

Luke chuckles, low. "I love it. Let's do that."

"Done," I agree, feeling shy, but I try for a reassuring smile as I tuck a strand of loose hair behind my ear.

He nods once. "Right. So, that's the bell."

"My lunch!" I say, and I move past him. "I'm sorry; I need to save my mom's Tupperware."

"See you at work!" he says.

I wave a hand over my shoulder and keep walking, but

I definitely feel Lindsay Turton's eyes shooting lasers at me as I go.

Your loss.

It's a rowdy Thirsty Thursday at the Loud Lizard, and Meg is perched on a stool at the end of the bar, chatting it up with Ben and sipping on a lemonade like it's her job. Dozens of coeds mill around the small tabletops, most with significant tabs, and my glittery best friend has the best seat in the house. Anyone else might think she's smitten, but I know better. Meg and Ben are like brother and sister, growing up on the youth group circuit together. They even play in a band together. Not the bluegrass band that requires a beard to participate but a church band.

In fact, I've never seen Meg interested in anyone in that way. More like she's interested in everyone in a more eternal kind of way. She's the most joyful and generous person I've ever known, and people are attracted to her like flies on syrup, but she doesn't do crushes. At least, not yet. One day, someone with those faux pointed ears will waltz into her life and make her head spin.

Tonight, however, the door opens and Cullen walks in, carrying the weight of the world and the smell of impending spring. He sees me and makes a beeline. "Is my brother here?"

I tip my head to the side, taking in his entirety. Cullen's more flustered looking than I've ever seen him. His black hair is windswept, but not in an artful way, and he's wearing gym shoes. Like running shoes. I don't think I've ever seen Cullen Greenly in anything athletic. Behind him, Zack follows. In contrast, he appears . . . patient.

"Vada," Zack says.

"Social Media Manager Zack. You've been busy," I respond back. "And no," I say to Cullen. "He's not on the schedule tonight."

Meg flutters over as I pull out two mugs. "Sit down," I say. "Coffee? Or juice? Maybe ginger ale? Nothing fancy, though."

"Coffee, please," Zack says, and he settles on a stool. Cullen sits next to him and runs his hands through his hair. I pour them both a steaming cup. Zack dives in.

"I'm such a fucking idiot," Cullen groans.

I raise my brows to his boyfriend, who sighs heavily and explains. "Have you been online lately? It's Luke."

Meg pulls out her phone. "Gosh, I adore Luke," she gushes. "He's the sweetest, and his song is the literal best I've ever heard." She looks up at us wide-eyed. "Am I allowed to say that?"

I roll my eyes. "It's out now. Besides, you don't love him because of his song; you were already a fan because he feeds your Shirley Temple addiction."

Meg lifts a dainty shoulder. "Guilty as charged." She scrolls on her phone, her eyes widening. "Holy . . ." she mutters.

"Exactly," Cullen says. "Lionel Best retweeted 'Break for You' to his billion followers. RIP, me."

"RIP, Luke, you mean," I say, not even trying to hide my annoyance. "Why didn't you guys take it down days ago?"

Cullen moans dramatically, and Zack rubs his shoulder. "Because," Cullen says, "I'm a fucking prat who cares more about numbers than my family."

"In your defense," Zack says, "you didn't really understand how adamant he was about his privacy."

"I don't know how," I say. "I've only been hanging out with Luke a short time and know how much he hates attention. You've known him literally since the womb." Cullen looks hurt, but he should have known better. Of all people, *he* should have known better.

"I just wanted the girl, whoever she is, to know how he felt!"

Well. My heart thuds at that.

"It's not about anyone!" a voice says behind me, and I jump. *Luke.*

Cullen's head jerks up, and he looks admittedly terrible. I almost feel bad for him, but I feel worse for Luke.

"What part of that don't you get?" Luke says, exasperated, shoving his blond hair from his eyes. He's holding his board and still wearing his leather jacket, so I don't think he's been there long. "It was only a song. It's not about anyone. It was never meant to be heard. It's none of your business!"

Everyone is quiet.

"Anyway," Luke continues. "I was just dropping something off for Phil. Glad to see everyone got the latest update. Thanks again for cluing me in to *my* life, Cull." With that, he slams the half door to the bar, and with barely a glance at me, he leaves.

Meg settles next to Cullen, rubbing small circles into his back, and Zack is clicking around on his phone, probably trying to get Luke to come back.

I take care of a few customers, a pit in my stomach. Luke's words stabbing in my brain. *It was only a song. It's not about anyone.*

It was never meant to be heard.

Except he was supposed to be writing a song for someone. Me. For the spring showcase. Which we haven't mentioned at all since the Song was released. I'm dying to know if "Break for You" was meant for me. Every time I wonder, it seems ridiculous and presumptuous. Even in the safety of my head. We held hands, once. That's all.

It was never meant to be heard.

Even by me? Of course even by me. It's what he said, wasn't it?

21

LUKE

Cullen went through this phase when we were like twelve where he lived for those Worst-Case Scenario / Would You Rather games. Like, "If you were stranded on a desert island and you hadn't eaten in three days, and you were millimeters from death, would you rather eat a pound of squirming centipedes or a single raw squid tentacle that is still twitching?"

Neither option is great, but when the hypothetical alternative is death, you choose the one that makes you feel like puking the least. (Death, obviously. I never said I was brave.)

I feel like I'm living the live-action version of Worst-Case Scenario, titled "Absolute Worst-Case Scenario for Very Private and Introverted Luke Greenly Where There Is No Winner and Also He Will Always Lose."

After five years, you finally start songwriting again and bam! Your first effort is found out by your brother.

Then your brother posts it on your podcast. On the internet. Which is easily accessible by the majority of the planet.

And then a major website picks up the now-viral hit!

And a major celebrity decides it's his favorite and retweets it to a zillion people.

And those zillion people speculate about *who the song was about in the first place.*

And your ex-girlfriends hate you.

And you're nominated for the prom court even though you weren't planning on going unless . . .

Unless the one girl—the girl who the song is about and who is the *only* one not speculating so clearly she doesn't care—unless maybe *she* wants to go to the prom. But she probably doesn't, and how the hell do you ask someone you secretly (and very creepily, let's face it) wrote a viral love song about after watching her dance (again, so creepy, *God*)?

"Oh, hey, sorry about the stalker vibes, but I really do actually like you, and now that I'm low-key locked into this prom thing, do you wanna go with me?"

So, you do the only thing you can, and you deny, deny, deny.

There's a knock at the door, and I don't bother to look up from the geo trig homework I'm not finishing. "Yeah."

"Can I come in?" Cullen says.

"Nah," I say into my textbook.

My twin releases a long, dramatic sigh that lasts about thirty seconds longer than it should. I feel my bed compress with his weight. Wanker.

"You can't ignore me forever."

"Four hundred seventy thousand hits says I can."

He flops back. "Look, I said I'm sorry."

"Somehow this feels bigger than 'I'm sorry.'"

"What else can I say?"

"It's not about what you can say, Cull. There's nothing you can say *now*. It's about what you shouldn't have done in the first place."

"My intentions were honorable."

I sit up, tossing my pencil down on the comforter and chucking my graphing calculator at his head. He ducks easily. "They weren't your intentions to have, honorable as you think they were. It was never *my* intention for that song to be heard by anyone, ever. Christ, Cullen, it was a rough draft at best!"

"So, that's the problem? That it wasn't a clean cut?"

"Among other very major, far more important things, such as my pride and my private business, yeah! You don't even like Zack seeing you without showering first."

"So, this *is* about a girl."

I throw my hands in the air and lift up my heavy textbook, ready to throw it.

"This stopped being about a girl the second you uploaded it to the internet. You don't tell a girl you have a crush on her with four hundred and seventy thousand likes." I fully intend on throwing the numbers in his face every chance I get.

"But you would have with a song?"

I slump, the book falling with a bounce on my mattress. "I don't know. Maybe I would have eventually. With the right girl. But now I can't. I can't tell her that song was for her. No girl in her right mind wants that kind of pressure."

"But you said yourself, the right girl might be okay with it."

I shake my head. "I'll never know. This isn't anything I wanted. I'm not like you and Dad. I don't want to sing. I don't want to perform. I don't care about the media attention, and I'm not playing that song ever again."

"That's so stupid. What a waste."

"Fortunately for me, I'm too busy worrying about what *four hundred and seventy thousand* other people are saying about me to care if I'm not meeting the expectations of my twin brother."

"If you'd just play your music instead of hoarding it and building it up like something precious, this never would have happened."

I get up and walk to the door, opening it, suddenly exhausted. "No. If you'd respected my privacy, this never would have happened. Please leave."

Things are worse by dinner. Much worse.

Apparently, my dad's bored with his retirement and decided to venture into real estate. He'd been approached ages ago about opening a nightclub in downtown Ann Arbor. At the time, he turned it down, saying he was happy to be a house husband.

It seems home reno shows and upcycling wood pallets have lost their luster.

While this is the first Cull and I are hearing about it, I'm getting the sense things have been in the works for a while. At least, long enough that the so-called partners have acquired an interest in dad's quasi-fame. And mine.

"They only mentioned that since you two have had quite a lot of recent success with *The Grass Is Greenly*, maybe you could talk up the club? Like a regular market-ing spot," Dad is saying. Cull mutters under his breath something that sounds like, "Only a daft idiot . . ."

"I had no idea you were even into that kind of thing anymore, Dad. I thought you gave it up when we left Brit-ain," I say, my brain racing as my stomach squirms un-comfortably at the gleam in his eyes.

"I wasn't, but this time they really seem to have their ducks in a row, and I'm taking a larger percentage, so I won't be at the mercy of the Man."

"What will you call it?" Mum asks.

"Not sure, but I'm liking the Bad Apple."

Very original, Dad.

"Oh, I like it," she says. Clearly, they've talked about this already. She's taking this way too calmly. I can't get past the queasy clench in my gut when I think of Phil and the Loud Lizard, though. Phil's place has been around forever, but it's no secret that it's a dive. It's not like we pack in crowds worthy of Pearl Jam these days. From what I can tell, it's a miracle Phil's in the black most nights.

Could he survive my dad?

The investors are smart to recruit him. Even though we know he's a big old nerd who'd rather craft a bench out of driftwood and falls asleep before ten thirty most nights, he's still got a lot of credibility in the industry. Not to mention, so many of the guys who were around during the decade he was actively making music are gone. Like, *gone* gone.

Rock and roll isn't for the faint of heart. Neither is heroin.

It makes perfect sense to sign on my dad. What's shady as fuck to me is the whole "and could you sign your kids on, too?"

Particularly this week.

"You didn't tell them we would do it, did you?" I ask.

My dad looks up from his rice noodles. "Do what?"

"The marketing spot, the mentions or whatever, on the podcast."

He puts down his fork and takes a sip of water. "Why wouldn't you do it?"

Because of Phil, I think. *And Vada and Ben and Kazi and my job.* But that would be pretty douchey to say to my *dad,* so instead I say, "Well, we need to talk about it. We have a pretty, um, strict policy on marketing."

"You don't have a problem giving the Loud Lizard a shout-out," my dad says slowly.

"Well, yeah." I look to Cullen for help, but he's playing with the food on his plate. "That's a deal we worked out with Phil. In exchange for recording there."

"You can record at my club, then. Anytime you want. I'll have a custom sound booth made for your podcast or *whatever else* you might want to use it for." His tone is far too casual to fool me.

I stab at a shrimp. "What else would we use it for? We don't need to build a whole new studio for our podcast. It's not that popular."

"Well, after last week—" my dad starts, and I raise a hand cutting him off.

"That was a fluke. Once they realize I'm not going to be playing any other songs or declaring my love for kittens or Cullen's not running for Senate, they'll die down."

"What do you mean, you won't be playing any other songs? 'Break for You' is a hit."

I want to scream. "That's not even the name!" I insist. "It doesn't have a name because it's not a real song."

My mum puts down her fork with a clink, as if making

sure her hands are clear if she needs to move. Cullen finally raises his head, his eyes narrowed, but I can't tell at who. This is not the first or even thousandth time we've had this conversation.

I lower my voice. "Nothing's changed, Dad, just because my daft brother posted a song on the internet."

"I beg to differ," my dad says, his eyes clouded over. "Explain to me. You are writing lyrics, yes? That was your song, wasn't it?"

"Well, yeah," I start, "but—"

"And you composed that incredible melody as well? I've never heard it before."

"I did, but—"

"But nothing. I refuse to allow you to deny your gift. This stage fright you have is a phase. All musicians go through it. The bloody miracle in your case is your brother helped you out. You get to skip right over the years of toiling for name recognition and playing in dingy clubs and shoot right for the top. I've already fielded three calls from agents looking to represent you. Not to mention Eddie over at Abbey Road is ready to cut an album yesterday."

For a full minute, we sit in silence. I can't speak. An adequate response escapes me. Finally, it's Cullen who says in an even tone, "Dad, you didn't make any promises, did you?"

"Well, sure I did!" My dad blusters as he looks at me. "I said you were in the middle of your senior year, but I'd book a ticket after graduation, and we'd hear Eddie out. Maybe arrange for some collaborators."

And looking at my dad, at the gleam in his gray-blue eyes, at the ruddiness in his cheeks, everything he passed down to me, for the first time, I see him as Charlie

Greenly. As the former punk rock icon. As the man who found his worth in the music industry. I don't see him as my dad, because as much as he might think it is, this isn't about him being my dad. This is about me being his legacy.

And I don't want it.

My brother looks at me, stricken. I can read his face perfectly. He finally, *finally* understands. That, somehow, is enough to propel me to say what I've needed to for a long time.

"Dad," I say. My voice is firm. I'm tall in my seat. Not as tall as Cullen, but taller than our father. "I don't want to go to England. I don't want to meet with producers or collaborators. I don't want to sing. This isn't stage fright. This is a rejection of all that goes along with being a singer. I love music. I want to make it and write it and share it. But I don't want to perform it. Ever."

My dad shakes his head, the light reflecting off his white-blond hair, the hints of silver more apparent to me than before. "You'll change your mind," he says. "And by then, it will be too late."

The following night, I arrive to work fifteen minutes ahead of my scheduled start. I didn't bother stopping home, boarding straight from Zack's house after school. As of this morning, my dad was giving me the silent treatment, and anyway, it's Zack and Cullen's three-and-a-half-year anniversary, whatever that means. When I left, they were baking rainbow sprinkle cupcakes together.

"I come bearing gifts!" I say, holding out a Tupperware with half a dozen cupcakes inside to Ben and Kazi at the bar. Ben takes one immediately, and I pull out another, dropping it on a cocktail napkin for Kazi.

"Everyone else in the back?"

Ben nods, wiping frosting from his beard. "Vada's in with Phil, but the door's shut. I wouldn't go in."

"What? Why? Did something happen?"

Kazi jerks his thumb to a guy at the end of the bar who is slumped on his stool and shouting at the TV. "Marcus," he says.

"Why does that name sound familiar?"

"Vada's dad," Ben says in a low tone. "He's been here all afternoon getting sloshed and cussing out Phil."

"What? Why?"

Ben fiddles with his sleeve, unrolling and rolling it again. "I'm not a psychologist, but I would guess it has something to do with jealousy and Vada's near hero worship, however warranted, of Phil. Also, about her mom. And Phil?"

"Oh, Jesus," I say.

"Yeah."

"But isn't he remarried?"

Kazi nods. "Yeah. His wife is gorgeous." He makes a face. "I don't know why I said that. Not that it makes a difference. In his mind, dude peaked in high school."

"Apparently, Marcus and Phil were in a band together," Ben adds. "Marcus was the lead singer and got the girl. Then he blew it, became an insurance salesman, and has resented Phil ever since."

I consider them both shrewdly. It seems Vada's dad is common knowledge around this place. Right up there with mixing pitchers of margaritas and hitting the ice machine in the top-left corner when it's sticking. I decide to forgo clocking in for now, since I'm technically early, and hop behind the bar, prompting Ben to count out his tips early. I grab a rag and start busing tables and wiping down anything sticky, a never-ending job around the bar. After Ben clears out and waves goodbye, I slide into his spot.

Kazi is taking care of a few people, and Marcus raises a finger for a refill, so I meander over. I can see where Vada gets her coloring. "What're you having?"

Marcus shuts one eye, appraising me. "Did you have a beard before?"

"Nope," I say cheerfully, not bothering to explain.

"Another Jack Daniel's," he says dismissively.

"On your tab?" I ask.

He straightens. "My daughter works here. Vada. Family doesn't pay."

"I'm sorry, I didn't realize you knew Vada. I do, too. She's one in a million. Can I start a tab for you? All I need is your debit card."

Marcus's smarmy smile slips. "My drinks are free."

"I'm new," I say, holding out my hand. "Luke Greenly. And no one ever told me drinks were free for family. So, I'll just get your tab started."

"My name is Marcus Carsewell; Vada Carsewell is my daughter."

My grin is blinding. "I don't recall Vada having a father."

"Not having a . . ." Marcus shakes his head, his fist hitting the bar. "What are you talking about? Of course she has a father. I'm her father. Marcus. Marcus Carsewell."

I keep my hand out for the payment. "That's strange," I say, tipping my head to the side. "See, Vada and I were talking about college, and I remember her telling me that she couldn't afford to pay for school because the man she called Dad said she wasn't his daughter. *That he already had two kids.* So, you can understand my confusion. You couldn't possibly be her dad. She's doesn't have one."

Marcus blinks.

"That about sums it up," Phil says, startling me from behind. "You should probably hit the road, Marcus. I called you an Uber, and it's almost here."

Marcus slides off his stool, wobbling a little. He takes in Phil's imposing figure and, with measured movements, slides his wallet into his back pocket without bothering to leave so much as a tip. "You think you're all high and mighty with your disgusting bar and your snot-nosed bartenders, but I know you, Phil. And I haven't forgotten how you couldn't hack it playing professionally."

"That's true," Phil says dryly. "And believe me, I'm so grateful you're here to remind me of how far I've fallen. Take care, Marc. This one's on the house. Don't come back, or I'll call the police."

"You can't call the police on me! My daughter works here."

"Debatable!" I say.

Kazi jumps in front of the bar. "I think I see the Uber driver, Mr. Carsewell," he says in a placating voice. He leads Marcus through the tables of curious spectators and out onto the street.

"Vada okay?" I ask as soon as the door closes behind them.

Phil pats my shoulder. "Yeah, she's good. Annoyed as hell and has broken a few glass bottles out back, but she's back to herself and sweeping them up. Afraid the raccoons will get cut up if she leaves a mess."

"I had no idea what a proper dick her dad was," I say, feeling sick. "I mean, I guessed, but he far exceeded my expectations."

"And you've exceeded mine. You handled him like a pro."

"He didn't pay," I grumble.

"He never has. I could call the police if I really wanted to, but I think you scared him away plenty, and this way, Vada doesn't have to see her dad in handcuffs."

"He really shows up just to get free booze?"

"I suspect it's his asshole way of seeing his daughter, but yeah, at least once a month, he shows up here and drinks himself to the floor, berates his daughter, berates me, and then we kick him out."

I stop short. "What do you mean, 'berates his daughter'? What did he say to her today?"

"Nothing. He didn't get the chance. She came in only minutes before you did, and I was about to kick him to the curb when I saw you were handing him his balls."

I slouch back against the counter, relieved. "Right. Good. I'm glad."

"Me, too," Phil says. "Did I see rainbow cupcakes by the register?"

"My brother's anniversary. Want one?"

"I already snuck one, actually. But you could bring one back to Vada, and while you're at it, tell her the coast is clear and I expect her back to work."

"Ten-four, boss."

A minute later, juggling two cupcakes on a beverage napkin, I nearly smack right into Vada, leaving Phil's office.

"For me?" she asks. Her cheeks are rosy from the cold, and she smells like the color green and fresh air.

"Well, one is. I was hoping to share. I'm a little early for my shift."

Vada backs into the office, holding the door for me. I place the cupcakes on Phil's desk, and she moves around to our boss's chair and sits, folding a jean-clad leg underneath her.

I take the seat across from her, passing a lurid, multi-hued dessert across the desk.

"I didn't know you bake," she says. She picks at the rainbow wrapper and frowns. "Ah, wait. Cullen?"

"And Zack. It's their anniversary."

Her fingers pause midway to her mouth. "They baked them *together*?"

I nod, peeling my wrapper away. "I know. They're one of those disgusting couples."

"They are. Disgusting and adorable. How do you stand being around them?"

I raise the bit of cupcake I haven't already stuffed in my mouth. "This helps."

She licks frosting off her finger, and I swallow hard, tracking the movement. Twice.

"You didn't just get to work, did you?" she says after finishing her cupcake. She doesn't meet my eyes, instead folding her wrapper neatly into half and then thirds, pressing it flat with her fingers.

"Ah, not quite."

She nods. "Did you meet Marcus?"

I decide on honesty. "I did." And I tell her about our conversation, watching her face change from aggravated to hurt and finally, happily, to amused.

"I can't believe you said that to his face!"

"Yeah." I adjust in my chair, first sitting back and then uncrossing my legs and curling forward. "Should I apologize?"

"To me?" she asks, surprised. "Fuck, no. I'm just sad I

missed seeing his expression when you asked for his debit card to open a tab."

I sit back again, pleased and more than a little relieved. "Still, it wasn't my business. It's not like you can't take care of yourself. I was just—"

She cuts me off, grinning. "It's honestly fine. More than fine. Sometimes I wonder if I'm overreacting, you know? Like, maybe my dad's not that much of a dick. He's not physically abusive. He's just neglectful. Like, to the extreme. It hurts me, obviously, but it's sort of validating when someone else besides Meg gets all puffed up in my defense."

"Phil was plenty puffed up, if that helps."

She nods. "It does. But—and I know this sounds stupid— I feel like Phil gets to be defensive for my mom's sake. Not mine."

"Because he loves her."

"Right."

"But it's okay for me to be defensive for you?" I check. I can't help but sit a little taller at the implication—the idea that I could be that person for her. That she might need me to be.

Vada ducks her head, tucking some strands behind her ear and tracing the edge of Phil's giant desk calendar with her fingertip. "Sure. I mean"—she allows her brown eyes to meet mine for barely a blink before they shift away—"if you want."

Oh, how I *want*. I want so much I can taste it. Or her. Taste her. *Stay on track, brain.* I swallow again, trying to think of a response that isn't creepy or weird. To play for time, I clear my throat and cross an ankle over my knee. Verrry casually. "Good," I say. "That's good."

22

VADA

Late last night when I arrived home from work, it was to an unusually dark house. Apparently, I wasn't the only one Marcus went after yesterday. Except, while I had Luke and Phil at the bar to run defense for me, my mom was alone. It's interesting—and by *interesting,* I mean fucked to high heaven—how he doesn't want anything to do with us until he remembers how disappointed he is in himself and then has to remind us how he holds us responsible for his many failures.

I found my mom sitting in our dimly lit kitchen, her Bible open in front of her and an entire kettle of Sleepy-time tea resting on a crocheted hot pad. Her tears had already been spent, and she looked peaceful. "Had a little talk with Jesus," was all she said before smiling generously and pouring me a mug of steaming liquid.

It's obvious my mom's way of dealing with Marcus's shit is healthier, but she's had more practice. Or maybe she hit the end of her rope, and at the end, there's only God. I'm not sure. I haven't tried everything else yet. Which sounds stubborn. I guess it is. Or maybe it's just curious. All I know is I don't want to borrow faith. I want something I own wholeheartedly, and I'm not in the business of buying yet.

Mom communes with a deity. I commune with music.

Which explains why, the following afternoon, when I enter dance class, Madame takes one look at me and cuts short our barre time. I'm pretty positive *I'm in my fucking feelings* is written in cursive between the creases on my forehead.

"It's minutes till the weekend," she says. "I'm too antsy for conformity. Vada?" she calls me over.

I fidget with the waistband of my leggings, tugging it higher before settling it down over my hips. Her face is a picture of beatific understanding, and I struggle to meet her eyes, not sure I'm in the mood for a poised sort of pep talk today.

"Have you ever heard of an artist named Ke$ha?"

I freeze. "With the dollar sign in her name? Sure."

She bends easily, digging around in her tote bag. "Sometimes I can't properly feel a thing until a pretty melody or ferocious bottom line plays me through it. I suspect you relate."

"Yeah. I suppose."

She nods. "I have a song for you. It's helped me work out all sorts of demons. Find your space, and maybe it will help you work through yours as well."

I don't hesitate to claim my shadowy corner. A soft melody, bittersweet and caressing, plays over the sound system, washing over me.

My eyes shut against the hot tears that rush against my lids, and I release a shaky breath before my limbs stretch and lift weightlessly away from me.

When I dance, I don't always hear the lyrics, but today it's like they are coming from inside me—like they were made for me in this moment.

Lyrics do that sometimes. They find their home at just the right time. Like a secret message in a bottle, floating on a current for decades, only to wash up at someone's feet when the words are needed. This is my anthem. No matter the original intent of this song. No matter what Ke$ha wrote it about. It was sent to Madame for her pain, and now, it's been given to me.

Ke$ha screams her heart out, and as the song builds, my feet pound on the floorboards, my knees absorbing the shock, my ankles crying under the stress. I twist on the balls of my feet and drag my toes along, relishing in the burn. Thriving in the pain. The aliveness of it. My core throbs, and I know this isn't a pretty movement. This is as ugly as it gets. I itch in my skin. I want to peel Marcus from my DNA, strip away the parts of him that grow inside of me. Erase my father completely, from my life, from my memories. Every aching thing starts with him and his rejection.

I want to change the narrative. I want to reject him and everything he unwillingly gave me.

Except my father gave me music. And I hate him for it. I hate that he's not only entwined in my genetics but in everything I love that makes me so essentially, irrevocably Vada. He doesn't deserve credit for my favorite parts of me.

But it's what keeps me dragging my bones back to him—the insane gratitude that he accidentally gave me the exact coping mechanism for dealing *with* him and being my ticket *away* from him. The (admittedly) distant memory of the days he would spew music trivia to me and talk about bands like he knew them personally and what their process was for creating. His hobby became my obsession, and I idolized him for it. Now I know better.

The weirdest part is when he gives Phil grief. Like, you were there first, dude, and you walked away. *You walked away.*

It's all very fucked up. I'm positive there's some Shake-spearean study on this particular Venn diagram of father issues, and I bet it has something to do with self-loathing.

Add that as reason #785 why I hate Marcus: he's turned me into an amateur psych major at eighteen. I scrub my hands down my face with a loud groan. After class, I slink off to the locker room and take my time splashing icy water on my cheeks until they feel cool to the touch. Hands still damp, I scrape my hair into a top knot and change back into my skinny jeans and T-shirt.

By the time I shove out of the locker room and into the relatively fresh air of the hallway, it's empty. I stop at my locker to grab my phone and puffy vest, and finally it's the weekend.

The air has the wet, almost rainy feel of early spring in Michigan, and even though there are barely any real buds on the trees yet, everything seems greener. It's as though I walked out of school and entered into the Clarendon-filtered version of the world.

I inhale huge lungsful of air, holding them, absorbing them, and every time I let them out, I swear I shrink an inch. It's incredible what a difference being outside makes. I pull out my phone and plug in my earbuds, scrolling to Amy Shark and playing it nice and loud. Readying for battle, armor settled back into place. I recite my five-year plan.

Loud Lizard, Behind the Music, Liberty Live, UCLA
Loud Lizard, Behind the Music, Liberty Live, UCLA
Loud Lizard, Behind the Music, Liberty Live, UCLA

I repeat the litany with each step, mouthing it as if to stamp it into being.

Loud Lizard, Behind the Music, Liberty Live, UCLA
Luke.

Gah. Luke Greenly is definitely not in the plan.

A very quiet part of me, the part that can still feel his hands on my waist the night we slow danced, and can hear his "good" reverberating in my ears, thinks he could be part of the plan.

I don't know what I'm doing with you.

Like an addendum or something. Just . . . every good plan allows for addendums. Like the Bill of Rights.

Unless that's not what he wants. Like, literally every girl on the planet is falling over themselves for him and his swoony vocals after that stupid (amazing) song, and maybe the last thing he wants is . . . a relationship.

Maybe he likes that we're really good friends who held hands once. My strutting falters, and I skip a step. Maybe it's a relief for him to think he can just be himself with me and I'm not angling for an Instagram post.

Jesus. What if I've been friend zoned? My brain scrambles backward, cataloging all our interactions and . . .

Holy hell, he's seen me in spandex, flailing like a chicken. He met Marcus. I groan. Marcus, that fucker. Who wants in on that whole mess?

And his song! That perfect song! He straight-up told Cullen it wasn't about anyone.

Who cares that I want it to be about me? Every girl wants it to be about her. I've officially become like every other girl.

My phone buzzes in my pocket, and I pull it out. Of course it's Luke. That charming bastard.

I consider ignoring it. Reading it when I get home. Like that will show him. *I won't even know what you sent me for the next fifteen minutes, so there.*

But of course I don't because I'm helplessly in love with him.

(Just kidding. I'm kidding. I'm totally not in love with Luke.)

LUKE
Just checking in on you after the
other night. Also, happy weekend!
YouTube: Sponge "Molly"

This time, I take a minute to click on the link and let it play me home before responding. Sponge is a favorite of Phil's. One of the first bands he made me study. Every LP of theirs somehow comes off sounding like it was recorded in a church basement, but you can't help falling for their jaunty drumbeats.

I'd say the best modern-day equivalent I've found is the British band The Wombats, which Phil unequivocally denies but I'm pretty sure is dead-on. His ears are old. He doesn't know.

As I round the corner to my house, I see not only my mom's car in the drive but Phil's old beater Chevy S10, too, and for the very first time in my life, it occurs to me that I could walk in on something.

Like, *something* something.

Not that I'd be opposed. I love Phil, and he's so good to my mom. And Lord knows she deserves someone good. But, also, it'd be pretty squicky if, like, their tongues were in each other's mouths. Yes, they've been together for over a year, and yes, I know they are sexing it up. I just don't need to see it.

I fling open the front door, making sure to be extra loud. I hear the clatter of dishes and water running, so I head to the kitchen. My mom's at the table, coffee in her cup and a smile on her face, and Phil's at the sink, rinsing a plate. The utter domesticity of it all catches in my throat.

"Hey, baby," my mom says, not looking caught in the slightest.

"Hey, Mom. Heeeeeeey, boss," I say, raising an eyebrow at Phil.

"Afternoon, kid," Phil says, unperturbed. I swallow hard, and he puts down the dish. "Oh no, what happened?"

I shake my head, speechless, even as my eyes well up. He crosses the room toward me, uncertain, but holds out his arms. I dive into them burying my head in his chest, a sob breaking free.

"Vada!" my mom says, alarmed. I hear the scraping of her chair, and she's next to me, her hand at my hair, stroking.

But I can't stop crying. I hold on tighter, and to Phil's credit, he doesn't let go. This is definitely not something we do on a regular basis. Our relationship is mostly professional, except when he cusses at me for throwing out his cigarettes.

Something in me broke, though, seeing him at my kitchen sink looking for all the world like he belonged, calling me *kid*. So stupid, I *know*. But it was sort of everything. After a long while, he gently presses me back. "I have to get to work."

I wipe at my face and nod.

I see my mom reach for his arm and rub it reassuringly. He's stunned, and I feel terrible. This is probably more emotion than he's experienced in his entire life.

"Vada, look at me."

I lift my swollen eyes. I must look terrible. Phil looks crushed.

"I'm sorry I have to go, but I'm already late. I can't leave Kazi in charge. He'll have the place reeking of incense and Regina Spektor will be playing and it's a whole thing."

I nod, smiling at the image. He's not wrong.

"But you know I'm not running away from you, right?"

How can I possibly have more tears to give?

My mom comes up behind me and wraps her arms around my shoulders, leaning down. My breath hitches, and I nod.

"I'm not leaving you because you cried. I'm leaving because I have to. But if I didn't have to, I wouldn't. You understand the difference, right? You know what I'm saying?"

I do. I also don't know what to think about it. I'm not . . . equipped for this. I manage a nod.

"Okay. I'll call you later, Mary," he says, and I hear him drop a kiss on my mom's head. She's holding me tightly, and I'm still trembling.

After the door closes behind Phil, my mom asks if I want to talk about it.

"Not yet."

She seems to understand that it's not a closed door. I'm just spent and confused and so tired.

"I have to tell you something, Vada."

I turn, and she releases her grip. She is smiling again.

"You know how Phil and I have been seeing each other for a while."

I choke as a laugh gurgles out. "Duh."

"Oh. Well," she says, smoothing out the nonexistent wrinkles of her blouse, revealing something sparkly. "He asked me to marry him today."

My jaw drops clear to the floor. "Wow," I say. "I thought maybe you were more serious than you were letting on, but—"

"We are. I'm sorry we've kept it so private. Phil worried that you might not be too keen on another guy around with all the Marcus bullshit."

"Mom!" I say, shocked. Mom never, ever swears.

"Well, that's what it is. Anyway, we wanted to tell you together, but . . ."

"I started sobbing all over him?"

She tilts her head, her eyes shining with unshed tears. "Right. And as I watched you, I wondered if it would be okay. Maybe *you* would be okay with Phil around *permanently*. And I really love him. He makes me so . . ."

"Happy?" I say. "Duh," I repeat. "You are radiating kittens and sunbeams, Mom."

"Well, I think I've loved him most of my life, to be honest. We almost got together in high school, but he chickened out. Then I met your dad and convinced myself it wasn't what I thought it was, but . . . I think it's been there all along."

My mind can't help but go to Luke.

"For him, too, right?" I say, no longer sure who I'm asking about.

She nods, her dark hair bouncing. And something calms inside of me.

"It's incredible, Mom. Truly. I'm so happy for both of you. My two favorite people in the world love each other."

"And you, Vada. We're both crazy about you."

I bite my lip, trying not to cry again. "Mom," I say finally. "Mom! You're going to be a bride!"

She slips into a chair at the kitchen table, and I sit across from her.

"I know! I need to find a dress. You'll come with me, right?"

"Of course."

"We're thinking something small. I don't want to wait."

"Okay."

"Vada," my mom says, her hands reaching for me but stopping short as if she's unsure. "Are you really okay with all of this?"

I lean back against my chair and meet her gaze. "Absolutely."

She bites her lip in a way so familiar to me that I know she's playing for time. "That was fast. I really want you to think about it."

I press forward and take her hands. "Mom. I have thought about it. I've been thinking about it, wishing for it, even, for years."

"For a dad?"

I shake my head. "I have a dad. He sucks. I've been wishing for a Phil. For a man who will love you the way you deserve."

"But he'll be your stepdad, you realize."

"Yeah. I know. And I'm"—I swallow against my tight throat—"grateful. But I'm eighteen. I don't need a step-dad. I've always just needed a Phil, and he's been that since the day he let me follow him around the club."

"You don't think things will change?"

"Not in a bad way."

She sniffs. "I hate how grown up you sound about all this."

I shrug. "Not your fault."

A tear runs down her cheek, and she sniffs louder. "I can't hate him because he gave me you, and I love you more than anything in the entire world, but sometimes I hate him."

I stand up and wrap my arms around her from behind. We cry together, and it's at once the saddest and happiest thing.

Finally, I straighten and swipe at my eyes. "I need to stop by the club. Is that okay? I want to congratulate him. You're a prize, Mom."

"I think he'd like that."

"Wanna come?"

"Nah, I think this is between the two of you."

I don't cry this time. I walk right to the jukebox and put in a dollar, scroll to Brad Paisley's biggest hits, and find the song I've waited my whole life to play. When "He Didn't Have to Be" starts up, I meet Phil's gaze from across the room, and even in the dim light of the bar, I can tell his eyes are misty. I blow him a big theatrical kiss and leave before I get carried away. He's not going anywhere. I'll see him later.

23

LUKE

I'm at work when Zack finds me. I should've known something was up since it was my best friend, alone. The place is deserted, being early Saturday afternoon, and it's only Ben and me at the bar.

He sees Zack perch on a stool, and I wave him off. "Go to lunch. He's not drinking."

Ben grabs his coat and heads across the street, and I turn to Zack. I pass him a glass of Sprite with a cherry garnish.

"Classy," he says, smirking. He picks out the tiny plastic sword and pulls all the cherries off with his teeth. I roll my eyes at his exhibition. "Sorry," he says, still grinning. "Works on Cull."

"Fuck off."

Zack's face grows serious, and he removes his messenger bag. He pulls out his laptop and opens it, turning it on the bar to face me.

"Whatever it is, I don't want to see it."

"You don't, but you have to."

It's an article. People.com. I dry my hands on a clean rag and tap the scroll. My stomach churns at a picture of my family, taken four years ago in England. The caption reads, "Punk rock legend and entrepreneur Charlie Greenly with his wife, Iris, and twin sons, Cullen and Lukas (14), outside Marigold Theater on 5 August."

"Okay . . ."

"Keep going," Zack prompts, chewing on an ice cube.

Son of Former Punk Rocker Releases Viral Hit for a Mystery Girl

Chances are, you've heard the viral hit "Break for You" from Lukas Greenly, podcast star and son of legendary lead singer of the Bad Apples, Charlie Greenly. If you haven't, comment below with the name of the rock you live under. After releasing the insta-hit online, thousands of fans, mostly but not all, of the female persuasion (twin Cullen is in a long-term relationship with his boyfriend, after all) are clamoring for a hint at just *who is the lucky girl*?

The interwebs have always championed a good love story, and this is no exception. Not long after Greenly released his song, polls cropped up all over, speculating as to the identity of the girl eighteen-year-old Luke is willing to break his heart over. The answers ranging from seventeen-year-old British child star Veronica Nelson, who is a rumored longtime love of Greenly's—

"Who?" I yelp.
"Ah. I wondered about that. Keep going."
"Is that a real person?"
"Keep reading."

—to ex-girlfriend, Lindsay Turton—

"Well, she'll be thrilled."

"Keep. Going."

—to his American coworker, an up-and-coming eighteen-year-old music blogger, Vada Carsewell.

My voice is strangled. "Holy shite."

"There it is."

"How did they even come across her name?"

"Journalists be nosy motherfuckers, man."

"Oh my god. This is going to kill her. She doesn't want this."

"Hold on." Zack closes the laptop with a click and sits back.

"I didn't finish."

"That's all there was. Speculation. The point is, it's not going away like you thought."

"And now it's affecting Vada."

Zack narrows his eyes shrewdly. "I don't know that it is. I mean, she might get more traffic on her blog, but that's already been the case."

I grab at my hair and then remove my glasses, wiping them frantically on the edge of my T-shirt. "But she didn't ask for this."

"True. But neither did you. And that's not why I came here. I knew you'd be beating yourself up when you heard. And that's bullshit, Luke."

"How?"

"In every possible way. But think about it. The most recent photo they had permission to use was from *four years ago*. They couldn't even get more than your blurry profile pic because you're so private."

I think about it for a minute. "Are there comments?"

Zack pulls his laptop out of the way before I can grab it, stuffing it back in his bag. "Always. You know how that kind of thing works. Nothing more than what you're getting on the podcast, though."

"I stopped reading them," I admit.

"Well, Cullen hasn't. He's obsessed with redeeming himself and makes himself read and respond to nearly all of them in defense of your honor, and now Vada's."

"Really?"

Zack rolls his eyes, standing. "Yeah, really. You know, for two guys who share DNA, you can be pretty dense about each other."

"I didn't know."

"Exactly why I came. You're selling yourself short. Them, too. This is a sucky situation that can have excellent repercussions if you let it. I'm not saying you need to do anything. Stay private and keep living your life. But stop looking at everything as if it's the literal end of the universe."

"Lindsay is loving it, I'm sure."

"No reason for her to be the only one."

"Ladies and gents, as we wrap up, I want to take a quick moment to discuss what happened a few weeks ago."

I wince, shaking my head rapidly back and forth, mouthing, "No."

Cullen presses forward. "I promised my brother I wouldn't bring it up, and I won't, except for this: I messed up. More than that, I fucked up. I invaded my twin's privacy, and I feel terrible. Yes, he's massively talented, and I'm not ashamed every person on the planet knows. But posting a personal clip, unauthorized, was a violation of the worst kind, and I've apologized in private, but I also want to apologize publicly."

I exhale. "Thanks, Cull."

"Anything you want to say before we close the doors on the discussion forever? Call me out or anything? I offer you the floor," he says.

I think for a minute. This is my chance to turn something terrible into something good. "Only this: since I have everyone's attention, you've heard Cullen and I say we record at the Loud Lizard in downtown Ann Arbor. This place is legendary, and we're so grateful to Phil Josephs for letting us use the space each week. If you're a local listener and appreciate good music, I highly recommend you check it out. And if you're not local, our very own Vada Carsewell has a fantastic music review blog called *Behind the Music* that you have to check out. It's my first stop for new music, and while I don't love sharing my work on a public stage, I *am* passionate about finding good talent to support."

Cullen shoots me an amused look over his mic. "Okay, then. Do what he says, listeners. The Loud Lizard in Ann Arbor, and *Behind the Music,* our very talented friend's music review blog. Believe me, if it's good, Vada will tell you about it. Girl's about as tough on the industry as she is easy on the eyes. She can be found manning the spigots at the Loud Lizard alongside my dorky brother. Two local celebs for the price of one."

After he logs us off, I drop my headphones and round on him. "Why'd you say that?"

"Say what?" he asks, eyes wide.

"That part about Vada being easy on the eyes. It's irrelevant and offensive. She's a goddamn genius, and you made it sound like they should all show up to see how she fills out her skinny jeans."

"Hm," is all he says.

"What d'you mean, 'hm'? You need to go back and change that."

"Okay."

"Okay?" I huff, confused at his easy acquiescence. "Okay. So, what was that about?"

"Let's just say it was an experiment."

"An experiment?"

"Something I wanted to test out. A hypothesis of mine. And Zack's, to be frank."

"You're telling me you were, what? Testing me to make sure I wasn't a sexist asshole?"

He waves me away, closing his laptop and gathering up his notes. "I know you aren't sexist. I wanted to see if you'd rush to Vada's defense."

I stare at him and blink once. "What?"

"Come on, Luke."

"Of course I rushed to her defense. You're setting her up to be visited by any number of creepy guys where she works, which is a bar, in case you forgot."

"I haven't forgotten. Listen, Zack and I have noticed you getting closer to Vada is all."

"So?"

"So," he counters blandly.

"We're friends."

Cullen rolls his eyes, slinging his black messenger bag over his shoulder. "You and Zack are friends. You and Vada are clearly more."

"I didn't write the song about Vada," I blurt. "If that's what you're implying." My brother freezes in his tracks and slowly turns back to me from the doorway.

"*Wow,*" he says, dragging out the word into multiple syllables.

"Oh, fuck off. I know you were thinking it."

"Maybe." He grins. "You've been pretty insistent, but all signs pointed to the ginger music nerd. But now I *know* you wrote it about her. Holy shit, Luke. How long?"

I shake my head and sink back down in my chair. "Go away."

Cullen hesitates and sits back down. "Are you going to tell her?"

"No."

"You should tell her."

I glare. "No."

"Why?"

"I already went over this with you."

"Yeah, but that was before I knew it really was about a girl, and not just any girl, but Vada. She's amazing, Luke. You guys would be great together. Who else understands your music nerdiness?"

I narrow my eyes but don't respond. My brother's lips crush to the side, thoughtful.

"Fine. The song is off the table. But what about asking her on a date? Just because you aren't dedicating a viral hit song to her doesn't mean you can't let her know you like her."

"Maybe. I might."

"Huzzah!" Cullen says. He's about to leave again when he turns back, looking mildly outraged. "Zack knew all along, didn't he?"

My dad's (very mature) unending silence has only succeeded in making me more adamantly anti–music career, so first period finds me sitting outside the guidance counselor's office. Enough is enough. If I'm not going to do a thing, I might as well commit to not doing it. Even though Phil's words about writing music come to mind, I mentally give myself a shake. Better to cut it off completely—shove my composing back into a secret place until years down the line, when it will rise up again and become overwhelming.

Hopefully by then, I won't live with my twin, and he won't be able to secretly record me and post it online.

I'm sitting in a plastic chair, phone in hand, scrolling through Vada's latest blog post when I feel a rush of air as she sits down beside me.

"Hey," she says. "What are you doing here?"

I quickly close the screen on my phone and tuck it away. "Seeking guidance. You?"

"Same. Well, sort of. I have an appointment to turn in some financial aid paperwork." She holds a stack up.

"Right."

"So . . . dropping Spanish?"

"Huh?"

She grins, and my stomach clenches when I realize she's wearing some sort of lipstick that makes her teeth look blinding and her freckles stand out and *God* I love gingers.

Her brown eyes crinkle in the corners. "Sorry. I have this theory that if you aren't seeing a guidance counselor about college, you're dropping Spanish senior year. Most colleges only require three years."

"Is that what you did?" I ask, mostly to keep the conversation going. Is it possible to never grow tired of talking to a person?

"Yup. It's why I'm in that embarrassing but therapeutic dance class." She huffs out a small laugh and removes her backpack, dropping it on the floor between her Converse. "I think Madame finally caught on to me, too. She's started bringing in a lot more angsty music. Who needs counseling when you can just wrench all the anger and hurt out?"

I feel my lips quirk in a smile, and I push up on my plastic frames. "I never thought of it that way before."

"Really?" she asks, surprised. "I figured you'd know all about it. That's what making your music is about, isn't it? What's that Annie Mathers's quote? Something about not really knowing what she felt until she put it to music?"

"Wow, that's . . . profound."

"Country singers, man. They get to the heart of the matter."

"Yeah. So . . . I'm actually here to quit Senior Composition. I mean"—I hurry to assure her—"I'm still 100 percent writing your showcase music. If you want me to, that is. After, you know, the whole viral thing."

"Of course I do! I haven't wanted to bring it up, but I would be honored."

I nod. "Good. I'm definitely still in. I just need to drop the class."

"But why?"

I shrug, fidgeting with my frames again. "I don't know. We have to perform live . . ."

She nods.

"Well, um. Yeah. After the aforementioned 'Break for You' thing, I don't feel like it."

"You don't feel like it?"

"Well, okay, more like I don't want to play for a crowd, and I don't need my dad seeing it as a victory—"

"So, don't tell Charlie. I'm not telling anyone."

"But people will be there, and they'll have cameras."

She sits quiet a moment. Finally, she says, "Okay. Tell

me one thing. Have you already started writing something for the showcase?"

The guilty look on my face confirms it.

"That's what I thought! You could have told me!" she says happily, smacking me on the shoulder. "What if you didn't have to play it live?"

"How would that work?"

"Duh, record it. You don't have to play it live. Just record something and send it my way. I'll choreograph something worthy to it and perform the piece for both of us."

The idea is so appealing, I can barely breathe. "But you haven't even heard it yet. How d'you know it will move you?"

"Easy," she says. "I know you." Her cheeks flush a little, and she tucks a loose wave of fiery hair behind her ear. "And I know your gift. Think about it?"

I already have.

When the administrative assistant calls my name a minute later, I tell her I've changed my mind.

I've been given a second chance. This time, Vada will know my song is for her and only her.

VADA

Hey, Greenly, I need a wedding date. You in? YouTube: Sheppard "Geronimo"

LUKE

Duh. YouTube: Vance Joy "I'm with You"

VADA

It's the night of the prom. Do you
mind?

LUKE

What prom? New phone who
dis?

VADA

You're a nerd. I like you.

24

VADA

As previously explained, I'm not a church girl. But Meg is.

Because of this, I am under certain obligations to attend some services. It's in the friendship contract I signed when I first met Meg in the church preschool our moms brought us to. That sounds like an exaggeration, but it's not. Meg literally drew up a letter of "Will You Be My Friend Yes/No," and while it didn't contain anything more than that, she's added to it over the years.

But it's not terrible. Listening to worship music, especially sung by someone I hold dear and who believes so easily, feels different and easy. More powerful.

Meg thinks it must have something to do with the emotion I attach to lyrics. But I think it's that *and* the emotion I attach to her. Regardless, it's a rare Sunday night that finds me in a dark theater instead of closing the bar. I listen to the message halfheartedly, but I'm itching for the moment the stage brightens and the opening chords start up. I can appreciate the darkness here. Have you ever noticed how concerts are always dark?

Some might say it's because darkness helps people hide and let go of their inhibitions and have a better time.

I think it's something else. It allows the person in the audience to experience the show as if it were meant only for them. One-on-one. No one ever looks around if they're really having a good time. They don't need to see who else is having a good time. They don't care. They have eyes only for the performer. They have ears only for the music. And, yeah, if they are really doing the thing correctly, they can close their eyes and wish the rest of the universe away.

It's not different tonight. I can pretend it's only me here, along with my hurt and frustration and insecurities. I can be real with God, and I can almost mostly believe that he's listening and being real right back.

Each time I come to one of these, it gets a little bit easier to want it to be real because wouldn't that be amazing? Maybe it's my desperation talking. Like a ten-year-old still clinging to the last Christmas with Santa Claus, I'm grasping for anything that could make me feel better.

But, I don't know, isn't it objectively better to grasp for the supposed creator of the universe than for a fallible human?

Anyway, Meg asked me along tonight because they are trying out a new song. I did my research, and to be frank, it's not my scene. Pretty enough vocals, but breathless and Stevie Nicks-esque.

I hate Stevie Nicks.

But I love Meg. (I feel like now is a good time to reassess the sheer number of things I've done in my life out of love for Meg. *Stevie Nicks*, I tell you. Ugh.)

The lights dim, and I hear the rustling of the band setting up onstage. As far as youth groups go, I'm not an expert, but I think this one is pretty well stocked. What I mean is, they aren't just a group of kids sitting in a church basement talking about the dangers of slow dancing. I'm sure there's some of that, too, but this Sunday-night service seems to focus on a message and music, and afterward, junk food.

Meg walks to the mic, sans wings. Her rainbow-striped hair is tucked behind her ears, and she perches on a small stool, folds her hands in her lap, resting on her white denim skirt. She doesn't play an instrument. Her voice is enough. While Meg is on the small side, her range is ginormous.

Her eyes find me, and she gives a light wave. Ben is highlighted in the blue light upstage, holding his violin. This evening, Ben and his violin are wearing their serious faces. I haven't had a chance to talk to him since the latest Marcus incident, and now I wish I had taken the opportunity to clear the air so he wasn't looking at me in that pitiful way.

I'm fine, I want to say. *Whatever you're thinking about me, don't. I don't want it.*

It's a lie, but I still wish I'd done it.

"We're trying out a new song tonight," Meg says. "Jesus laid it on my heart, and I haven't been able to shake it since. I think it must be meant especially for one of you.

It's called 'Rescue,' and I'd love it if you'd follow along on the screens behind me." That's the thing about Meg. She talks about Jesus like he's her broski. Like he's been texting her brain all week with his playlist. Like he's her Luke, actually.

I never know how to take it. It's this club she and my mom are in, where they have meetups with Jesus, and I get the feeling they are talking about me. It's unnerving and, frankly, embarrassing.

This feels like a setup. Does God do setups? Objectively, he built the world, so he's probably cool with premeditation.

Damn it, Meg.

The following night, I've exchanged the darkened theater— where I'm pretty sure I left my pride in a puddle on the sticky floor alongside the discarded popcorn kernels—for the mall.

The contrast is just as jarring and surreal as one would imagine.

After my sort-of come to Jesus, I talked to Meg, trying unsuccessfully to unpack all that had happened. Mostly what it comes down to is—I don't love the whole "God wants to be your father" thing. Probably because *father* is synonymous with *selfish asshole* to me, and the only thing my "father" has ever inspired in me is distrust and loneliness and rejection.

It's more than a single night of pretty singing can cure.

But I'm willing to try. Or at least try to try. Feel what I'm feeling. Search what I'm searching. Keep an open mind or whatever. Which Meg is over the moon about.

Then I told her about asking Luke to be my wedding

date, and she insisted on coming shopping with me, because according to her, asking a boy to be your wedding date is like Big League Chew big. And since we were already headed to the mall, my mom tagged along so she could find herself a dress. We found the prettiest ivory lace cocktail dress that is going to knock Phil on his butt when he sees her. Mom ran it to the car, promising to meet Meg and me in Macy's after she called her fiancé.

"So, how does it feel to know, definitively, your mom and boss are borking?" Meg asks in a hushed voice after double-checking my mom isn't anywhere near us. "I mean, we knew, but now we *know* know about the borking."

I shoot my best friend a look across the rack of dresses. "Meg."

"Probably while you're at work," she continues casually, holding out a fire-engine red minidress and replacing it just as fast, all the while wrinkling her nose. "Nice of you to cover those closing shifts," she says.

I make a face. "*Stop* it."

"Oh, come on. You must have thought about it."

I flick through more gowns, each floating up in a cloud of pastel tulle. "Honestly, I haven't. As far as I know, she hasn't dated anyone since my dad left when I was ten, except for Phil. That's a long time to be alone. So, if there's borking"—I wince at the mental picture—"good for them. In fact, if they aren't, Phil needs to work on his romantic-stylze. But they must be because I've never seen my mom so glow-y"—I stifle a shudder—"and if that's Phil's doing, well, great. *Furthermore,* using terms like *borking* isn't doing you any favors if you're hoping to dispel any of those homeschooler clichés."

Meg raises a brow and bounces on her toes, causing her fairy wings to flutter behind her.

"Whatever," I say, hiding my grin. "You get what I mean."

"Are you going to be a bridesmaid?"

I move on to another rack of metallic dresses. "Maid of honor. But it's a super-small wedding. Like, courthouse small. Last I heard, Phil was trying to talk my mom into eloping. It was supercute, actually. He said he'd been waiting since he was seventeen and didn't want to wait another week."

"Phil said that?"

I nod, plucking out a glittery gold number.

"*Phil* Phil?"

"I know, it's weird. But sweet. I even saw him eating a salad with his Big Mac the other day. Like, what? Who is he, even?"

"Smitten is who he is. Ooooooh. Vada." Meg's voice turns reverent. "That one. You have to try it on."

I hold the dress under my chin. It's a glittery golden strapless dress with a full-out tulle princess skirt that ends at the knees. "I don't know. It's a lot."

"It's your mom's wedding. Isn't it supposed to be a lot?"

"Yeah, but even this is like *extra* a lot."

"Just try it on. If you want, we'll grab some less flashy ones so you can compare."

After pulling another half dozen dresses, we smush into a tiny dressing room, and Meg perches on a stool in the corner, holding our purses.

I should try on the others, but I'm too curious about the gold one. The thing is, I haven't had much opportunity to wear dresses before. No one's ever asked me to a school dance, and all my good friends are either homeschoolers or work at the bar. But I've never been against the practice. Just, you know, no reason to be all dressed up with no place to go.

But this wedding is going to be magic. By default. My two favorite people in the world are in love.

And having Luke as a date feels like magic.

And this dress looks like magic.

Its shimmery gold glints pull out the red in my hair and set it on fire. I've always been a little self-conscious about my extra pale, freckly skin, but somehow my shoulders look creamy instead of transparent. The cut gives me curves, enhancing what little is there in a way I never realized I could like. I swish side to side, and the full skirt sways around my knees. Even the terrible halogen lighting of the dressing room somehow makes the little sparkles on the tulle glitter and dance. Magic. Pure magic.

"You look like Cinderella."

"I'm getting it."

"Duh," Meg says.

"Vada?" I hear my mom's voice. "You girls in here?"

Meg dangles her arm out the top. "This one, Mary!"

I unlatch the door and step out to the three-way mirror. My mom gasps, clasping her hands together under her chin. "Oh, Vada. Oh my word. You are lovely. That dress is perfect."

"You think?" I ask. This is something new, too. Dress shopping with my mom. Hot tears prick in the corners of my eyes when she nods wordlessly. She shakes her head after a minute, sniffing.

"I absolutely think. I can't believe I made anything as beautiful as you."

I turn back to the mirror, not sure how to respond. Not uncomfortable or anything. Just very loved.

"Luke is going to fall over when he sees you."

"Oh," I say, pleased, a split second before my brain catches on her words. "No. Wait. Who?"

My mom's reflection rolls her eyes. "Seriously. Vada. You think I didn't know?"

"Um."

"Girl, I knew the second he turned up at our door fifteen whole minutes early for your *study date*. You two are stupid for each other."

Meg snickers loudly, and I shoot her a glare. "What?" she says. "She's right."

"Not to mention," my mom adds slyly, "I heard all about how he saved your behind at the club *and* told off your father."

"Ah," I say, smoothing the tulle at my waist, comprehension dawning. "Phil."

She doesn't deny it. "He says Luke's a good kid."

"He's the best, Mom."

She nods. "He'd better be."

I turn back to my reflection. "I don't even want to take it off. Can I just wear it out of here? And for the rest of the day?"

"Don't you work tonight?" Meg points out. "That dress will make quite a stir at the bar."

I huff an affected sigh. "Fine. I'll take it off. In a minute. Take a picture." My eyes flicker to my mom. "I want to send it to Luke!"

Meg pulls out her phone but pauses. "Isn't that bad luck?"

"I'm not the one getting married," I say lightly.

"Not yet," she mutters. She shakes her head at her theatrics. "Smile!"

I make my most ridiculous supermodel pose, and Meg takes several shots, sending them to me immediately after.

"I'm going to put these back," she says, gesturing to the pile of untouched dresses.

"Thanks, Meg."

She flings her arms around my neck and noisily kisses my cheek. "I'm so glad you're doing this. You're going to have a fabulous time, I can already tell."

Meg walks out, and I spend another minute spinning in my dress. My mom watches, her eyes sparkling, radiating sunshine.

"Did you tell Phil next Saturday is a go?"

She nods. "Yep. He's closing the club for a 'private party,'" she says, making air quotes. "First time ever."

"Wow," I tease, "he must really be serious about you."

She shrugs, sort of bashful. Adorable. "Guess so."

"Have I told you lately that I'm super happy for you?"

My mom pulls me close, kissing my forehead. "Thanks, baby. I'm happy for me, too. For both of us, even." She leaves me to change, and I turn to the mirror one final time, ogling my dress.

It doesn't even need to be altered. I could probably get away with wearing my Converse, honestly.

Or, like, new Converse. Or flats. Pretty, glittery flats. That's probably better. I can clean up for a night. It won't kill me.

I hang the dress back up on the hanger and slide back into my jeans and hoodie. Picking up my phone, I scroll through the photos Meg sent, and I can't keep the smile off my face. I look equal parts ridiculous and glamorous. Perfect. I choose the goofiest one and send it to Luke.

> VADA
> No backing out now.

> LUKE
> . . .

> LUKE
> . . .

I chew my lip, ready to jump out of my skin. What if he is trying to think of a way to back out? Or what if I read that last text wrong. What if he wasn't saying yes? I scroll back, my heart in my throat. I mean. He said, "Duh." And sent the link to "I'm with You." That seems like a yes. But oh my gosh. *This. This is why you don't broach important topics via text like a freaking coward, Vada.*

I glance at my screen. We're still at the gray dots. An eternity lives in those gray dots. I'm not being dramatic. It's fact. There is a universe of possibilities in those three little blinking dots, and I feel like throwing up.

> LUKE
> I'm sorry. I'm just . . . I'm
> speechless, Vada. That's how
> incredible you look.

> LUKE
> Cullen just asked if I was having a
> stroke. I might be.

My eyes well, and I giggle. Again with the giggling!

> VADA
>
> Oh no. Can you feel your face?
> I hear that's a warning sign.

LUKE
I don't know. Maybe?

> VADA
>
> So, I should definitely buy this
> one?

LUKE
Definitely. I'll just have to stare at
your picture three full minutes every
hour until I can look at you and still
function properly.

> VADA
>
> I really like you, Luke Greenly.
> You know that?

I'm headed out with Meg and my mom, shopping bag happily in hand, when my phone chimes again.

LUKE
YouTube: Counting Crows "Anna
Begins"

My hand covers my mouth, and I wordlessly pass the phone over to Meg, who squeals in a way I'm not physically or emotionally capable of. My mom raises an eyebrow.

"Vada. Think," my best friend gushes. "Did you ever tell him about this song? In all that sexting you do? Ever?"

"It's not sexting," I insist, glancing at my mom, who is *smirking,* of all things. Meg makes a face. "No, never," I say.

Meg shakes her head and whistles low.

"Maybe it should be sexting. Up your game a little. Dude sends you Adam Duritz, you'd be silly not to have his babies."

I smack her arm, feeling my face flame. "Okay, that's enough, you weirdo."

"I'm just saying. That song has been your adorable Achilles' heel since the second grade. You used to make me listen to it on repeat and perform it in your front yard for your neighbors as they drove by. People would stop, thinking we were selling lemonade."

"I remember."

"And it's not, like, a cute song for kids to perform. We sounded like deranged potheads. Isn't that your first tattoo? 'Anna Begins' lyrics?"

"Okay, okay. Settle down. I'm not getting a tattoo. What is it with you and tattoos?"

She barrels on, "And of the bajillion songs in the world he could have sent, he picked that one. It's fate."

"We don't believe in fate."

"True. But wouldn't it be fun if we did?" With that, she flounces off after my mom, her wings flapping behind her. I glance at my phone again, Luke's last text still lit, and I write back before I lose my nerve.

VADA

> Damn. Now you've officially done it. Just when I thought you couldn't be sexier, you send me Duritz.

LUKE

You know Adam Duritz.

VADA

> *fans self*

LUKE

Interesting. And what if I told you I might know how to play "Long December" on the piano?

VADA

> I thought you didn't perform in front of others.

LUKE

I might make an exception.

VADA

> *fans self again*

LUKE

runs off to practice on nerdy—I mean super cool—keyboard

I click off my phone and see my mom and Meg waiting for me at the exit. When I catch up, Meg rolls her eyes at me.

"Kids and their sexting these days."

I press my lips together to keep the smile from seeping out. Sexting is a bit of a reach, but Luke is definitely flirting with me. This time I'm sure of it.

And I've decided that I really, *really* like it.

25

LUKE

"Think, Luke, think."

I'm sitting in a quiet, darkened classroom outfitted with better acoustics than my bedroom and far away from my brother's secret recording skills. I still owe Vada a song. The absolute *final* final deadline for my portion is Friday—truthfully, I should've given Vada something earlier—and I've never written under deadline before. I've gone from refusing to write, to forcing it, and it's absolute shite.

I start over at the beginning and try again. This may be for Vada, but it's an expression of both of us. Not together, but it could be. It's an anthem—about how we can ignore the rest of the world, parents and work and relationship expectations. We're eighteen. On the verge of the rest of our lives. I can just see Vada onstage, with a back glow of soft light, looking as if she's about to take flight, because she is. I am, too. It might not look the way my dad wants it to, but I'm finally walking toward the future I want.

That's where I'm getting hung up. It's easy to believe Vada can do this. She's brilliant. She can do anything. It's far more difficult to see myself as the kind of person who can shake free from my family and accomplish my dreams the way *I* want. I considered not adding lyrics. Composing only the melody. Lots of people do that. A million composers don't sing a word of their own.

But that felt like a cop-out. A concession. I *can* sing, and I have the words I want to say. Words I want Vada to hear and that I hope will inspire her. Anyway, my voice is just another instrument. Playing it over piano adds depth to the track as it weaves over and under the bass line. Honestly, a drumbeat would be perfection on this. For me, and for Vada.

I've never played around with it before, but I have the software. Or Cullen does, and I'm using his laptop. Am I still taking advantage of his guilty conscience every chance I get?

Too fucking right I am.

I scroll through his software, looking for the drum tracks, picking a speed that fits the melody in my brain. It takes a few tries, but I lay it over, starting with the chorus, and the result gives me chills. I'm on the right track.

Over the heavy bass line, I layer on a cymbal track, and want to cry at how right it feels.

Drums. Who knew?

This, *this* will move Vada. It's like the bass line is my heartbeat, achingly patient and consistent. My vocals are strained, but not in a bad way. In a slightly mad way.

Because that's how I feel. How she makes me feel. Off balance and slightly mad.

And devoted. Dedicated. Over the moon for the girl.

Yeah. This is good. Really, really good.

When I finally walk through the door that night, my parents are waiting in the kitchen for me. I halt at the sight of them, still holding my longboard.

"Am I late?" I ask.

My mom smiles reassuringly. "Not really. Though we did text wondering when you'd finally make an appearance. We ate without you. I was just putting it away." She holds out a stack of Tupperware and a fork. I drop my stuff, grabbing them and sitting down at the island to dig in.

"After you're done, we're all gonna take a little drive. I want to show you the warehouse we're remodeling for the Bad Apple." I guess he's talking to me again.

I choke on my bite. "You're still doing that?"

My dad stares at me, dumbfounded. "What d'you mean? Damn right I am. Invested money and everything. Used your college fund, didn't I?"

"You're shitting me."

"About the college money, maybe. But not about the place."

I look at my mum. "You knew about this?"

She looks at me like I've lost my mind. "Of course I did. So did you. We talked about this weeks ago, Lukas."

"But, Dad, you got all mad that we wouldn't advertise on the podcast," I point out.

"Well, yeah, I did. But that's not keeping us from

buying the place. No offense, but a stubborn teenager isn't enough to halt business."

"Better a stubborn teenager than a sullen old man," I can't help but say.

"Watch it, youngster. I was kidding about the college money, but I'm not above holding back your allowance."

"Dad, I have a job."

"Right, right. The job. The ever-important bartender gig."

I shove the Tupperware away. "I ate before I got home," I lie. "I have homework to do."

"Not so fast. You and your brother are coming with. This is family business. You're both old enough to contribute and participate."

"Dad, we're a month out from graduation. Cullen is going to school in New York, and I'm going out west. We won't even be here to contribute."

"You don't leave for several months, and anyway, I plan for this place to be around after you finish university."

"That's fine, Dad, but this is your thing. Just like punk bands and refurbishing pallets and writing that YA novel about aliens and teaching pottery at the community center. All very valid and amazing pursuits, but they are *yours*. Not Mum's, not Cullen's, and not mine."

"Is this about the podcast thing? I talked to my partners. I told them you weren't comfortable advertising while employed by Phil. It was tacky of me to ask. Son, it's fine if you want to wait until after the Bad Apple is built to quit."

I slam my fist down, impatient. "Who said I was quitting?"

My dad huffs out an exasperated laugh. "What're you talking about? Of course you'll quit. You can't work at a competing club."

"Then don't compete with Phil!"

My mum fills a glass with water and hands it to me like my outburst is from dehydration. I ignore it. I appreciate how uncomfortable our fighting makes her, but I'm tired of being bulldozed by my dad for the last eighteen years. From playing music, to skateboarding, to liking the right girls. He's always standing over my shoulder, feeding me his opinions. It's stupid, but working at the Loud Lizard is the first decision I've made 100 percent on my own. I don't want to give it up just because, once again, Charlie Greenly has a grand idea.

"You think I'm trying to replace Phil?"

"I don't know," I reply honestly. "I mean. No. I don't think *you* are trying to replace Phil, but I wonder if your investors are. Think about it, Dad; there's not enough capital in this town to fund two rock venues."

"It's not my fault the Loud Lizard is a failing club."

"I realize that."

"I'm not going to keep away out of courtesy so someone else can limp along."

"Fine."

My father's sigh is long suffering, and he rakes a hand through his hair. "What would you have me do, Luke?"

"I'd have you think of someone besides yourself for once," is all I say, and I turn for the stairs.

Minutes later, I hear the front door slam, and I watch the car back out of the driveway, my entire family inside, minus me.

The next day, during a lull at work, I knock on Phil's office door. I wait for the muffled "Come in!" and push open the door.

He's at his desk, just hanging up his phone when he sees me. He leans back in his chair, which gives a loud creak, his face impassive.

"I have something to tell you," I say.

"Is it about Vada?"

I lift my eyes, surprised. "What? No. Why?"

He raises a brow over his bifocals and settles back in his chair with a creak. "No reason. So, this is about your dad's club, then. Are you coming to offer your resignation?"

"How'd you know about the club?"

Phil gestures at his desktop. "It's been all over the news, kid. What do you guys read on your phones all day?"

"You know, and you haven't fired me?"

"Why the hell would I fire you? You've given me no reason."

"Except my dad's investing in a rival club that could put you out of business."

"Correction," Phil says, exhaling painfully. "It will definitely put me out of business. It's honestly a shock we've made it this far, Luke. I would've gone out of business years ago, if not for the sentimentality of this town."

"But you're not firing me."

"Luke. If I haven't fired Kazi yet, I'm not about to fire you. You're not quitting? I'd think Charlie would want his internet-famous offspring on staff."

I grimace. "Like most things between us lately, it's a sore subject. But no. I'm not quitting. I'm determined to go down with the ship."

Phil lifts his dirty coffee mug and raises it in a salute.

"So, what's the plan?" I ask.

"I'm not sure. There's something to be said for going

out with dignity and just closing our doors one afternoon with a sign that reads, 'It's been fun. Fuck the establishment.'"

"Or . . ." I prod with a smile.

"Or"—Phil smiles in return—"we come up with a way to limp along a bit further. Liberty Live is still set to run this summer, and it can't if we're closed. Vada's been depending on it for a half a decade."

"I remember."

"Right, and as Vada is about to become my stepdaughter—"

"I heard. Congratulations!"

His grin widens. "Thank you; I'm a lucky bastard. But as I was saying, Vada is about to become my kid, so I would really love to keep it running one more summer."

"You'd do that? Keep the whole thing running just for her?"

"Wouldn't you? It's incredible the things we do for people we love, isn't it?"

"Right." I feel my neck getting hot. "Well, this might be a mess, but I have an idea."

Once Vada arrives an hour later, things start falling into place.

"You think you can convince them?"

She shrugs, flicking her hair over a bare shoulder. The weather is unseasonably warm today, hitting eighty for the first time since last summer, and I'm distracted by the freckles dotting her clavicle. There must be a hundred at least, and I want to press my lips to every . . . single . . .

"I think so. I just heard from them, actually. Or I heard from their PR person anyway. They were super grateful for the boost my review gave them. Said they were filling up venues all over the place after that. I figure now is a good time to ask them for a favor."

"A 'favor' is putting it lightly," Phil says. "We're asking them to play practically for free."

"Yeah, but Ann Arbor is a fantastic touch point. Particularly if they squeeze us in during the next three weeks. If they can do that, the college students will still be within reach and looking to burn off final exam steam. Not to mention, the podcast is hitting peak numbers, right?"

I nod. "As far as I know."

"You think Cullen would be cool doing some advertising?"

"Yup. Even if he weren't, he owes me."

Vada turns to Phil. "Is this bananas? This is really short notice. Like, we can't pull this off, can we?"

Phil nods thoughtfully. "Last minute is the best kind, sweetheart. Not enough time to get tangled in the details, and it doesn't allow anyone to forget what's happening. We used to pull off things like this all the time back in my day, and that was when we had to paper the town in flyers and word of mouth."

Vada's lips push to one side. "Well, we might still need to rely on word of mouth, and papering the town in lurid flyers sounds like as solid a tactic as any. If we can get (Not) Warren to sign on, I'll even rerelease my review."

"I can make some calls to the campus paper and see if we can get it published in print ahead of the show," Phil offers.

Vada sinks back in her seat with a small smile. "Don't think I don't know what this is all about, Phil, but for the record, Liberty Live has been a tradition in this town for decades. I'm not the only one who wants to see it survive another summer." She turns to me. "How does your dad feel about you helping with this?"

"He might not know."

"Might not?"

"There's a very small chance he knows and even smaller chance he'll be happy with me."

Vada frowns. "You don't have to help."

"Well—" Phil says.

"Well," I interrupt. "Aside from the part where it's the right thing to do, I want to help. And while I'm pretty sure papering downtown will spread the word, the podcast's reach is a bit wider."

Vada watches my face and must find the answer she's looking for because she turns back to Phil. "So, that's that. We're off to save Liberty Live. No problem. Of course, you also have a wedding to plan for in two days."

"And we . . . er"—I glance at Phil—"have that thing at school the day after that," I add, thinking of the showcase and steadfastly ignoring the hot feeling in my face at the mention of the wedding. Our *date*.

"And graduation in four weeks," Vada offers with a knowing smile.

"Right," I say. "No problem. None of this is life altering *at all*."

"At all," Vada repeats. I can't believe it, but she looks completely jazzed by the challenge.

Or maybe I can believe it.

Or maybe I just believe in her.

26

VADA

I get right down to business planning the Save Liberty Live concert. I haven't forgotten what's at stake; *Rolling Stone* is staring me down from my in-box. They promised to snail-mail me the formal application and program details, but I've been (almost) too busy to care.

First up, an amazing band.

"We can do two weekends from Sunday," (Not) Warren's manager, Jenn, says in an almost apologetic tone. They are almost fully booked—a catch-22 of just how sought after they'd become since my review. Sunday isn't ideal, but I'll take what I can get.

"Great! Put us down. Thanks so much for doing this," I say. "I wish I could promise more funds, but as it's a fund-raiser—"

"No problem, sweetie. You bring the crowds, and we'll bring the swag."

"Excellent. Crowds I can promise. We're already on it. Thank you!"

I hang up the phone and stand up, stretching. Making a check mark on my list, I look over the rest. I still need to talk to Ben about opening for (Not) Warren. For free. Luckily, Ben is working tonight. I can catch him on the floor and convince him to play the show and then convince everyone else they want to order tacos from Enrique's next door.

I swing open the door right as Luke is raising his hand to knock. "Hey!" I say.

"Hey back," he says tightly.

"What's wrong?"

Luke tilts his head. "Marcus is here."

I start to walk, and Luke puts a hand on my shoulder. "Not for you. He doesn't even know you're here, Vada."

It's stupid how that stings to hear. "How long?"

"Thirty minutes, give or take, but he's being pretty belligerent. Phil had to call the police."

I deflate, and Luke tugs me back into the office. I've known this was coming. Phil's let Marcus get away with far too much already.

And yet.

"He really tried, Vada. I'm sorry. But Phil asked me to come warn you so you didn't have to see."

"Of course."

"I mean, it's a place of business and—"

I hold up a hand. "You don't have to justify it. I told Phil to do it years ago, and I know he and my mom have discussed this." I sigh, thinking. "I have to go out there."

"Vada, come on. You don't need to see that."

"But I do. Don't you see? I need to see this, and he needs to see me see this."

Luke's tone is soft. "He's pretty drunk. I don't even know if he'll remember, Vada."

"Well, I'm not," I say blithely, heading past him for the door. I open it and turn, holding a hand out. "You coming?" What I really mean is, *Please come. I don't want to do this alone.*

I know I need to face this—it has been coming for a long, long time—but I still don't want to see it. Not really.

Luke's face is unreadable as he joins me, but he takes my clammy hand in his warm one. We walk down the back hall together.

The scene is worse than I'd imagined, and I've imagined it plenty. Glass is shattered everywhere, and the place reeks with the heady fumes of alcohol. Marcus is holding a bleeding hand to his chest, surrounded by uniformed officers. The back wall is lined with patrons and curious onlookers. Phil is talking to another police officer, who's taking notes. He looks terrible. Resigned and tired. I stare between the two men, and for a half second, I'm torn.

On one side, there's my dad. A fucking asshole, but he's my dad. In my head, he's "Dad." He might've ruined the title, but it's his. I can't change that.

On the other, my Phil. The man who gave me a job and encourages my dreams. The man who loves my mom and has somehow made us both feel like we deserve better. The man who won't ever leave me.

Luke squeezes my hand, and I squeeze back, pressing my palm to his. When the police officers move away, I let go of his hand, giving him a reassuring smile. "I'm okay," I mouth.

I approach Phil and stand by his side. When he feels my presence, he glances at me, his eyebrows raised in concern. Seeing I'm okay, he wraps me in a side hug. Except, instead of fortifying *me*, it feels like we're holding each other up. And that's the difference, isn't it? All my life, I've been trying to grasp any and all love from my dad where I could, scraping the bottom of the barrel of his affections.

But I don't want to fight for it anymore. And I won't.

Marcus, if he notices me, doesn't say a single word as they take him away.

Before bed that night, I'm lying across my comforter, earbuds in and my eyes closed. With everything that's been happening lately, I haven't had a ton of time to choreograph my senior showcase piece, but I decided it didn't matter. Not really. Luke's challenge was to create something beautiful and full of intent, despite knowing it would be listened to and judged for what it was. And holy hell, did he ever deliver. It took me three tries to listen to the song all the way through without breaking down into a hot blubbering mess of emotions.

My challenge is different, though. Mine is to put myself quite literally out there. Onstage. Feeling all zillion and a half of my feelings and making sure every single one of them can in turn be felt by the audience.

In short, I want to own that shit, and I want to share it.

Luke gave me the perfect soundtrack; it's stark and lonely at first, but then reckless and hopeful. I tried to choreograph, I did. I wanted to produce something shiny and clean to honor his hard work. Something refined. But the feelings his song gave me weren't any of those things, and every time I listened, I responded differently. Eventually, I realized the best choreography was no choreography at all. I would improvise. It was, after all, my favorite part of class. Unplanned and raw. That felt right. Painfully so. I don't want to be distracted by memorizing steps; I want to be singularly focused on what this song inspires in me the moment my feet touch the cool, hard surface of the stage.

I inhale carefully on my bed, eyes still closed, letting Luke's vocals smooth my edges and squeeze my heart just like a hundred times before. Onstage, in front of all those strangers, will only be one more.

27

LUKE

I pull up short at the sight of a sleek black SUV in the driveway. We aren't a very swanky family, so *sleek black SUV* isn't really in the Greenly vocabulary.

More like banged-up, forest-green Subaru. Or used-to-be-white ten-year-old Corolla. That sort of thing.

Let's just say it's no tragedy to commute via longboard.

I pick up my board and carry it under my arm, careful not to skim the gleaming surface of the Land Rover. When I get to the front door, it's open to the screen, and I can hear voices inside, along with the clinking of glass and laughter. My mom is employing her tinkling hostess laugh, which is the higher, falser version of her usual deep chuckle.

The first person who sees me is Cullen, and he's subtly shaking his head, the meaning of which should be obvious because of twin speak, but it's not, and the screen door closes with a slam, alerting everyone to my presence. My dad peeks his head around the corner, his smile grander than I've seen in weeks. That alone should scare me.

"Here he is!" he booms. I prop my board with more care than it warrants and shrug off my jacket, hanging it over the banister before walking into the kitchen.

"There's the star!" A man in a pin-striped shirt and pointed black shoes says, winking. *Winking,* I tell you.

Another man I'd missed reaches out his hand, and I shake it automatically. Cullen looks pained, and my instinct is to move closer to him. A united front.

"Clyde Morgan," he says. "We were just talking about you. Did you know, as of this morning, your little audio clip has over 1.2 million listens? It's been uploaded to Imperium."

"I'm sorry," I say, ignoring for the moment that someone has illegally uploaded my song onto a sharing app. "Who are you?"

He laughs, and it doesn't meet his eyes. "My apologies. Coming off like a fangirl, am I? I'm Clyde, and that's Steven. We co-own the Bad Apple with your father."

"Right," I bite out. "Cool."

"And I bet you already know your numbers. I'm sure you're tracking them the most. If it were me—"

"Sorry, no. I, um, muted the link. It was a misunderstanding and won't be repeated."

"But surely you plan to take advantage of the fifteen minutes of fame."

"No, actually. As I said, it was a misunderstanding."

"But it's gotten you a ton of interest in your little podcast," Steven breaks in. "You've hit the top downloaded podcasts for the month on iTunes."

My head shoots up, looking for confirmation from

Cullen, who nods, shrugging, as if to say, *Welllll, you didn't ask.*

"I wasn't aware of that," I say. "But it doesn't matter. For the podcast, sure, but I'm not looking for a career in singing."

Clyde shakes his empty glass at my mother like she's a bartender, and more than anything else, that irritates me. No one treats someone like that in their home. My mum's gaze is steely, but she refills it because she's British and fucking polite. My dad clears his throat uncomfortably.

"Thank you, my love," he says in a low tone.

"Don't mention it," she says tightly.

"Well, now maybe you can understand why a few well-placed plugs for the Bad Apple would go far," Clyde says to me. "Particularly in the local community, though we've been tossing around the idea of global reach. Want to take advantage of a good situation, am I right?"

"How would that work?" Cullen asks. "You plan to ship booze?"

"More like ship swag. Take, for example, the business model used by the Hard Rock Cafe and Ron Jon Surf Shop. All locally owned and operated with global reach. The Bad Apple can become a brand for whatever we want, honestly. Whatever *you* want, even. We can start with some photos on T-shirts and some other swag. Famous podcast twins Luke and Cullen Greenly of the Bad Apple Inc. Obviously, we'd cut you in. We'd pay you for the rights to use your song, too, Luke."

And there it is. "No."

"No to the swag?"

"No to all of it. No to the swag, no to the exploitive marketing, and definitely no to the song rights."

"No offense, Luke," Steven says, giving a smarmy smile,

"but you haven't even heard our offer. We could make you very rich with that one song."

"It's not for sale."

"You wouldn't have to pay for college."

I look to my dad, but he's staring into his glass, swirling the ice. "Dad," I say, and I hate how pleading my voice is. But if ever there were a time to step in, this is it.

He sighs heavily, putting down his glass. "Mates," he says to his partners. "If the lad says no, he says no. It's his song."

"You said he would help," Steven reminds my dad.

"No," my dad says, more firmly. "I said you could ask him. It's his music, and he's an adult. If he doesn't give you permission, my hands are tied."

"What about the plug?" Clyde says. "Forget the rest for now. Maybe we're getting ahead of ourselves." He laughs shortly. "You'll have to forgive us. We're big dreamers."

"This vintage is excellent, Iris. Would you mind getting some more of it? It seems I've used the last." Steven digs in his wallet, pulling out a bill. My mum's eyes grow enormous, and my dad looks a little green. "Go ahead with her, Charlie. I'd like to get to know the boys a little better and lay out more of our business plan in living color."

I about choke on my own tongue. This is ridiculous. They can't dismiss my parents like that. My dad looks legitimately torn, and I want to scream.

I glance at my brother, and this time his meaning is clear. *It's up to you.* The thing is, it wouldn't be hard to hear them out. Play along for my dad's sake. I could even go so far as to plug the venue. We could easily work it to plug both venues in the same podcast. One at the start and one at the end.

It'd be cake, and everyone would be happy.

But as my mum goes to get her purse, I lose my cool. Because this stupid club has turned my family inside out in such a short time, and while I love my dad, I'm not about to go along with this. Not for these guys. Clyde and Steven and their smarmy shoes and their patronizing smiles. No one dismisses my brilliant mum.

"I've been abundantly clear about my view on this. Never once have I encouraged your enterprise in town, and most definitely not at the cost of my own privacy. Now you've come into our home, insulted my mum, and taken advantage of my dad. I'm not interested in plugging your club. Furthermore, I will most assuredly be plugging competing clubs every chance I get. And I wouldn't be so sure the Loud Lizard is going down so easy. Things are really rolling for their fund-raiser concert, and the talent they've booked is out of this world. (Not) Warren? Ever heard of them? *Behind the Music* predicted them to be the next big thing."

By their stony expressions, they have, and it sends a thrill of pride through me that Vada got to them first. Genius girl.

I turn to my dad. "I'm sorry, Dad. This isn't about you or your club. I'm just not here for exploitation."

I turn on my heel, grab my board, and leave.

The following morning, I find my dad sitting at the table, drinking his coffee. The rest of the house is quiet. My mum is probably on her run, and Cullen's in bed. Of the two of us, I'm the early riser.

"Morning," I say.

My dad holds out his mug, and I top him off before

pouring myself a cup. I'm a weekend coffee drinker, with the rare exception. I like it enough when I'm sitting with my parents, reading the paper, and I can drink it super-hot. To me, coffee is only any good if it's burning my tongue.

Plus, my slurping annoys the shit out of Cullen. It's a twofer in that way.

I sit across from my dad. "Look, Dad, I'm really sorry about last night."

He sips his coffee, raising his brows over the rim of his mug. Then he places it down in front of him. "Are you apologizing for saying no or for losing your temper like a child?"

I grimace. "Um, the second part."

He waves me away, exhaling with loaded patience. "Luke, you *are* a child, and Steven and Clyde are first-rate pricks."

I smile at his cussing. His habit of swearing at the breakfast table is probably the most punk rock thing about my dad these days. "Then why're you working for them?"

"I'm working *with* them, not for them, and after last night, I'm not even sure if I'm doing that."

"Are they mad at you?"

"Mad? This is business, son. No one gets mad. That's where you went wrong last night. You gave in to your emotions. Not that I blame you. I was ready to dump your mother's glass of wine on their heads. She's a saint, she is. I owe her a million and a half back rubs after that disaster."

"Okay, well, did I mess things up for you?"

He's already shaking his head, his eyes crinkling in the early-morning sun that streams into our kitchen. "No. I should be the one apologizing. I'm the one who let them ask you. I knew you were going to say no, but I was so tired of their harping. Figured it was best to show them, once and for all."

"I think I did that," I say.

He belts out a laugh. "Sure as shit, you did."

"Are you going to have to deal with what I did?"

"If I do, it's fine. It's my job as your dad. Speaking of, we need to talk about your song."

I groan. "Dad, I told you—"

"I know, I know. But Steven's remark made me think. Your song is out there on the internet, and anyone can steal it. You need to copyright the lyrics."

"Oh."

My dad grins. "Yeah. *Oh.* Unless you don't care if other people steal your grand gesture."

"I don't—wait. Grand gesture?"

He rolls his eyes. "You still pretending that wasn't about a girl?"

"Oh, he's admitting it now. I got it out of him," Cullen says, groggily slumping into the chair across from us and stealing my coffee.

My dad leans back, narrowing his eyes. "Hm, who could it be about? Ginger?"

Cullen snorts into the mug.

"Dad," I start. The screen door slams, and my mum comes in, panting, heading straight for the sink to fill a tall glass with water. She turns and rests against the counter, facing us.

"What'd I miss?"

"Luke's grand gesture," Cullen says. "Dad's trying to guess who the lucky girl is."

My mum smiles. "Oh, I know."

"You do not," I insist.

"Redhead?" she asks.

I huff and steal my coffee back, sloshing a little on my brother. "You deserve that," I say.

"I'm so daft," my dad says. "It's that Vada bird he's always going on about, isn't it?"

"I'm not *always* going on about her," I say. Waspish.

My mum pretends to be texting and giggles like a little girl. She looks up, shrugs, and says in a fake deep voice, "Oh, just something Vada said."

"Vada said you sang better than Morrissey, Dad," my dad pipes in.

"Of course you would remember *that*."

"I think I'm just gonna pick up this Springsteen book for Vada."

"For her blog," I say.

"Point being," my mum says, "you talk about Vada enough that we've noticed."

"Fine. He'll tell you anyway," I say, gesturing to Cullen. "I wrote the song about Vada Carsewell. I really like her."

"Just like?" My dad presses.

"I don't know. For now. Probably."

"Uh-huh," my mum says, straightening from the sink and dumping the rest of her water out. "I'm getting in the shower." She waggles her hips at my dad. "Wanna join me?"

"Ugh. Stop," I say.

Cullen grimaces. "Gross, Mum."

"Absolutely," says my dad. "Be right there."

My mum shuffles off, and my dad watches her go. I suppose it could be worse. My parents could hate each other.

"So, the copyright, Luke. Want me to look into it for you?"

"S-sure."

He holds out his hands, placating. "Nothing more. No calls into contacts, no demo tapes, no nothing. This is purely to protect your interests. One day down the line, you may want to sell it or produce it or whatever, fine. That's your choice. Scout's honor." He holds up his hand. "Mum made me swear."

"Okay," I say. Relieved for once that my dad knows about these things.

"Excellent. All right, lads. Don't come up for at least twenty minutes." He winks at me and slaps Cullen's back. "Your old man's not as good as he once was, but he's as good once as he ever was."

I pound my head on the table as Cullen makes gagging noises.

28

VADA

I've never been to a wedding before, so I can't really draw a comparison, but I can tell you that a courthouse jam, with a giant fancy dinner afterward, feels right, particularly when you close out the night in a dive bar, and the couple has their first dance to a song played on a jukebox.

I can't imagine anything better.

Well, except that we get to keep Phil now.

That's pretty wonderful.

If I thought I was picky about songs for significant moments, Phil took it to another level. He literally loaded the entire jukebox with preapproved tunes, and "not a single drop of Stevie Nicks to be found."

(There're even *three* Britney Spears songs on tap: "Lucky," "Baby One More Time," and "Toxic.")

It's late, and Phil and my mom have been swaying slowly around the dance floor with eyes only for each other. Ben is manning the bar, but only casually. Aside from a champagne toast, no one's drinking. I have a cupful of cherries and lemonade in front of me.

Phil doesn't have a lot of family. His mom's still bedridden in Ohio, so she couldn't come. Mom and Phil have been talking about moving her into our place and setting her up in the downstairs guest room.

They aren't traveling for their honeymoon, but they are planning to make a trip to Mackinaw tomorrow. Mom wants to tour the island and eat at the Grand Hotel.

Phil wants fudge.

I told him to bring me home some of the peanut butter kind. It has these swirls of melty peanut butter in every square. Yummmm.

Anyway, everything is low-key and perfect.

Well, almost perfect.

Luke's been over at the bar talking to Ben for the last twenty minutes, and I want to dance. And sure, it's great to see him talking with Ben like old friends. Ben's awesome, and it's good for Luke to have a friend he doesn't have to share with his brother all the time . . . but Luke's been smiling my way, and while I'm not super great at picking up cues, I'm pretty sure he's giving me the signal.

The signal for what? That part is less obvious.

So, I need to choose my selection very carefully.

"Hold Me Now" by the Thompson Twins? Ugh. Stalker vibes, much?

"Do You Want to Dance" by Bobby Freeman is pretty on the nose. And adorable, but only in that teenybopper, bobby socks, french fries served by a girl in roller skates kind of way. So, that's probably not good. Plus, fast music. I have two kinds of dancing: frantic contemporary and slow and swoony. Pass.

"I'll Make Love to You" Boyz II Men. Ew, Phil. Gross.

"Lazaretto" by Jack White. WTF, Phil. How is that wedding appropriate? Like, "I Think We're Going to Be Friends" would have been *adorable* given their past of growing up together. But mother-loving "Lazaretto"?

Long, artistic fingers reach over me and punch in a request before I can see it. Luke holds out his hand.

"Dance with me?"

It's not a slow song, or a fast one, but it's perfection. "Just Like Heaven" by the Cure. *Well done, Phil,* I think. Luke pulls me to the center of the floor and bounces a little with the music, swinging me so my floaty tulle skirt twists around my knees. He's singing along, and this is my new favorite song because of how seriously cute he is. His cheeks flushed, his wavy blond hair falling across the frames outlining his stellar gray-blue eyes. I'm on the balls of my toes as he spins me out once, and pulls me in, closer than before, and his breath brushes my face, and it's all cinnamon gum and whispered singing.

Next to us, Mom and Phil are dancing like maniacs,

and Cullen and Zack have just walked in, straight from the prom and still in their tuxes. Luke wasn't kidding. He really didn't care about missing the prom. They join us on the floor, and Meg hops off a stool, dragging Ben over, and they start jerking around, singing at the tops of their lungs.

All my favorite people are in one contained space. I take it in, my cheeks aching from smiling so widely. My eyes are teary, watering from laughter or sweetness, I can't tell. But everything at this moment is so lovely I want to preserve it just . . . like . . . this . . . in my mind. The music bouncing off the rafters and echoing off the concrete floors. The smell of the stack of pizzas Cullen and Zack brought to share. The way the lights sparkle off Phil's glasses, so I can't see how he's looking at my mom, but Jesus, I can feel it.

I exchange looks with my mom, and she holds out her arms and I move into her embrace. She pulls me in and whispers, "I'm so lucky, baby."

I kiss her cheek and whisper back, "You both are."

We all are.

After the party wraps, Ben and Kazi offer to clean up, and Luke drives me home in Phil's shitty truck. "Hungry?" I ask.

He smiles. "We just ate pizza."

"Yeah," I say. "I guess I'm not really ready to go home. I feel too . . . electric, or something."

Luke purses his lips and pulls into a small public lot. We're still downtown, and the warmer weather has people out and about. "I know a spot, if you want."

"Sure," I say. My voice is too eager, but I'm wearing a glittery gold dress and I'm with a cute boy with a British accent and my parents just got married. *Eager* is par for the course tonight.

He opens the door for me and immediately reaches for my hand. "Warm enough?" he asks, gesturing to my cropped jean jacket.

Holding his hand has my face extra flushed. Like, yeah, I'm good. Just hold my hand forever and winters should be a breeze. But I play it cool-ish and nod. Enthusiastically.

Like, my head is swimming and ready to bob right off my shoulders and roll down the sidewalk.

He squeezes my hand and leads me down the road a few blocks, stopping in front of a softly lit all-night coffee shop with quiet guitar music strumming through its speakers. He tugs me inside and orders two hot chocolates with extra marshmallows. After we have them in hand, we sit at a small table outside. The shop blocks the wind, and twinkle lights zigzag across the large awning. We sip our drinks, staring out into the street, people watching, until Luke says, "So. Your boss is your stepdad."

I blow on the top of my drink and watch as Luke's eyes follow the action, feeling a little thrill. "He is."

"Weird?"

"A little. But only because he's moved into our house. It's been Mom and me for so long that having a guy live with us is strange. He's always been like a dad, though, so it's not a huge stretch."

He blinks and shakes his head a tiny bit, and I tilt my head in question. His cheeks flame. "Sorry. I told you. You're very distracting."

This boy. *Gah.*

"Let's walk," I say, finding it hard to sit still under his gaze. "The breeze is warm."

This time, I take his hand. He seems uncertain after my abrupt change, and I want to reassure him. And I just want to.

We walk for what seems like forever. We weave up one block and down another. Loud college students barhopping breaking through the silence, but dulling as I lean closer to him. At one point, he slows, looking up, and drags me to a stop.

"What?"

"This is it."

I look up. It's a darkened warehouse with cardboard up in the windows, but the unlit sign clearly reads *The Bad Apple.*

"Wow, it's . . ."

"Pretentious?" he says dryly.

I snort. "I was going to say *big.* It's hard to tell if it's pretentious yet, but I would venture anything seems uppity compared to the dive that is the Loud Lizard."

Luke exhales slowly, taking it in. "He acts like he's not, but I think he's still annoyed with me."

"Because of the song?"

His gaze finds mine. "The song, the disregard for his latest career choice, the refusal to plug his club on our podcast, me, in general."

"He loves you, though."

He nods. "I know."

"I get the impression that Charlie's a good guy. He'll come around. He's just disappointed."

"D'you think he's right?"

I'm already shaking my head. "Luke, no. It's like when

you say you're cold and someone else tries to tell you it's hot. It doesn't matter what they think; *you* feel cold. It doesn't matter how talented he thinks you are, and believe me, Luke, you're . . . exceptional, but if you don't want to perform, you shouldn't. What do *you* want to do?"

He faces me full on and takes my hands in his. He's not that much taller than I am, so I can look straight into his eyes. I search them, losing myself easily in the calm gray blue. I'm feeling dizzy, but his hands are holding me steady.

"I want to write songs."

I smile. "That sounds perfectly *you*."

He tilts his head. "You don't think it's a waste?"

"Never. Unless you decide one day you want to be the voice behind your lyrics. Then seize the moment, Greenly."

The corner of his lips draws into a lopsided smile, and I'm somehow attached to the movement. At first, I think I'm going to kiss that one little spot where his smile is still quirked. But the closer I get, the more I want every bit of his mouth.

Every song lyric about tasting someone cycles in my brain, and I'm so curious to taste Luke Greenly. Which is super weird, I know. I've barely kissed anyone ever, and I've certainly never tasted them, but . . . oh my gosh, he's moving closer.

He's so close that, despite his frames, I can see the navy specks in his irises, and navy has always been my favorite color and I wonder if this very moment is why.

"Vada?" His voice is barely above a whisper, and I can smell the hot chocolate on his breath. It's delicious. When I swallow, it's loud in my ears.

"Yeah?"

"D'you think . . . I mean, is it okay if I . . ."

I can't speak because I don't want to waste my mouth on words when I can close the distance between us and show him just how okay it would be if he kisses me.

Or, I suppose, when I kiss him, because that's what happens.

At first, we're all soft, closed lips and tentative fingertips. Like butterfly wings or a brush of feathers against sensitive skin. But then there's a shift, and my skirt floofs between us as his hands circle my waist in a way that feels like he's possessing me.

I don't hate it.

I possess him right back, sliding the palms of my hands up his jacket, over his shoulders and around his neck, my fingers tangling in the corn silk blond hair at his nape as his lips open up and gently pull my bottom lip between them.

Oh my *gosh*.

Something in me comes alive at the sensation of his warm cocoa mouth, cautiously insistent, and almost inside of mine, and well, since he's there . . .

Update: french kissing is the best thing *ever*.

I don't know why tongues make everything so much more . . . *everything*. But they do. It's hot and wet and his hands are tangled in tulle and my legs are pressed to his and my heart is thudding in the back of my throat but I can feel his heart beating in his neck and *now* I want to kiss his neck because I want to feel what that is like and I do and did he just make that sound or did I? Why would you ever do anything else when you could spend every moment of every day kissing Luke?

Every moment before now has been a wasted opportunity, and when I'm done kissing Luke, I will be having a stern talk with myself about that.

Too soon, he pulls back, grinning like an idiot. His

mouth is red-stained, and a thrill of pride rushes straight to my toes because *I* did that. I'm sure my mouth matches, idiot grin and all. We stand there, inches apart, on a chilly, darkened street, smiling at each other, me dressed like a country music ballerina and he like the skater boy he is and then there's applause?

Luke's head slowly turns, his smile freezing as he takes in our audience.

"Shite," he murmurs, and the cuss has my mouth watering all over again. What is wrong with me? My entire body is buzzing with awareness, and I'm so baffled and in love with the feeling.

I lick my lips surreptitiously in the hope that there is enough of his taste lingering to cool my jets.

There's not.

His eyes are wide, but he must read something in my expression, because his mouth quirks in an adorably proud way. "Vada," he says, his eyes laughing. "God, you're beautiful. We need to get off this street, though."

I follow his gaze to the crowd gathered in front of the trendy collegiate bar called 21 across the street. "We've been caught by the smokers," I say.

"I'm afraid we have a bit of a walk of not-quite-shame, but—"

I take his hand impulsively and throw it in the air like we're on final curtain call. "On three," I say. "One, two . . ." Together we bow, to wild enthusiasm. Some smarty yells, "Encore!" and I'm not gonna lie, I'm tempted, but Luke shakes his head.

"Let's go, you little exhibitionist."

The nickname pulls me up short. "Oh God," I say. "I didn't even think. I'm sorry, I wasn't trying to . . ."

There's a wrinkle between his eyes as he tries to follow, but when it finally dawns, he shakes his head. "Ah. No, not the same. You didn't post that on Instagram. You weren't half attending to your social media while kissing me. Were you?" He lifts a single blond brow.

"Please, I couldn't have told you my name if you'd asked me while you were kissing me."

That was clearly the correct response. He wraps my hand in his and keeps walking. *"Excellent."*

After a bit, I confess. "I could almost understand, though." Luke looks curious, and I plow on. "I mean, that was literally the best moment of my entire life. I wouldn't mind the memento."

His smile is relaxed and happy, and he brings my hand up to his mouth, pressing softly. "Best moment of my life, too. But you don't need the memento. We'll be repeating that, and often."

LUKE

Hey, girl, are you a parking ticket?

VADA

Wut.

LUKE

'Cause you've got fine written all over you.

VADA

Oh em gee.

LUKE

Kiss me if I'm wrong, but dinosaurs
still exist, right?

VADA

Luke.

LUKE

Hold on, hold on. I have one more.
Pretend we're in class for this next
one, though, okay?

VADA

Okay. Important question.
What class?

LUKE

U.S. history. Obviously.

VADA

Obviously.

LUKE

Do you have a pencil?

VADA

Y-yes?

LUKE

'Cause I want to erase your past and
write our future.

VADA

Why are you the way you are?

LUKE

You like me, though?

VADA

I do. <u>YouTube: Taylor Swift
feat. Ed Sheeran "End Game"</u>

LUKE

<u>YouTube: Taylor Swift "You Belong
with Me"</u>

VADA

Hot damn. Just when you
thought he couldn't get any
cuter, the Brit sends you
country music–Taylor Swift.
heart eyes

29

LUKE

The next morning, I'm woken by my brother banging on
my bedroom door. I'm only given half a second before he
bursts in, shit-eating grin in place.

"And how was your night? Took you an awful long
time to drive Vada home."

I sit up, rubbing my face. "What time is it?"

"Nearly noon. Mum wouldn't let me in to steamroll you. Said it was 'uncouth.'"

"I'm surprised you're awake, honestly."

Cullen sits down, uninvited. "Zack's on his way. We're going to head downtown and do all the classic post-prom stuff. Dinner and a show."

I snort. "Yeah, because most seniors are heading out to the theater to see something off-Broadway after the prom."

He nudges me halfheartedly. "Sorry about the other night. With the partners. I tried to warn you, but . . ."

I shrug. "Eh, it wouldn't have mattered. They would have tracked us down eventually. And Dad was right. I shouldn't have lost my temper."

"Dad said that?"

"Among other things."

"What kind of other things?"

I reassure him. "Not *those* things. He hasn't mentioned the club or advertising since. Maybe they got the point."

"Hopefully. Anyway, not to ruin your day, but I thought you ought to know . . . someone caught you and Vada making out in front of Dad's club last night. It's all over Instagram."

My stomach lurches, remembering the standing ovation we'd gotten from the smoking college students. "No shit."

"No shit," he confirms. "It's a bit grainy, but they recognized you. No one has tagged Vada yet, since your face, and likely tongue, are blocking her from view, so she should be safe."

"Ugh, you arse. Why didn't you lead with that?"

"Why? It's not like you can do anything about it. I just wanted you to know. And to congratulate you on *finally* getting your act together. You guys looked really happy last night. I'm proud of you," Cullen says in a lofty voice that makes me want to punch him. But I'm either too tired or too blissed out on Vada's kisses to care. He continues, raising a well-shaped black brow. "The Cure? Excellent choice. Well done."

I flop back on my pillow with a groan, but secretly, I'm pleased as fuck. "Whatever. Go be all cultured with your boyfriend and leave me alone."

That night, I sit in the crowd, slumped in my seat and wearing Cullen's Detroit Tigers hat, which is maybe Zack's now that I think on it, because there's no logical reason my brother would know anything about baseball. At any rate, I'm definitely on the down low tonight. After being spotted by the camera-hungry smokers, I'm prepared.

I didn't tell a soul Vada would be performing tonight, but I couldn't stand the idea of staying away. She's dancing to *my* music. How often does an artist get the opportunity to see someone respond to their work, live and in color?

Which sounds like a very sophisticated and creative and, I don't know, noble reason to show up. Really, I just want to see her. I know. I saw her last night. I kissed her last night.

I want—*need*—to kiss her again.

That *should* be enough. A kiss should have released this mountain of tension and chemistry between us, and all it did was make me want her more. It ought to have tided me over a few days. Instead, I barely slept last night. Could barely think today. I wasn't kidding when I told her I was saving that picture of her in the dress to desensitize myself to her.

That's legit.

I'm kind of an idiot for her.

Several dancers from her class take the stage. Thank God they are doing the dance class first. I don't plan to stay all night. Even though I'm not performing, I have sympathy hives just thinking of getting up in front of all these eyes and having my hard work assessed, live.

Madame whatever-her-name-is finally calls up Vada. She's dressed in a simple black pair of loose-fitting linen pants and a loose-fitting black tunic, and she looks radiant under the lights. I suck in my breath as the song starts, hearing the familiar chords.

Her interpretation is incredible. I watch, rapt, my breath held in as she slowly removes the tunic and pants, revealing a simple black one-piece bodysuit. It's not meant to be seductive but like she is removing a part of herself. The song is about shedding others' expectations and being your own person, and I know without her telling me that it's not so much a piece of her but a piece of *him,* Marcus, that she's discarding. She's gleaming and glowing, her pale skin a striking contrast against the dark curtains and stage. An apparition borne out of my words. As my voice sings about taking a risk and fighting fears, she spins across the entire stage, tossing expectations away. Ignoring the weariness of the world. Fuck the rest of the world.

Fuck 'em.

A smile spreads across my face as I watch her, so proud of her and what, or who, she's overcome. Grateful. To witness this moment. I might have sung those words and even believed them, but I realize I thought more of what they would mean for *her*. All my bullshit about standing up to Charlie and being my own man and whatever else was only that. Words. No action.

The action is there on the stage. Vada's left her entire self up there, bared to the world, and I'd hidden behind my keyboard and laptop.

I'm not changing my mind about singing. I'm just saying . . . I don't know what I'm saying. I guess maybe I want to be more like Vada. Listen to my own lyrics, probably.

Take some risks.

After the show, I'm waiting in the lobby for Vada, stalking the exit since she doesn't know I'm here, when my phone vibrates, one, two, three times. I shuffle the flowers I brought and dig it out.

CULLEN
Fuck. Where are you?

CULLEN
I swear I had nothing to do with this.

CULLEN
Pick up your phone. Seriously,
where are you?

CULLEN
Luke. I'm not kidding. Answer your
phone.

I'm startled as it rings again, and I answer. "Christ, Cullen, I was"—Oh. I can't tell him—"busy," I finish quickly. The lobby is loud, and I automatically raise my hand to cover my other ear, only to hear the crinkle of the bouquet. "Hold on," I say. "I can't hear you. Let me find a quieter place."

I shove through the glass doors and out into the cool night. "Okay. Start over. What's wrong?"

"(Not) Warren backed out of Liberty Live."

My stomach clenches, and my arm sinks, flowers and all. "What? Why would they do that? It's only a few days away!"

"They got a better offer, apparently."

"What the fuck? They promised Vada."

"That's not the worst part, Luke. The other bidder was the Bad Apple."

I groan. "No. No way. He wouldn't do that. They aren't even open yet."

"Apparently, they're opening the same night."

I'm spinning, but I can't tell if it's all in my head. "What? But. That's insane. They can't do that. There's no way. That's such shady business. What is Dad thinking?"

Cullen releases a slow breath over the phone, and it's static over the roar in my ears as the implications of everything sink in.

"I don't know. He seemed surprised at my reaction. I don't think he realized it was the same night. Or the same band. Maybe it was those idiot partners of his? He stopped listening to the podcast, apparently; it doesn't matter. What matters is the benefit concert is fucked."

"Luke?" I swing around. Shite. It's Vada.

"I have to go, Cullen." I crush the phone in my hand.

"Hey," she says. "I didn't know you were here. Did you watch?"

I swallow. Trying to grasp on to the feeling from a few minutes ago. Before I answered the phone, when I was high off Vada. But I can't. I'm sunk. She's sunk. The club is sunk. Liberty Live is sunk.

And it's my fault. *All my fault.* I was the one who'd bragged to Dad's partners about the Loud Lizard getting (Not) Warren. I'm the one who'd told them exactly what they'd needed to take Liberty Live out—what would crush Vada's plans.

I muster up something that hopefully resembles a real smile. "Yeah. I did. You were brilliant."

She closes the distance between us. Her hair is already down around her shoulders, and the scent of her shampoo covers me, making my stomach pitch painfully toward the dirt below my feet. "Are those for me?"

I look at the flowers in my hand. They don't even feel attached to me anymore. I pass them to her. "Definitely. Vada." I shake myself. I need to get this out first. Before the rest. Before I lose my chance. "That was incredible. I've never seen anything like it—"

"Twitching. I told you," she jokes, but I shake my head, needing her to hear this.

"No. Incredible. Moving. Spectacular. The best thing I've ever seen, and to have it to my song, it's like . . . I don't know what to say. I can't tell you what that meant."

She presses a finger to my lips. Her eyes are bright in the glow of the parking lot lights. Then her lips are replacing her finger, and I can't stop myself from kissing her back. Feeling every part of her against me, her scent overwhelming me. She tastes like nothing in this world, and I'm desperate to memorize it.

For such a short time, she was mine.

I pull back and wish I could smile at the slightly dazed look in her eyes. I clear my throat.

"Vada, that was Cullen."

"Yeah?" she asks. Her hands are tracing circles on my shoulders, and they burn through my shirt.

I step back, putting distance between us. "Vada, I have bad news."

She blinks, and her brows crease in concern.

"The Bad Apple is opening the same night as Save Liberty Live."

"Oh," she says. "That's . . . well, not ideal. But we'll have (Not) Warren, so—"

I'm already shaking my head. "We won't have (Not) Warren. The Bad Apple outbid us. They dropped out."

"What? Why would they—"

"Vada, we were outbid by my dad."

Her face tightens. "Your dad? Charlie did this?"

I nod. "More likely his partners, but still. It's his club."

"But why?"

"I'm not sure. Cull thinks my dad didn't know, but—"

She takes another step back. "But?"

"But I'm not that confident. Maybe Charlie didn't know, but his partners had to. I think they did it because I refused to cooperate."

"You?" she asks, her voice wooden. "Why do you think this is about you?"

"I don't know. The last time I talked to the partners, I lost my temper. I threw the Loud Lizard in their faces. I was *so* angry, Vada. They were talking about using my song and all this global brand marketing, and I told them I wouldn't pitch them on the podcast, and then I bragged about how the Loud Lizard had scored (Not) Warren—"

"You told them about (Not) Warren?"

"I did, but I never dreamed they would go after the band. I didn't even know they were ready to open. I haven't been paying much attention . . . I was busy with you, planning for—"

"Right," Vada says flatly. Cold, like when she talks about her dad. "And somehow you just *missed* the fact that your dad's partners were out to get Phil?"

"No," I insist. "Not completely anyway. I knew my dad's club was a threat to Phil. Even Phil knew it was a threat. It's why we were planning this fund-raiser in the first place. But to be honest, I thought it was just business." I choke out the words.

"Just business? To shut Phil down?" Vada sounds close to tears, and I want to die. "You're as bad as Marcus, calling him a failure just because he's soft on his employees."

"Stop. Vada," I plead. "That's not what I meant at all. You know I don't think Phil is a failure. I think he's incredible. This wasn't about him. This was about me and my song. That's it. My dad's partners were looking to exploit the song, and Christ!" I yank at my hat, accidentally ripping it from my head. "I was selfish, okay? But I wasn't trying to hurt anyone!"

Vada shakes her head slowly, her hand combing through her hair at the roots for a moment before dropping heavily to her side. "I don't understand how this happened."

I open my mouth, and she holds up a hand, stilling the words in my throat. "That wasn't—I know what you said. I get it. You threw a tantrum and revealed our cards. It was an accident, and you didn't mean it. I know. Luke, *I know*. Okay?" Vada's eyes are shining with tears, and one spills over onto her cheek. She swipes at it angrily, sniffing loudly. Her voice breaks, and my chest cracks open with it. "But it's shitty. You know? Everything we worked for, down the drain. Everything I've worked for, for years, gone. Marcus wins."

"Marcus does not—"

"He does, though. I've been naïve to put all my stock in Liberty Live. It's just a show, and I'm just a kid. I was stupid for believing I could pull off something special. I'm not special. Phil's not special. Hard work only takes you so far." She grimaces, and her shoulders slump, defeated. "Marcus, the asshole, was right."

"Stop. He's not right. Not this time. Listen, I'm sorry," I say, my voice a croak. "I'll talk to (Not) Warren. Get the band back—"

"Jesus, Luke." She laughs humorlessly. "It's too late for that. We can't outbid them. Whatever the cost, it will be way beyond our means. No, I need to talk to Ben. Maybe his bluegrass band . . ."

I try to step closer, and she holds her hand out. "No. I can't think with you . . ." Her voice rings hollow. "Please go. You've done enough. I need—I need to try to fix this." Vada closes her eyes, compiling a mental list. "Without the fund-raiser, the club will close. Maybe not right away, though. Maybe Phil can coast another summer at least. But Liberty Live will be gone. I'll still have the blog, but not the access to shows. And Jesus, *Rolling Stone* . . ."

"Wait, what about *Rolling Stone*?"

Her brown eyes pierce me as if just realizing I'm still standing here. Tears roll down her cheeks in earnest now, and she swipes at them furiously. "Never mind. It doesn't matter anymore. I'll have to figure out another way."

"I can help you. Please. Vada—"

"No. Seriously. You've done enough. Go. I need to do this alone."

But it's not me who leaves. It's Vada.

30

VADA

LUKE

<u>YouTube: Vance Joy "Like Gold"</u>

LUKE

<u>YouTube: Tom Odell "I Know"</u>

LUKE

<u>YouTube: Twenty One Pilots "Car Radio"</u>

LUKE

<u>YouTube: Dramarama "Anything, Anything"</u>

LUKE

Vada. I know you're there. I know you can see my calls.

LUKE

Fine. Text it is. Please let me help. I
need to help. I want to fix this.

> VADA
>
> YouTube: Demi Lovato "Stone
> Cold"

> VADA
>
> YouTube: Noah Cyrus &
> Labrinth "Make Me Cry"

> VADA
>
> YouTube: The Civil Wars
> "Poison & Wine"

> VADA
>
> YouTube: Counting Crows
> "Colorblind"

> VADA
>
> I'm turning off my phone now.
> Please stop calling.

I shut off my phone with a sob and throw it at the wall, watching the screen splinter as it skitters on the hardwood floor. Fuck. I'm going to regret that.

I listened to every single song he sent me. Twice. And the ones I sent him. Twice. I don't have time for this bullshit. I need to be making plans, and yet.

And yet. I'm not stupid. I know what I feel for Luke transcends petty arguments. And I know he never meant for this to happen. I'm not angry so much as hurt. And my hurt isn't all his fault, but everyone's. Life in general's fault. Nothing is fair. I can plan and fix and plot and schedule and dream all the fuck I want, and it will still come unraveled no matter what I do.

And I'm not completely self-centered. I realize this goes beyond Liberty Live and me. This is everything Phil has ever had. And is Phil pissed at Luke?

Nope. When I came home late last night, tearfully sharing that everything had fallen apart, he pulled me to his chest and told me to go to bed. "I'll head in early tomorrow. See what I can come up with. It might not all be lost," he said.

But it is. Still, if Phil isn't giving up, I can't either. After scrubbing my face clean of yesterday's tears, I scrape my hair into a messy knot and throw on my Loud Lizard uniform of skinny jeans and T-shirt. Jogging down the stairs, I nearly tumble straight into my mom in her bathrobe. She passes me a cup of coffee and smiles gently.

"I know you don't drink it, but you might need the boost. It's mostly coconut creamer. You can take my car today. I have an overgrown garden calling my name."

I sigh. "It's not going to work. I can't fix this."

She shrugs and wraps an arm around my shoulders. "It's not your job to fix everything, Vada."

"But it's *my* future," I say, feeling my eyes well.

"And it's as bright as ever, my girl. If anyone can pull something out at the last minute, it's Phil. He's been at it for hours already. But life's unpredictable. Part of the ride is learning to roll with whatever comes our way. So, that's what you're going to do. Roll with it. Change what needs to change and make the best of what you're handed. Think I planned to finish out my doctorate with a baby?"

"No."

"Think I planned to fall in love with my best friend?" I smile. "No."

"Nope. The two best things to ever happen to me were completely unplanned."

I let that sink in. "You make a lot of sense, Mom."

"Good."

"I don't see how that will help anything today, but—"

"It might not. But it's just one day." She hands me a mason jar with something green inside. "Bring this with you. Phil forgot his smoothie this morning. He's probably starving. Poor guy," she murmurs fondly.

Fondly.

I bite my lip at the pang of regret behind my eyes. *Luke.*

"By the way, I broke my phone," I say. "Um. Threw it against the wall. So, that's on me, obviously. I'll have to get a new one, but in the meantime, if you or, um, anyone else needs to get ahold of me—"

"You're at work."

"I'm at work," I agree with a sigh. For better or worse, I'm going to work. But first, I have a bearded bluegrass bartender to plead with and a future to readjust.

31

LUKE

I try all night to call her. I text her a thousand times. I wasn't sure if she read my messages until she sent songs back.

I should have taken them as a fuck-you, but I know Vada. *I know her* now. So, I took it as, "I'm angry but still care enough to send you agonizing yet handpicked heartbreak songs, so."

I mean. She sent me Duritz. *Duritz.*

I confronted my dad about it all last night, and he seemed genuinely shocked and upset. That's all the confirmation I needed. This is my fault. I did this.

And I need to fix it.

Cullen feels terrible, moping all over the damn place, which makes everything worse. He's reaching way back to take credit for everything, and I'm inclined to let him, even though I'd let the band name slip. Not that I want to be absolved, but if it makes him shut up about it . . .

I've tried everything. I went to my dad's partners, but they are intent on making me suffer for my obstinacy. Which, fine. I didn't really want to cooperate with them, but I would've. For her.

Cullen, Zack, and I brainstormed ways the podcast could help out, but aside from creating buzz, it's not good for much. What good are thousands of new followers when they live in different countries and are only there for the singing?

Which brings me to my final option. One that I *really* don't want to do, but it's the only thing I have.

It's time to be brave.

I knock on Phil's door first thing the next morning.

"This looks familiar," he says, and I sink into the chair across from him.

"I fucked up," I say.

"So I heard."

"I need to fix it."

"I'm all ears." Phil leans forward, his elbows on his desk as he peers over his bifocals.

I inhale heavily. Once I do this, I can't go back. I wipe my hands on my jeans and inhale and exhale deeply again. Sweat prickles on the back of my neck.

"(Not) Warren, thanks to Vada's blog, is bigger than anything around here. Bigger than Ben's bluegrass shit anyway. No offense to him."

"I agree with you."

"Right." I wipe my hands again. Fuck, it's hot in here. I wouldn't put it past Phil to be sweating me out on purpose. "Right."

"Luke," he says. "You look ready to hurl. Just say it."

"If we want to make the money, and potentially beat my dad's club on opening night, we'll need a really big act. One that can bring in numbers."

He nods, raising a brow.

"Like internet-famous numbers."

He sinks back in his chair with a loud *whoop,* startling me. He laughs and leans forward again. "Man, she's got her hooks in you."

I swallow back the bile and nod.

"You sure?"

"I already told Cullen. He's out covertly papering the internet as we speak. I'd appreciate it if you could help me find a way to keep Vada away from the internet for the next thirty-six-ish hours."

"You have enough music to make a show out of it?"

This, I've thought about. "Plenty."

"You don't have to do this," he says. "You can still back out."

"I'm doing it. One night, and one night only, Luke Greenly, son of British punk star and lead singer of the Bad Apples, Charlie Greenly, will perform his viral hit at the Loud Lizard."

"You looked a little pale when you said that." He hands me his trash bin just in time for me to puke my guts out in it. Twice.

He grimaces. "You gonna get a hold on that?"

"Better put a bucket on the stage," I say, wiping my mouth.

"This is a good thing you're doing, Luke. I won't forget it."

"You'd better not. I need you to market the shit out of it. But remember, don't tell Vada. I already talked to Ben. He's going to play it cool with her, so she won't know. I can't . . . I'm not ready for her to know."

"She's going to be there. She'll find out eventually."

"I know. I'm . . . I know."

The Saturday of the show, I'm at the club before it opens. Early. Really early. To practice. The show will be in Liberty Square, but I needed a private place to practice my set.

My mother-loving *set* of all the ridiculous . . .

I'm cuing up when the door opens, cutting me off. The daylight filters in, and my breath catches.

"Dad," I say. The mic in front of my face amplifies it. "Shouldn't you be at your club? Opening night and all."

He shakes his head. "I quit."

"What?"

He shrugs, looking sheepish and much younger. "Not my scene, it turns out. I didn't love how they were doing business. Not to mention, your mum threatened to cut me off, *if you know what I mean,* so I took my part and walked. They're still opening tonight. I only owned a third, so it won't sink them, but—"

"What are you doing here?"

"Your brother told me you were here, and I thought, well." He runs his hand through his short blond hair. "I wasn't always a lead singer, you know. I started off playing guitar. Thought maybe you could use some backup."

My throat is suddenly thick. "Dad," I say. "It's only one show."

"I know," he says quickly. "So, I'd better take advantage of the occasion."

"I thought you might be needing a second-rate drummer, as well?" My boss is standing in a dim corner, drumsticks in his hands.

My dad crosses the room. "Good to see you, Phil. It's been years."

"Likewise, Charlie. The pleasure is mine, believe me."

I'm too overwhelmed to respond, but these two aren't ones to wait for a response. They take the stage behind me. Phil sits on a throne.

"I was wondering about the drum set," I say.

He lifts a shoulder, slamming on the cymbal. "Haven't had a chance to move it to Mary's yet."

"That's lucky."

"Sure is. All right, kid. Show us what to do."

There's been a last-minute change of plan, listeners, so spread the word far and wide. As we speak, my twin brother is in sound check. That's right. The tortured piano-playing prodigy is singing for one night, and one night only. Tonight, he'll be in downtown Ann Arbor at the Liberty Square stage at 8:00 p.m. sharp with special guests you'll have to see to believe. We're setting out to save Liberty Live and the Loud Lizard tonight, friends. I repeat, this is a once-in-a-lifetime chance, and I have it on good authority that if you ever found yourself curious who the lucky girl was that inspired his runaway hit . . . well, all will be revealed.

Tickets are twenty dollars at the gate. All for a good cause, folks. Bring your friends. This is Cullen Greenly, signing off.

32

VADA

I spent all morning prepping for the concert, moving speakers and setting up the stage, dealing with vendors and issuing orders. It's fantastic, to be honest, and the first and possibly last time I'll ever do it, so I soak in every moment. At least until we're five hours prior to the start and Phil sends me home.

"You need to get some rest, kid. You've done all you can. All that's left is for the band to sound check. I can handle that."

I'm not sure, and he can tell.

"Go! I'll call you if I need you."

"Fine. But don't forget I broke my phone," I say. I've been repeating it to everyone today. Even though I've been too busy to really miss it, I feel naked without contact with the outside world. I almost dug out my mom's iPad last night, but I stumbled into bed instead, nearly sleeping through my (borrowed) alarm this morning. Ben's stupid band kept me running all day yesterday. Who knew a bluegrass band could be so high maintenance? They're playing for free, though, so I've been trying to play it cool.

"If you need me," I try again, "call the landline." I don't remember the number to our landline, but I assume Phil does. Probably. "Maybe I should stay."

He rolls his eyes and shoves me toward my mom's car.

I'm far too keyed up to nap, so I beg Meg to come over, and she brings episodes of *Teen Wolf* to distract me.

It passes the time but doesn't really help. It's making me think of Luke and his DVDs. I definitely would have texted him by now were my phone not broken. Meg offers hers, so I send out a quick I'm sorry. Can we talk after this is all over? But he never responds, and it's just as well. I'll force him to talk to me tomorrow, if I have to.

There's still the whole *Rolling Stone* thing, but I haven't felt witty enough to write. Ben's bluegrass band isn't exactly going to be anything to rave about. At least not to

Rolling Stone. I have to try, though. Like my mom said, make the best of what I'm given or whatever. Even if what I'm given is a bunch of hairy college juniors who smell like pine trees and don't wear socks under their old-man shoes.

"Think it's too early to get ready?" Meg asks.

My mom knocks on the door. "I thought we could pick up some dinner before the show. I told Phil I'd bring him takeout. It's gonna be a long night for everyone."

"Give me fifteen, Mrs. Josephs," Meg says, using my mom's new last name. My mom's face flushes like a teenager's, and she waves her hand in a useless way.

"Gah, that woman is starry-eyed," I say.

Meg smiles, shuffling through her duffel bag. "I think it's nice."

"Me, too," I say.

"Straight hair or beachy waves?" Meg asks.

"Side braid."

Meg sighs. "I knew you would say that. No hat, though."

"Fine."

"What are you wearing?"

I look down at my flannel and jeans. "This. And my Docs."

My best friend frowns. "I realize this is banana pants to even suggest, but maybe you could change into a flannel that doesn't have holes and isn't seventeen sizes too big."

"It used to be Phil's," I say.

"And that's adorable, but Phil's not an eighteen-year-old girl. Let's just have a look." Meg flips through my closet and pulls out a short black T-shirt dress and a fitted purple-and-green flannel. Here." She says. "It's called a compromise. Still the flannel and boots but put on some leggings and a dress. You deserve to look good. This is your night."

"Technically, it's Phil's night."

"Technically," she repeats louder, "it's your best chance at saving the club and Liberty Live. So"—she shakes the dress—"put this on, and you'll look like you care."

"Fine," I say. "I happen to love this dress," I grumble. "It's comfortable. I just forgot about it."

"That's the spirit," Meg says, not bothering to hide her exasperation.

After getting dressed, I put on a little light makeup and pull my long hair to one side, braiding it loosely enough that strands fall around my face, how I like it. I'm pretty sure it's how Luke likes it, too. Not that it matters. I don't even know if he'll show. After blowing him off, I deserve it if he goes to his dad's club instead. Thinking of him at the Bad Apple, listening to (Not) Warren without me, is depressing, though, so I push it away.

"Perfect," Meg says, and I nudge her shoulder in our reflection, grateful she's here. For better or worse, whatever happens tonight, I'll still have Meg.

"Let's get this over with," I say.

We arrive late. Okay, not late. On time, but it *feels* late. I wanted to run the show, but Phil put his foot down. My purpose tonight is to watch and write and talk it up tomorrow on my blog. All my work was in the prep and marketing. By the time we arrive, it's dark and crowded on the street.

"Holy shit," I say to Meg. "They closed Liberty?"

Meg shrugs. "They had to. Look at this. People are packed in like sardines."

"This is incredible. Who knew people loved bluegrass so much?"

Meg lets out a high-pitched laugh and pulls my hand along. We arrive at a barrier, and my mom says, "We're expected. I'm Mary Josephs."

"Of course," the officer says, letting us past. I gape up at my mom. "Did you just name-drop?"

She smiles. "I've waited my whole life to do that."

We push up to the stage right as the lights shut off and the crowd gasps before screaming.

"There are a lot of girls here!" I shout to Meg.

She shakes her head, mouthing, "What?"

I can make out some movement in the dark, the band getting set up, but I can't make out anything they are saying. It looks like three figures and a piano? I don't remember Ben's band having a pianist, but good for them. They're obviously branching out.

"Turnout's great, isn't it?" I look to my left, and it's Ben.

"What are y—"

The lights flare on, and I gasp.

It's not Ben and his bluegrass band onstage.

It's Luke. *My* Luke. His piano is raised in the center of the stage, a spotlight making his white-blond hair stand out like a halo around his face. His eyes are closed, and his fingers are steady. He inhales once, sharply, a rise and fall of his broad shoulders, and opens his eyes to stare directly at me. He smiles his sideways, crooked smile and begins to play the showcase song.

What if this is all we're going to be?
What if we just did what they expected
And we let them take the lead?

I'm not sure I have it in me,
More than maybe is all I'll be
But I know it's not how I see you,
So, it can't be what I believe
And if that means that we're falling short
If we're missing all the marks
Then our potential, we abort,
Then, baby, quitting's just the start
We weren't meant for ordinary,
We weren't meant to wait
Our lives aren't supposed to be ordinary
I'm no longer leaving us up to fate

The crowd is breathless in anticipation. His voice echoes through downtown like it was meant for this. For all the times I've heard Luke sing, I've never had the privilege of watching him play, and *mercy*, it's the most sensuous thing I've ever seen in my life. His entire lithe form pours into the movement, from his legs pumping a perfect rhythm against the pedals to his long fingers dancing confidently along the keys. And the way his face scrunches up at the words? His intensity terrifies and thrills me. I know this beautiful, talented, awkward boy. I've kissed that face. I've loved that face.

And he wrote this for me.

Oh *God*.

Luke's shoulders bunch and sway along with the chorus, and he barely sits on his bench, as if he's incapable of staying grounded. The words, already tattooed on my heart, bring hot tears to my eyes, but I swipe them away. I don't want to miss a second of this.

My hands yearn to reach out and touch him. Feel if he is real, and just when I wonder if maybe he's not—maybe

I've imagined this entire scenario, the drums cut in, and I remember he's not alone up there.

Phil is perched behind a polished set of drums, looking like he's a kid again. My mom is screaming. Oh, geez, they're gonna be impossible to live with after this. I scream along with her. My mom clutches my hand, her face shining.

Luke's voice is joined by another, and it only takes me a half second to realize Charlie Greenly is singing backup. He's got an expensive guitar strapped across his chest, and he's beaming at his son as if he's been given the best gift of his entire life.

How.

How did I not know this was happening?

How did they ever convince him to do this?

Why?

This time, I sing along with the chorus. The only one in the whole place singing along because I'm the only one who's heard it enough times to memorize. The words get caught in my throat as I frown. He's blowing everyone away, but deep down, this isn't where he wants to be. He's closing his eyes, and not because he's intent on the music. He's shutting out the crowd.

I'm starting to think he's doing this for me.

Which is bananas, right? Like, how arrogant am I?

He transitions into another song. A cover, this time. Vance Joy's "I'm with You." It takes me until the next song to understand. He's playing them *all*. The songs we've been sending each other all these months. He plays Led Zeppelin and Kodaline and Mt. Joy and Tom Odell and, gah, Counting Crows (where I spend the entire song gritting my teeth to keep from running onstage and licking him). He even plays a Bad Apples hit and lets Charlie take the lead for a toned-down but nevertheless stellar version of their biggest hit, "Who's That Girl?" Phil gets in on the act, too. When Luke plays the Cure's version of "Just Like Heaven," Phil takes a second to dedicate it to his "lovely bride," and my mom dies all over again.

I lean over to Meg and yell, "Can I crash at your place tonight?" over the roar of "Aww!" ringing out in the crowd at his declaration.

Playing covers seems to suit Luke. It's less about him, so he can hide inside it. The crowd knows all the words, and their voices join his at every turn. It's the most fun I've ever had at a concert, and that's saying something. I don't want it to end, but it has to be wrapping up soon because it's late. I swallow hard. He hasn't played *the* song yet, and I can't help but wonder if he will.

I don't know how to feel if he does.

Somewhere along the line, Cullen and Zack found us and are dancing and singing along with the crowd. A few times, I've snuck peeks at Cullen and caught him watching his twin closely. As if willing him to get through this. He can see it, too.

"He's doing great," I say when the crowd gets quiet, trying to reassure him just as much as myself.

Cullen nods seriously. "He's doing brilliant. Beyond what I imagined."

"But this is it," I say firmly.

He looks down at me, his dark eyes holding something like approval or even affection. "This is it," he agrees.

"Why is he doing this?"

Cullen looks around, motioning at the crowd. "He knew he could get them here."

"But he hates this."

"He really does," Cullen agrees cheerfully. "Fucking can't stand the crowds. In fact," he says, pulling me gently by the shoulders, "maybe you should be right up front. Give him friendly support as he finishes up."

Cullen performs his magic, and the crowds part, allowing me even closer than I was. From here, I can practically touch Luke.

"Oy!" Cullen yells, and Luke's head jerks up, and I wave. Stupidly. Luke's entire face smiles, his shoulders lifting as if he's been given a new lease on life.

The lights dim, and the crowd seems to hold its collective breath, knowing *this is it*. This is the moment everyone has been waiting for since the second that song was leaked. A pale blue spotlight creates an eerie sort of circle around Luke and his piano, and I wonder if he'll say anything, or just play.

Luke turns on his bench, facing the crowd and pulling the mic nearer to his mouth. "Thank you all for coming out tonight to support a place that is very dear to me. I don't have the official numbers, but I think"—he raises a hand to shield his eyes, smiling—"that we've done all right. I hope to see you all this summer at Liberty Live, where we're gonna have a host of amazing new talents lined up for your enjoyment."

Luke wipes his hands down his jeans. "I have one more song for you. And I think you all know the one. My twin brother, Cullen, decided to do me a solid with the girl I was crushing on by releasing this song into the world. Turns out, it was bigger than either of us ever anticipated. So big, I never felt right telling the girl. I worried it might scare her away. It's a bit intense, because, well, I'm a bit intense, it turns out.

"But I messed up. By not telling the girl, I mean. And that girl went from the one I had a crush on"—Luke's eyes zero in on me, and I can't breathe—"to the one I fell in love with. So"—he exhales into the mic—"there it is. I wrote this song for a girl named Vada Carsewell, and it's called 'Break for You.'"

At first, he closes his eyes, but he changes his mind and opens them, looking back at me and winking, before turning to his piano. He counts it off with his dad and Phil and begins to sing.

Before now
Not the slightest inclination
Racked with
Hopeless indignation
Except when I sink into bed
Each night you're in my head
It's not
That I was born unfeeling
More like
I have some issues dealing
With the thought of offering
Them to you
Till now
Everything's been pale gray
Outlined with beige
and stony-faced whey
But what if
You misunderstood me
(Would you know
I meant this sweetly?)
That I might
Be willing to for you?
Perhaps that, my heart could break
For you
Fissures split

Along my surface
Snapping my
Carefully crafted courage
Echoes of
My former, brave self
I can't
Seem to bind all the pieces
What's left
What's revealed is the least
It's
All of me exposed for wanting you
Till now
Everything's been pale gray
Outlined with beige
and stony-faced whey
But what if
You misunderstood me
(Would you know
I meant this sweetly?)
That I might
Be willing to for you?
Perhaps that, my heart could break
For you
Every song I hear
They all bring you to mind
The way your hair falls
The way your eyes shine
The way my hands shake
When you say my name
And how I can't concentrate
Until you say it again
Every song I hear
I just had to give you mine

About the way your hair falls
Across the smile in your eyes

The song swells and stretches into the air, his face scrunched up and his hands slamming gracelessly against the keys. It steals my breath and makes my heart ache. This isn't the same as playing the song over my earbuds at night and wishing it was about me. About us.

Instead it's listening with all the knowing and understanding within me. It's hearing the words wrenched from inside of him and feeling them thrum through my veins with each beat of my heart.

It's something I will never ever forget as long as I live.

Till now
Everything's been pale gray
Outlined with beige
and stony-faced whey
But what if
You misunderstood me
(Would you know
I meant this sweetly?)
That I might
Be willing to for you?
Perhaps that, my heart could break
For you
But perhaps my heart could break for you
Perhaps my heart would break for you

When the song is over, I can't contain it any longer. Mike from the Loud Lizard is standing guard at the stage and doesn't even try to stop me from hopping up past him. Luke sees me coming for him and stands, knocking over his bench in his haste, and before he can say a word, I'm flinging my arms around him and choking the life out of him. He doesn't seem to mind, pulling me against him just as hard.

"I'm so sorry—" he starts, and I cut him off.

"Oh my gosh, shut up. I wanted it to be about me. So badly. I love you, I love you, I love you, you ridiculously selfless boy."

This time, he's the one ending the conversation, kissing me hard, and lifting me clear off my feet, swinging me around with a whoop.

"I'm sorry I didn't tell you sooner."

"I'm not," I say, kissing him one last time on the cheek. "This way I got to hear you sing Duritz, too."

Behind the Music

By Vada Carsewell

(submitted for consideration)

Last night, I had the privilege of witnessing magic. My own personal total eclipse or super-ginormous moon or Halley's Comet. One of those blink-and-you'll-miss-it, once-in-a-lifetime, home-before-the-stroke-of-midnight kinds of magic.

It was so very special to me and to everyone in attendance that I can't tell you about it. I know what you're thinking. What the actual fuck, isn't this a review? Well, yes. I realize that's, in general, how I roll.

But here is why I can't share: it's not mine to tell. Luke Greenly (yes, that Luke Greenly) didn't mean to release his hit song. He didn't want to share it with the world. It slipped out of his hands and tumbled onto the world's stage without his permission. There was no intention behind it. Even last night, when he performed for a giant crowd, it wasn't for his benefit. It was for, well, mine, actually.

I know. Get fucked, Vada. Right?

I know, I know. Believe me.

ahem *Anyway,* what am I doing here? I'm painting a picture, folks. I can't tell you about the music—which was brilliant, by the way— but I can tell you what that music did to those listening.

After all, that's what we really care about when it comes down to it, isn't it? We care about what we felt. We want to be moved and changed and knocked over and pieced back together. We want to swoon and taste and cry and scream to the sky, *Yes, this.* We want ninety-minute relationships encompassing a lifetime of feels. We want the fantasy, the reality, the immorality, the salvation . . . we want to be seen.

Well, friends, I was all those things and more. *And more.*

Oh. And remember a few months ago when I went apoplectic over (Not) Warren?

Psh. Greenly was better. My eyes were basically glued shut through the entire thing, which is a damn shame because he's a sight to behold.

Opportunity with Rolling Stone Online

Lori Kephart-Spinks Jun 10
to me

Dear Ms. Carsewell,

Welcome to *Rolling Stone.*

Lori Kephart-Spinks
Director of Musical Review for Online Publication

Rolling Stone

EPILOGUE

LUKE

THREE MONTHS LATER

People are packed in like New Year's in Times Square tonight. The summer is wrapping up, and we hosted our last performance of this year's Liberty Live season this afternoon. Apparently, no one wanted to return to work after that. Everyone just migrated from the Square, came in for happy hour, and haven't left. Phil's had to double the bar staff and even hire on new help. It's still the same old Loud Lizard. Same sticky floors, same graffitied walls, same grungy regulars. But it's also brand new with exciting bands coming through thanks to Vada's blog—and more capital from the success of my performance. Which feels good, even if I never want a repeat experience as long as I live.

Over the crowd and music and clinking of bottles, I hear a familiar laugh, and I look up from the table I'm clearing to take in Vada and Phil in conversation with a regular. Her freckles are a little darker, and her cheeks and tip of her nose are slightly pink from our weekend trip to Chicago so she could report from Lollapalooza. She's not technically working here anymore, but she offered to come in to help train the new staff.

We leave for the West Coast in five days. I have to

arrive a week before the semester starts for my composition program orientation. It sounds like a ballbuster, but I'm so grateful they let me in that I'm happy to comply. Vada's being sent to a private session with the Foo Fighters at the Starlight Theater, and if I didn't know she loved me, I would definitely be worried about her obsession with Dave Grohl.

I had no idea how deep it went.

Too late now.

She got two tickets just so I can stand next to her and watch as she melts into a puddle on the floor at my feet so I can then mop her up and take her home afterward.

"Oy, Greenly, stop staring at the ginger and grab these fellas a few pints, will you?"

I turn to a round of chuckles behind me and see my dad entertaining a group of soccer fans, Manchester United from the look of their jerseys. He has a clean rag slung over one shoulder and is leaning, propped against their booth, looking as if he's been painted into the scene.

May as well have been. After the benefit concert, my dad met with Phil and proposed a partnership. He'd gotten a taste for club ownership and liked it, but he preferred Phil's low-key, practically no-key way of managing things. In return, Phil got to keep his club. A clear win for the rock and rollers.

I take down their (extensive) drink order and promise to hustle. Instead of feeding the ticket to the bartenders, I duck under the flap and help myself to the spare row of spigots.

"Did you hear what song is playing?" Vada asks, nudging my shoulder with her bare one and causing me to nearly foam over at the tap.

"'Everlong,'" I say after recovering. I am perhaps un-successful at keeping the edge from my tone.

Her red lips spread into a wide smile, clearly ignoring my tone, and she nods. "Well done, you."

I narrow my eyes, my frames slipping down my nose a little. "Wait, did you play this for me?"

Her eyes roll, and she taps my frames back into place. "Duh. It's romantic."

"For who? You and me, or you and Dave?"

She takes two of the pints and nods for me to lead us to the table of waiting customers.

"*Mostly* you. I swear."

I try to glare at her over my shoulder and nearly trip over my own feet. She gets to the table first, distributing her half and passing out some of her signature smack talk along the way.

"Vada!" my dad says. "Light of my life! You aren't on today, are you?"

She gives him a side hug and plants a loud kiss on his cheek. When I first met Vada, she had one deadbeat dad. Now she has two rocker has-beens who dote over her every move, two meddling and overprotective gay brothers, and me.

Not that I'm like her dad or anything. Or her brother, for that matter. Thank God.

"You know I can't stay away, Charlie. I'm already go-ing through withdrawal. California can't compete with this crowd."

"Says you." He turns her to the group. "Have you lads heard? Our Vada writes for *Rolling Stone*."

"Just the online version," she demurs. "I got the gig writing about this genius," she continues, gesturing at me. "He deserves partial credit for inspiring me."

"Don't you mean *not* writing about me?" I tease.

She shrugs. "*Not* writing about *you not* writing a song about *me.*"

"That's a lot of denial. It's a wonder we ever found each other."

"All it took was one hot kiss on a street corner, and I was convinced," she says, stepping toward me.

"It's the Cure, actually. They're like a Vada-aphrodisiac," I reply softly so only she can hear.

Her brown eyes darken. "When're you done?" she asks, staring at my lips and licking hers. *Hell.*

"I'm not technically on. I came for you."

Her smile is blinding. "What a coincidence. Charlie!" she hollers. "I'm stealing your son away!"

Phil yells from the bar, "What are you talking about? Kid, you've owned that boy since the night you roped him into working for you." A great cheer goes up from the patrons, and I know my cheeks must be red because Vada is looking at me like I'm a puppy she found under the Christmas tree.

Adorable ginger.

I love her for it.

"True, but we don't need to dwell on it."

"Wanna get out of here?"

I tug her close, and even though I know we're making a scene, with her, it's always just us. I can't see anyone else. Her soft lips find mine as if they were created for that sole purpose, and I smile against them and whisper so only she can hear me.

"I'll go anywhere with you."

"Excellent," she whispers back. "Because I have plans."

Save Liberty Live Set List
(Holy fuck, we're doing this!)

"More Than Maybe" Luke Greenly

"Thank You" Led Zeppelin

"What It Is" Kodaline

"Silver Lining" Mt. Joy

"And Then You" Greg Laswell

"Just Like Heaven" The Cure—Phil gets to shout out to his new bride.

"I Know" Tom Odell

"Who's That Girl" Bad Apples—Give Charlie the lead so he can have a public midlife crisis onstage. I saw that, you ungrateful little shit. Doesn't mean it's not real, Dad.

"Anna Begins" Counting Crows (Be cool, it's just Duritz, man.)

"Break for You" Luke Greenly   After which Vada gets to kiss Luke forever.

ACKNOWLEDGMENTS

Writing your second book is terrible. It really is. Don't get me wrong. I am obsessed with Luke and Vada (and Phil and Mary and Kaz and Cullen and Charlie and Zack and Meg, etcetera, etcetera, etcetera . . .) but oh my gracious, telling their story took *all* of my magical unicorn powers.

It also took the hard work of so many others.

To my super-agent, Kate McKean, who read approximately seven thousand versions of Luke and Vada (ranging from bank heists to spurned best friends working in radio) and pressed me for just the right setting. I always knew who Luke and Vada were meant to be, but I didn't know *how* or *where* they would be until Kate said YES! That one! That feels right! And of course, as usual, she was spot-on. Thanks, Boss! I love our dive bar kids.

Vicki Lame, Supreme Editor and Lover of Lyrics. This book would've gone nowhere without someone who just *got it*. And *me*. And that's Vicki. Not every editor would have taken the time to actually listen to all the songs Luke and Vada sent each other over the course of the book, but Vicki did and that's hard-core. When I worried about too many songs, she replied with, "Actually, what if we added a playlist to the end?" See what I mean? She. Gets. It. Thank you, Vicki, for giving my adorable music nerds a chance to shine.

My Wednesday Books team. I have the best publisher in the world and I don't care who knows it. Thank you to Jennie Conway for always being the first to respond to my panicked emails with a calm and collected response, keeping me sane. I am positive the inside of DJ DeSmyter's brain must be a beautiful place because he creates the loveliest things I've ever seen. Natalie Tsay's enthusiasm has literally made my day so many times over the past few years and when I'm scrambling to figure out how publicity works, she will respond to my email on a Saturday morning like it's not even a thing. Who does that? The sweetest publicist in the world, Natalie, does, that's who. I'm very lucky.

To Karen McManus, who has stuck by me every step of this journey and was the first to fall in love with the British cupcake who is Luke Greenly. She even made a (photoshopped) T-shirt in his honor, which was exactly what I needed to press on through the early stages of drafting this book. I really hope I've done right by our boy, Karen. ☺

To Jenn Dugan, the Derek to my Stiles. Thanks for being broody and gorgeous while I get to play the role of the ridiculous one. That sounded sarcastic, but I swear I'm completely sincere. Your feedback made Vada stronger and your friendship makes me stronger. This is a tough career we've chosen and I'm glad to have you by my side. Or in my texts. Whichever. ☺

Kelly Coon. You offered to beta and ended up "just throwing together some light feedback." Girl, you are a frigging miracle-Hermione and I am so grateful for you. Your future is so damn bright, and I am extra grateful that I get to tag along and watch you soar. Let's change some hearts, friend.

I have two (super talented) author friends who have Lifetime Passes to my first drafts: Steph Messa and Samantha Eaton. I've known and loved them both since before *You'd Be Mine* and treasure their responses even while I cannot for the life of me understand why they would want to read my early messes. But whatever. I'm beyond grateful for them and their feedback and their encouragement. Thanks, ladies!

To all the book bloggers who have encouraged me and loved on my characters: I fucking love you guys.

To my sister, Cassie. She is always my very first reader, which means, she, too, read every one of those seven thousand iterations of Luke and Vada. Even when she was busy graduating and falling in love and raising her little girl, she read. I don't know that anyone on the planet will understand Vada the way my sister does. Cass, remember that night I sang to you under the covers while we shook and cried at the noise? Me too. This book is for the girls we were. I'm so proud of who we grew up to be.

To the Hahn, Jenkins, and Vrtis families. I am who I am because you were all who you were. Thank you from the bottom of my heart.

To Cate Unruh and Meg Turton, my Themed Sleepover besties: Looks like Tom Selleck with a side of toe-mah-toe, sea birds, and I want to buy a boat! Nicely, nicely thanks. (I realize that doesn't mean anything to anyone else. That's the thing about best friends who've been around since you were fourteen and fifteen years old, you have a secret language of movie quotes and nonsense.)

To Ryan Kearley, in the immortal words of Kurt Cobain, SEND ME WORDS, MAN. But also, thanks for being such an awesome friend. I can't believe I still talk to the guy who wrote a poem in eleventh grade about boobs, but I guess if it had to be anyone, I'm glad it's you.

To the radio station of my youth, Q101, out of Chicago. I don't know if anyone has ever thanked a radio station in their acknowledgments, but I was raised on grunge, alternative, and punk rock. I speak fluent flannel and I learned how to feel all the feels and navigate my teens from my deejay Sherpas, so thank you.

To my students, thanks for generally not caring that I'm an author.

To Mike. Every day I get to watch our kids thrive because they know they are loved by their dad. Phil and Charlie exist because of you.

To Jones and Al. Thanks for being my reasons, always.

And finally, to my Jesus. Thank you for giving your all for me. It defies logic, but I hope, in the end, I've done you proud.

Want more swoony romance?

Read on for an excerpt from *You'd Be Mine*

Available now from Wednesday Books!

1

CLAY

If I die, it's Trina Hamilton's fault. She's hard to miss; stat-uesque blonde with angry eyes and tiny nostrils wearing top-of-the-line Tony Lamas so she can kick my ass at a moment's notice. When the early-morning sun finally burns through my irises and kills me dead, she's the one you want.

"Christ, Trina, it's barely seven."

My road manager flashes cool gray eyes at me while pressing her matte red lips into a thin line. Her expression hasn't changed in the minutes since she came pounding on my hotel room door. She's a study in stone, but not for long. Better to get this over with.

I mumble another curse, yanking the frayed brim of my baseball hat lower. "At least slow down. I have a mi-graine."

Trina whirls around and shoves a manicured nail in my face. "Don't," she spits, "pull that migraine bullshit, Clay. You look like death, smell like sewage, and if you think those glasses are doing anything to hide that black eye, you're sorely mistaken."

I scratch at the back of my neck, playing for time. "Are those new Lamas? Because *dang, girl*, they make your legs look incredi—"

She grabs my chin in a painful squeeze, her sharp claws digging into my bruised cheekbone. "Don't even try it. What happened to you last night?"

I wrench my face away. "Nothing serious. A little scuffle with some fans after the show."

Trina stares at me a long minute, and I start to fidget. It's her signature move. I might be a country music star, but Trina makes me feel like a middle schooler who just hit a baseball through her window.

"A little scuffle," she repeats slowly.

"Yeah. A scuffle."

"Really. Just a few good old boys shooting the breeze, probably," she offers with a too-bright smile.

"Right."

She nods and starts walking, her heels clacking on the asphalt and ringing in my ears. A couple of middle-aged tourists halt, curious, midway through loading their golf bags into a rental car to watch us. I tug the brim of my hat even lower and hustle to match her strides through the hotel parking lot.

"So, that's it?" That can't be it.

"No, Clay. That's not it. Your face is all over TMZ this morning. We, as in you and me, because *I'm irrevocably tied to your fuckery*, are due at the label at 8:00 A.M. sharp."

I release a slow breath. "Trina, I have a contract. They already started presale on the summer tour. It can't be that bad."

Trina's cackle is edged with hysteria. "That guy you punched after throwing a beer in his face and waving a knife—"

"Knife? Really? It's a Swiss Army pocket tool. Every self-respecting Boy Scout owns one."

She plows on. "*He* was the SunCoast Records CEO's youngest son. His legally old-enough-to-drink son, as a matter of fact. Which you are not. How you manage to get served time and time again—"

I roll my eyes. "I've been playing bars since I was fifteen, Trina."

"—when you are so publicly underage—"

I lift a shoulder and wince as pain shoots down to my elbow. Must have tweaked it last night. "I'm a celebrity."

Trina grunts, her derision clear, just as my phone chimes in my pocket. I pull it out, ignoring her.

SAW TMZ. ON MY WAY.

"Is that Fitz?"

I nod, texting back.

TOO LATE. TRINA'S HERE.

"You can tell that good-for-nothing fiddler he's on my shit list, too. He promised he'd watch out for you after the last time."

SORRY, BRO.

"I don't need a babysitter, Trina."

MAYDAY, MAYDAY.

"Obviously. Just get in the car, Clay."

We pull into the lot of SunCoast Records fifteen minutes early. Trina slams the door with her bony hip and pulls out a cigarette, lights it, taking a long drag, and leans back against her outrageous banana-yellow convertible.

"I thought you quit." Fitz Jacoby lumbers over from where he's parked his crotch rocket and tugs the stick from between her lips. He stomps it out with his boot, and she glares but doesn't protest. Trina might have said Fitz was on her shit list, but she'd never hold to it. No one could.

"I did, but then Clay happened. He's fixing to kill me and my career. I wish I'd never agreed to manage you guys."

"Aw, now, Trina, that ain't true. You love us." Fitz pulls some kind of fudgy granola bar from his pocket and hands it to her. "Have some breakfast. Have you even taken a second for yourself today? I bet not," he croons. "Probably been up since dawn fielding phone calls and emails. You take five right here. Have a bite, find your chi or whatever. I'll make sure Boy Wonder here makes it up to the office, and we'll see you there."

Before she can protest, he silences her with a look and a waggle of his rusty brows and grabs my arm, tugging me along. "One, two, three, four . . . ," he mutters.

"Clay needs a clean shirt!" Trina yells, and Fitz holds up a plastic shopping bag without even turning.

"How the hell did you have time to stop for a shirt?"

"I have spares," he says, his jaw ticking.

I blow out a breath, trying to shrug out of his grip. He doesn't let go, just keeps dragging me to the glass doors of the lobby. "It wasn't as bad as they made it sound."

Fitz doesn't say anything. Instead, he leads me straight past the security desk to a men's room. He checks the stalls before locking the door and shoves the plastic bag at my chest. "There's deodorant and a toothbrush in there. I suggest you use them."

I remove my hat and glasses and pull my bloodstained T-shirt over my head before leaning over the sink. I turn on the *cold* full blast, splashing my face and rubbing the sticky grime and sweat from my neck. Fitz hands me a small hand towel, and I pat my skin dry. I use the deodorant—my usual brand—and brush my teeth. Twice.

"I like the shirt," I say.

"You should. You own three of them already."

"I have a contract."

Fitz laughs, but it's without humor. "Man, I don't care about your contract. You could've been seriously hurt. You could've been shot. You could've got in a car accident. You *did* get in a fistfight like some kid."

"He started it," I say, but Fitz is already holding up a calloused hand in front of his face, cutting me off.

"We don't have time for this. We're going up there, and you aren't gonna say shit in your defense. You're gonna say 'Yes, sir' and 'Yes, ma'am,' and you're gonna eat whatever crow they throw in your face and pray to God Almighty they don't sue you for breach of contract. Do you hear me?"

I sprint to the toilet. The coffee burns as it comes up.

"Christ," Fitz is saying when I come back to the sink, but he doesn't seem as mad. I splash more water and brush my teeth again, and then he holds the door open for me. As I pass, he grips my shoulder and gives it a squeeze.

Time to face the music.

I "yes, sir" my way through twenty solid minutes of lecturing done by three men in meticulous black suits. I manage not to throw up again. I manage to keep my contract. For now.

"Under one condition," the CEO, Chuck Porter, a balding man with wire frames says. "We have a little side job for you."

"Okay?"

"We've had our eye on your opening act for several months now. She's been giving us the cold shoulder, but we thought if we sent you in . . ."

I slump back in my seat, relieved. "You want me to convince some singer to come on my tour?" Piece of cake. Last year, my tour grossed higher than any other country act across the nation. Who wouldn't want in on that? It's the chance of a lifetime. "Who?"

"Annie Mathers."

A phone vibrates somewhere. Trina inhales softly. Fitz uncrosses his legs, sitting up.

I laugh. "You're serious?"

Chuck Porter's smile is all lips. "Perfectly. She's been hiding out in Michigan since her parents' untimely death. She's been touring the local circuit—"

"I know," I say. "I caught a show of hers last summer outside Grand Rapids."

This seems to surprise Chuck. "Well, then, you know she's special."

"She's talented as all get-out," I concede. "So why is she giving you the runaround?"

Chuck looks at his partners uneasily. "We're not sure. She's recently uploaded some clips onto YouTube and garnered quite a bit of attention, including from our competitors. Her mother, Cora, had originally signed with us. We'd love to have the pair."

I raise a brow at his wording. A *pair,* like they're collecting a matching set. Except Cora's been dead five years, so not much chance of that. I take my time, considering my odds. Annie Mathers is huge. Or, at least, she will be. It took approximately ten seconds of her performance for her smoky vocals to sear themselves into my memory.

And with her famous name, she might just make everyone forget my recent indiscretions. Next to me, Fitz pulls up her YouTube videos on his phone, and even through the poor phone speakers, her voice draws goose bumps on my forearms.

We all sit, listening, before Fitz lifts his head and looks at me. "They're pretty amazing." He passes the phone to me, and I watch her figure on the small screen pluck out the melody on an old guitar. She is framed by a tiny brunette playing a fiddle and a Puerto Rican guy with black curls and bongo drums.

"Jason Diaz and her cousin, Kacey Rosewood, round out her band. They've been playing together for years."

I can't drag my eyes from Annie's long fingers skillfully manipulating the strings as though they were an elegant extension of her limbs. Her wild brown curls spring in front of her closed eyes. Suddenly, she opens her eyes and stares right at me through the screen, and my stomach squeezes uncomfortably.

"So, what's her hesitation?" I ask again.

"The past few years, school. She wanted to finish high school in one place."

I nod. I was the same way, but the label wore me down my senior year. It helped that my brother died. I had no reason to stay home.

"More recently, it seems psychological. She's wary of the industry after her parents."

I shrug back into my seat, passing the phone to Fitz. "Not much I can do about that. I don't blame her."

Fitz presses the screen of his phone, turning off the voices and putting it in his shirt pocket. "Which is why you might be the best person to talk to her. You're currently in the industry."

"Yeah, but it's different. Singing was an escape for me, my ticket out."

Fitz shakes his shaggy head. "Maybe so, but you can see it, can't you? You recognize her passion? Because I sure as hell can, and I have maybe half as much as you and that girl. She's a performer. It's written all over her face." He sits back and re-crosses his knee over his leg. "Go up there and get her."

Chuck clears his throat. "You forget. We're not asking. We're telling you. Either you tour with Annie Mathers or you don't tour at all. I'm willing to take the loss on your contract. We have plenty of eager young talent ready to fill your spot."

I narrow my eyes as Fitz tenses next to me. I still him with a hand. The thing is, I don't think that's the complete truth, but I'm not willing to risk it. If that means I have to go to Michigan to convince a girl to tour with me, so be it.

"When do I leave?"